BOZO

FURY VIPERS MC: DUBLIN CHAPTER
BOOK 3

BROOKE SUMMERS

BOZO

FURY VIPERS MC: DUBLIN CHAPTER #3

USA TODAY BESTSELLING AUTHOR
BROOKE SUMMERS

Copyright @ 2025 by Brooke Summers

All rights reserved.

No part of this publication may be reproduced, distributed, or transmitted in any form or by any means without the prior written consent of the publisher, except for brief quotes used for reviews and certain other non-commercial uses, as per copyright laws.

This is a work of fiction. Names, characters, businesses, places, events, and incidents are either the products of the author's imagination or used in a fictitious manner.

Any resemblance to actual persons, living or dead, or actual events is purely coincidental.

Editor: Farrant Editing

Proofreader: Author Bunnies

CONTENT
PLEASE READ CAREFULLY.

There are elements and themes within this book that some readers might find extremely upsetting.

Please check out my website for that list of potentially harmful topics. Please heed these as this book contains some heavy topics that some readers could find damaging.

www.brookesummersbooks.com

DEDICTATION

This story is for those who have ever felt torn between love and fear, between the scars of the past and the hope for the future. May you find a piece of yourself in these pages, and may it remind you that love, though messy and imperfect, is always worth the risk.

ONE
BOZO

Eighteen Years Ago
Aged Seven

"Tell me, Maggie," Dad sighs heavily, running a hand through his hair, the other holding his beer bottle. "How the hell are we going to pay this shit?"

"I don't know, Craig," Mam hisses, her gaze darting toward me. She doesn't like arguing with my dad around me, but it happens anyway. I focus on building the Lego castle I got from Santa at Christmas.

"Look at this shit. Just look at it. We're ten thousand in debt. We barely have five hundred euro to make it to the end of the month. We have to pay the hundred-and-thirty-euro electricity bill," Dad snarls. "Not to mention buying groceries. That's usually another hundred at the very least. How the fuck are we going to make it to the end of the month and pay some money off the debt?"

"How much do we have left if we budget the one hundred and thirty for electricity and a hundred and twenty for groceries?" Mam asks.

"Two hundred and fifty euro," I say as I continue to build my Lego.

"What did you say, you little shit?" Dad snarls.

"Two hundred and fifty," I reply as I shrink further into the sofa. I hate it when Dad snarls at me. It means he's angry.

Dad's eyes narrow, his knuckles turning white as he grips the beer bottle tighter. "How the hell do you know that?"

I keep my eyes fixed on the Lego bricks, trying to make myself as small as possible. "I... I just subtracted the numbers you said."

"Craig, don't be mean. He's just trying to help. Honey, how did you manage to do it that quickly?" she asks, her voice soft. It usually is whenever Dad's mad.

I shrug, not really sure how to answer her. I've always been good with numbers.

"Help?" Dad scoffs and takes another swig of beer. "What we need is a goddamn miracle, not a smart-ass kid."

"Maybe..." Mam starts hesitantly. "Maybe I could pick up some extra shifts at the library?"

Dad snorts. "And who's gonna watch the kid? We can't afford a babysitter." He runs a hand through his hair. "Like the boy says, we've two hundred and fifty euro. If we use that money to pay off some of our debt, we'll be able to pay it off in..." He waves his hand in the air.

"In about four years," I mutter, still focusing on my Lego castle.

The room goes dead silent. I can feel my parents' eyes on me, but I don't dare look up.

"What did you just say?" Dad's voice is low, and dangerous.

I swallow hard, my hands shaking as I try to fit another brick into place. "If... if we only pay two hundred and fifty euro a month, it'll take about four years to pay off ten thousand euro. That's not counting interest."

Mam gasps softly while Dad slams his beer

bottle down on the coffee table, making me jump. "How the hell do you know that?" he demands.

I shrug, still not looking up. "It's just... math."

"Craig," Mam says softly, "maybe we should—"

"Should what?" Dad interrupts. "Listen to a seven-year-old about our finances? Christ, Maggie, we're in deep shit here!"

"I know that!" Mam snaps back. "But yelling isn't going to solve anything. And maybe..." She pauses, and I can feel her looking at me. "Maybe we should consider what he's saying."

Dad scoffs. "What, you think the boy's some kind of genius or something?"

"I don't know," Mam says. "But he's always been good with numbers. Remember how quickly he learned to count? And he's always the one who spots when we've been overcharged at the shops."

There's a long silence. I keep building my castle, trying to ignore the tension in the room.

Finally, Dad sighs heavily. "Alright, kid. Let's say you're right. What do you think we should do?"

I look up, surprised. Dad's never asked for my opinion before. "Well," I say slowly, "if we could make more money..."

"How?" Mam whispers. "How do you expect us to make money, honey? We're struggling. We're already spread thin enough. None of us are able to get a better paying job, let alone both of us taking on more hours. We're struggling with the workload and lack of money as it is."

"When Dad plays cards, I could go with him again," I suggest. I learned how to count the cards while he plays Blackjack. I watched as an old man did it at the casino when dad was there. He was drunk and explained the general rules to me. I've always been good with numbers, so it didn't take me long to understand what he meant. Soon I was able to count the cards. I'm really good at it now.

I see Dad's eyes light up. "You think you can earn me money, boy?"

I glance back down at the castle and nod.

"We don't have any money," Mam whispers. "We can't afford to lose any."

"We won't lose," I say quietly, still fiddling with my Lego bricks. "I can count the cards. I've been practicing."

Dad leans forward, his eyes narrowing. "What do you mean, you've been practicing?"

I shrug, not meeting his gaze. "When you play with your friends at the casino, I'm beside you. I count the cards in my head."

There's a long pause. I can feel the tension in the room, thick enough to cut with a knife.

"Craig," Mam says, her voice trembling. "You can't possibly be considering this. He's just a child!"

Dad ignores her, his eyes fixed on me. "How accurate are you, boy?"

I finally look up, meeting his gaze. "Very."

Dad's lips curl into a slow smile, one I've never seen before. It's not a nice smile. "Well, well," he says, leaning back in his chair. "Looks like we might have found our miracle after all."

"No," Mam says firmly. "Absolutely not. I won't let you drag him into this."

"Maggie," Dad says, his voice suddenly soft, persuasive. "Think about it. We're drowning here. This could be our way out."

"By exploiting our son?" Mam's voice rises. "By teaching him to gamble?"

"It's not gambling if you know you're going to win," Dad argues. He turns back to me. "What do you say, boy? Want to help your old man out?"

I look between them, torn. I want to help. I really do. But Mam looks so scared, and Dad... Dad looks excited in a way that makes me nervous.

"I... I don't know," I stammer.

"You don't have to decide now," Dad says,

standing up. "But think about it, okay? This could change everything for us."

As he leaves the room, Mam comes over and pulls me into a tight hug. "Don't worry, honey," she whispers. "We'll figure something out. You just focus on being a kid, okay?"

I nod, but as I hug her back, I can't help but think about the numbers. About how long it would take to pay off our debt. About how much we could win if I helped Dad at the card games. And I wonder, not for the first time, if being just a kid is a luxury we can't afford anymore.

I'M ALMOST FINISHED BUILDING my castle, mam is in the bath. She said she needed some peace and quiet and dad's been drinking. I've kept to myself, not wanting to anger dad any further than he already is.

"Come on, boy," Dad says, grabbing my T-shirt by the collar and dragging me out of the house. "What your mam doesn't know won't hurt her. We're going to make some money."

I stumble as Dad pulls me along, my heart racing. The cool night air hits my face as we step outside. Dad's grip on my collar is tight, almost painful.

"Dad, I don't think—" I start to say, but he cuts me off.

"Shut it," he growls. "You said you could do this, so you're gonna do it. We need this money."

We reach his beat-up old car, and he roughly shoves me into the passenger seat. The familiar smell of stale cigarettes and cheap air freshener hits my nostrils as Dad gets in and starts the engine.

The journey is intense as Dad teaches me signals to give him. I know Mam is going to go crazy when she finds out what's happened.

"Now listen up," Dad says, his voice low and filled with anger. "When we get in there, you keep your mouth shut. You just watch the cards and give me the signals. Got it?"

I nod silently, my stomach churning.

We pull into the casino parking lot and Dad kills the engine. He turns to me, his eyes hard. "This is our chance, boy. Don't screw it up."

As we walk toward the entrance, my stomach clenches with fear and worry. Dad steers me toward the Blackjack tables, his hand heavy on my shoulder.

"Remember," he mutters. "Just like we practiced."

We sit down at a table and Dad buys in with the

last two hundred and fifty euro that he has; the money that was intended to pay part of the debt off. I perch on the chair next to him, trying to avoid eye contact with anyone as I focus on the cards. As the dealer begins the game, I start counting, my mind racing through the numbers.

Dad plays hand after hand, following my subtle signals. At first, we're up a little, then down, then up again.

Hours pass in a blur of cards and chips. My head is pounding from the concentration, but I don't dare lose focus. Finally, Dad cashes out and I'm able to release a relieved breath.

In the car, he counts the money with shaking hands. "Five thousand," he breathes. "We did it, boy."

I should feel relieved, maybe even proud. Instead, I just feel tired and scared. As we drive home in the early morning, I wonder what price we'll really pay for this victory. Now my dad knows that I can win him money, I have no doubt that this will become a regular thing for him.

"We'll go again in a few days. Your mam's going to be pissed, but she'll relax once she realizes we don't have to worry about much this month."

As we pull into our driveway, Dad turns to me, still grinning, clutching the wad of cash in his hand like it's a lifeline. "Remember," he says. "Not a word to your mother about where this money came from."

I nod silently, my stomach twisting with guilt. I've never lied to Mam before.

We creep into the house, trying to be quiet, but Mam's waiting for us in the living room. Her face is pale, eyes red-rimmed from crying.

"Where have you been?" she demands, her voice cracking. "I've been worried sick!"

Dad steps forward, puffing out his chest. "Maggie, love, you won't believe it. I—"

"Save it, Craig," she snaps. "I know where you've been. Mrs. O'Brien from next door saw you leaving with him." She points at me, her hand shaking. "How could you?"

Dad's face darkens. "Now listen here—"

But Mam's not finished. She turns to me, her eyes filled with anger and disappointment. It makes me want to disappear. "And you," she says softly. "I thought we agreed you wouldn't do this."

I open my mouth to respond, but no words come out. What can I say? That I'm sorry? That I was just trying to help?

Dad steps between us. "Leave the boy alone. Look." He thrusts the money toward her. "Five thousand euros. Our problems are solved."

Mam stares at the cash, her face unreadable. For a moment, I think she might take it, might understand why we did what we did. But then she looks up, her jaw set.

"No," she says firmly. "This isn't the answer. We're not going to solve our problems by breaking the law and exploiting our child."

"Exploiting?" Dad scoffs. "He's helping the family!"

"He's seven years old!" Mam shouts, her voice breaking. "He should be playing with his friends, not counting cards in a casino!"

As they argue, I back away, bumping into the sofa where my half-finished Lego castle still sits. I slip away to my room, closing the door on the shouting. Crawling into bed, I pull the covers over my head, trying to block out the noise, the guilt, and the fear. I'm supposed to be good with numbers, but right now, nothing adds up. How can something that was meant to help us have gone so wrong?

TWO
GRÁINNE

Sixteen Years Ago
Aged Seven

I sit on the swing, my legs pushing me higher and higher as I watch the little boy laughing with his mam. Tears fill my eyes as I watch them. My mam used to do that with me. Not anymore. She's gone.

There was a car crash and she's gone, and she's never coming back. Dad hated being in the house we had, so we had to move. He couldn't stay there anymore without Mam. I'm seven years old and I no longer have a mam.

"Why are you crying?" I hear someone ask. I

turn to see a blonde-haired, green-eyed boy looking at me with a frown. "Why are you sad?"

I quickly wipe my eyes, embarrassed to be caught crying. "I'm not sad," I lie, looking away from the boy.

He doesn't leave, instead sitting on the swing next to me. "You look sad," he insists. "Did you fall and hurt yourself?"

I shake my head, still not meeting his gaze. The laughter of the little boy and his mam echoes across the playground, making my chest ache.

"Is it because of them?" the boy asks, following my gaze to the happy pair.

I nod slightly, unable to speak past the lump in my throat.

"Where's your mam?" he asks innocently.

The question hits me like a punch to the stomach. Fresh tears spill down my cheeks as I choke out, "She's gone."

The boy is quiet for a moment, then he says softly, "I'm sorry. Sometimes I wish my dad was gone."

I look at him in surprise. "You do?" I ask, hope blooming in my chest. I wish that too. My dad is mean now that Mam's gone. He doesn't play with me. All he does is shout and hurt me.

"Yeah, he's an asshole."

I gasp at him. "I'm not allowed to say bad words," I tell him.

The boy shrugs, kicking his feet in the dirt. "My mam says it's okay to use bad words if they're true."

I tilt my head to the side and watch him, then whisper, "My dad's an asshole too."

The boy grins at me, and I feel a small smile tugging at my own lips. It feels good to say it out loud.

"I'm Connor," he says, extending his hand like a grown-up.

I take it, shaking it solemnly. "I'm Gráinne."

"Want to play on the monkey bars?" Connor asks, hopping off his swing.

I hesitate, glancing back at the mother and child. The ache in my chest is still there, but it's duller now.

"Okay," I say, and follow Connor across the playground.

As we climb and swing from bar to bar, I find myself laughing for the first time in what feels like forever. Connor tells jokes and makes silly faces, and for a little while, I forget about the empty space where my mammy should be.

When it starts to get dark out, Connor takes my hand. "It's time to go home. I'll walk you to your house. Do you know where you're going?"

"I'm seven," I tell him. "Of course I do."

He gives me another grin. "I'm nine. Now come on," he says as he begins to walk out of the park. I tell him where I live and he laughs. "You live a few houses down from me," he tells me. "That's good. Now we can play again. Want to go to the park again tomorrow?"

I nod eagerly. "If my dad lets me."

"If he doesn't, I'll come find you," Connor says. "We're friends now, and friends stick together."

My heart races at his words. I have a friend. That's something I haven't had before.

As we walk home, Connor chatters away about his favourite games and TV shows. I listen, nodding along, but my mind keeps drifting back to what waits for me at home. Will Dad be angry that I'm late? Will he even notice I was gone?

We turn onto our street, and I feel my steps slowing. Connor squeezes my hand. "It's okay," he says softly. "Remember, I'm right down the street if you need me."

I nod, grateful to have a friend. We stop in front of my house, a place that doesn't feel like home to me. I can see the flickering blue light of the TV through the front window.

"This is me," I say, my voice barely above a whisper.

Connor looks at the house, then back at me. "Are you sure you'll be okay?" he asks, frowning deeply.

I force a smile. "I'll be fine. See you tomorrow?"

He nods, still looking uncertain. "Tomorrow. I promise."

I watch as he walks away, waving once before disappearing around the corner. Taking a deep breath, I turn back to my house. The path to the front door feels longer than usual, each step heavy with dread.

As I reach for the doorknob, I hear a crash from inside, followed by my dad's angry voice. I flinch, my hand freezing in mid-air. For a moment, I consider running back to the park, or even to Connor's house. But where else can I go? Dad will be expecting me and if I'm late, there'll be hell to pay.

I open the door and step inside. The house smells of stale beer and cigarettes. Dad is slumped in his armchair, empty bottles scattered around his feet.

"Where've you been?" he slurs, his bloodshot eyes narrowing as he spots me.

I swallow hard. "Just at the park, Dad."

He grunts, turning back to the TV. "Make yourself useful and get me another beer."

As I hurry to the kitchen, I think about Connor and his promise. Tomorrow, I tell myself. Tomorrow will be better. And for the first time in a long while, I actually believe it might be true.

I SIT on the swing and wait for Connor. My eye has a really bad bruise, and everyone keeps staring at me. I hate it. Dad was so angry last night when he ran out of beer. I didn't hide in time. I couldn't.

I close my eyes, trying to block out the memories of last night. The sound of shattering glass, Dad's angry shouts, the sharp sting of his hand across my face. I shudder, wrapping my arms around myself.

"Gráinne?"

I look up to see Connor standing in front of me, his green eyes wide with horror. He reaches out, his fingers hovering near my bruised eye.

"What happened?" he asks, his voice barely above a whisper.

I look away, shame burning in my chest. "I fell," I lie, the words tasting bitter on my tongue.

Connor is quiet for a moment. Then he sits on the swing next to me, his hand finding mine. "My dad hits me sometimes too," he says softly.

I whip my head around to look at him, wincing at the sudden movement. "He does?"

Connor nods, his eyes fixed on the ground. "That's why I said he's an asshole. Remember?"

I nod slowly, feeling a strange mixture of relief and sadness. Relief that I'm not alone, that someone understands. But sadness that Connor has to go through this too.

"Does your mam know?" I ask.

Connor shakes his head. "She works a lot. I don't think she notices."

We sit in silence for a while, gently swinging back and forth. The playground is mostly empty today; just a few younger kids with their parents on the far side.

"I've thought about running away," Connor says softly.

I look at him, my heart racing. "Running away? Where would you go?"

He shrugs. "Anywhere. I don't want to be a freak anymore."

"You're not a freak," I say adamantly. "You're my best friend."

Connor squeezes my hand. "Trust me, I'm a freak. My dad only likes me because I'm super smart and able to make him loads of money."

I smile at him. "You're a genius?" I ask and he nods. "That's so cool. I'm kind of dumb. At least, that's what Dad tells me. He says I'm dumber than a box of nails."

Connor's eyes narrow. "Your dad's an asshole."

A giggle escapes me. "Yeah, he is. He wasn't always. When Mam died, he became mean and hurt me."

"What was your mam like?" he asks.

I smile, remembering her warm hugs and gentle voice. "She was the best," I say softly. "She always smelled like flowers and cookies. She'd sing to me every night before bed."

Connor listens intently, a sad smile on his face. "She sounds amazing."

"She was," I whisper, feeling the familiar ache in my chest. "I miss her so much."

"I'm sorry," Connor says, squeezing my hand again. "I wish I could bring her back for you."

I nod, wiping away a stray tear with my free hand. "Me too. But..." I hesitate, glancing at Connor. "I'm glad I met you. You make things a little better."

His face lights up with a grin. "You make things better for me too, Gráinne."

We sit in silence for a while, gently swinging back and forth. The sun is warm on our faces, and for a moment, I can almost forget about the bruises and the fear waiting for me at home.

"Hey," Connor says suddenly, his eyes bright with excitement. "I have an idea. What if we made a secret hideout?"

I tilt my head, curious. "A hideout? Where?"

He jumps off the swing, pulling me with him. "I know the perfect place. Come on!"

Hand in hand, we run out of the playground and down a nearby alley. Connor leads me through a maze of backyards and narrow passages until we reach an abandoned lot overgrown with weeds and bushes.

"It's back here," he says, pushing aside a tangle of branches to reveal a small, hidden clearing.

I gasp as I step into the open space. It's like a tiny, secret world. There's a run-down old shed that's behind loads of big trees, keeping it hidden from the world.

"This is amazing," I breathe, spinning in a slow circle to take it all in.

Connor beams with pride. "I found it a few weeks ago. I've been coming here when things get bad at home. But I wanted to share it with you."

I feel a warmth spreading through my chest. "Really?"

He nods. "We can make it our own special place. Somewhere safe, just for us."

I throw my arms around him in a tight hug. "Thank you," I whisper.

As we spend the afternoon clearing space and planning our hideout, I find I'm not as sad as I was when I woke up this morning. I finally have someone who isn't going to hurt me.

THREE
GRÁINNE

Seven Years Ago
Aged Thirteen

"What's wrong, Sunshine?" Connor asks as he catches up to me. I'm walking home from the shop–not that I bought anything, I just needed to get out of the house–now I'm dragging my feet, not wanting to go home. Of course Connor saw me leaving the shop and decided to follow me. "You seem like you're about to cry. What's your dad done now?"

"It's not Dad," I whisper. "He's still the same as normal, still drunk."

Today has been awful. Everyone's been talking

all week about the teen disco that's happening tonight. I know that unless Dad's drunk and passed out, I won't be able to go, but I want to. And then today, Anthony asked me out. He's the cutest guy in our year and he asked me out.

I look up at Connor, feeling my eyes start to water. "Anthony asked me to go to the disco with him."

Connor's eyebrows furrow. "What, and you said yes?" he practically growls, sounding angry.

I shake my head, my voice cracking. "If I could go I would. But you know I can't. Dad will never let me, and even if he's passed out, I can't leave him alone. What if something happens?"

Connor's face softens with understanding. "You're too fucking soft for your own good, Grá," he says, his voice gentle. "Had that man been anyone else's dad, they'd have left that bastard to rot years ago. Not you though. You're too soft, aren't you?"

"He's my dad, Connor," I say.

He slides his hands into his pockets. "And?"

I smile, forgetting who I'm talking to. Connor doesn't care about his dad. Hell, he's getting to the point where he barely cares about his mam because she's always trying to make up excuses for his dad's shitty behavior.

"I don't see why you can't go to the disco. Surely your dad would be grand alone for a few hours?"

"I don't know. What will happen if he wakes up and I'm not there?" It's my ultimate fear. He'd be so angry if he woke up in the middle of the night and found I wasn't at home. He'd lose his damn mind and lash out.

Connor's eyes harden, a familiar determination settling over his features. "Listen, Sunshine, you can't keep living like this. Your dad's problems aren't yours to solve. You deserve a night out, to be a normal teenager for once."

I bite my lip, torn between longing and fear. "But what if—"

"No what ifs," Connor interrupts. "We're going to that disco tonight."

"We?" I echo. Connor's never been to a disco. He always says they're stupid and shit.

"Told you before, Sunshine: where you go, I go. I need to make sure you're safe."

My heart leaps at the possibility, but doubt still gnaws at me. "You'd do that for me?"

Connor's expression softens. "Course I would, Grá. You're my best friend. I want you to have some fun for once."

I feel a lump forming in my throat. I'm overwhelmed by his kindness. "But what about you? You won't have fun. You hate the disco."

He shrugs, a crooked smile playing on his lips. "Eh, you'll be there. So, we'll go and your dad is going to be fine."

For the first time today, a genuine smile spreads across my face. "You're the best, Connor. I don't know what I'd do without you."

"Probably cry a lot more," he teases, nudging my shoulder. "Now, let's get you home so your dad doesn't lose his mind as it is."

As we walk home, a mixture of excitement and nervousness bubbles in my chest. Maybe, just maybe, I can have one normal night. One night when I'm not constantly worrying about my dad. One night when I can just be a teenager. And it's all thanks to Connor.

But as we near my house, a nagging voice in the back of my mind whispers that things are never that simple. Not in my life. Not with my dad. There's always something. "Maybe—"

"Nope," he says. "That's not happening. We've made our decision. Now, go on in and I'll pick you up later. Be ready."

I give him a smile as I head toward the house. "Thanks, Con. I'll see you later."

"Later, Sunshine."

MY HEAD IS POUNDING and I feel dizzy. I'm unable to keep one foot in front of the other. I've never felt so out of sorts before. Panic crawls up my throat as I try to find someone to help me. I've been at the party for two hours, I was fine not that long ago, but I went outside to find Anthony after he disappeared and the next thing, I feel dizzy and I'm not in control of my body.

"There you are," Anthony says with a grin as he slides his arm around my shoulders as I make it to the top of the stairs. I think I've walked around this huge mansion of a house three times searching for him. I want to go home now. "I've been looking for you. Are you thirsty?"

I shake my head. "No. I think I should go home," I tell him, and note that my words are slightly slurred. Something is terribly wrong and I'm not sure what.

"Why?" he asks. "We're just about to have fun." His grip on my shoulders is hard and heavy as he steers me toward the bedroom.

My heart starts to pound and fear crawls up my spine. I need to get out of here, I try to pull away from him, but can't, he's too strong, and my body is so shaky and unlike my own that I can barely stand.

"I want to find Connor," I stammer. "Please."

His laughter is cold and sends chills throughout my body. "You're not going anywhere," he says thickly, his words filled with anger. "You're a little cock tease, Gráinne. You think you can flirt with me and then leave without giving me what I want. You've another think coming."

My heart races as panic sets in. This isn't the Anthony I thought I knew. His grip tightens, and I struggle to break free, but my limbs feel heavy and uncoordinated.

"Please, Anthony, let me go," I plead, my voice barely above a whisper.

He ignores my protests, pushing me toward the bedroom door. I try to dig my heels in, but my body won't cooperate. Tears spring to my eyes as I realize how helpless I am.

Suddenly, a familiar voice cuts through the haze. "Get your fucking hands off her."

Connor. Relief washes over me as I hear his angry growl.

Anthony's grip loosens slightly as he turns to face Connor. "Mind your own business, Connor. This doesn't concern you."

In a blur of movement, Connor's fist connects with Anthony's jaw. The impact sends Anthony staggering backward, releasing me. I stumble, my legs giving out, but Connor catches me before I hit the ground.

"I told you I'd keep you safe, Sunshine," Connor murmurs, his arms steady around me. To Anthony, he snarls, "If you ever come near her again, I'll do more than bruise your face. Understand?"

Anthony glares at us, rubbing his jaw, but says nothing as he slinks away.

Connor turns his attention back to me, his eyes filled with concern. "Christ, Grá, what did he give you? Can you walk?"

I shake my head, still struggling to form words. "I don't... I can't..."

"It's alright, I've got you," he says, scooping me up into his arms. As he carries me out of the party, I rest my head against his chest, feeling safe for the first time since I arrived.

"I'm sorry," I mumble. "I should've stayed home."

Connor's arms tighten around me. "Don't you dare apologize, Sunshine. This isn't your fault. That bastard... He'll pay for this, I swear."

As we step out into the cool night air, I close my

eyes, the world still spinning. "Take me home, Con," I whisper.

"Not to your house," he says firmly. "You can't go back there like this. We're going to mine. Mam will know what to do."

I want to argue, to insist that I need to check on Dad, but I'm too tired, too scared. For once, I let myself be taken care of, trusting Connor to make the right decision.

As he carries me down the quiet streets, I cling to him, grateful for his presence, for his protection. Maybe he's right. Maybe I am too soft. But right now, I'm just thankful to have him by my side.

"Thank you," I murmur, my words slurring together as exhaustion takes over.

"Always, Grá," he whispers, pressing a kiss to my head. "I've always got you."

FOUR
BOZO

I'm beyond fucking pissed. That motherfucker should never have tried to hurt Grá. No one hurts her. I won't let them. I wish I could get her dad to stop, but that fucker weighs around three-hundred pounds and is over six-foot-three. The man's drunk as a skunk constantly.

"Where are you off to?" Dad snarls as I head toward the front door.

I'm planning on finding Anthony. That motherfucker had planned on raping Gráinne. I know he did. The fucker drugged her and tried dragging her to the bedroom. I'll be fucking damned if I let him get away with that shit. He's lucky I didn't kill him earlier, but Grá needed my help. Right now, she's fast asleep in my bed. Mam was already asleep when we came home and Dad was busy doing fuck knows what.

I pause at the door, my hand on the knob. "Out," I growl, not turning to face him.

"Out where?" Dad's voice is slurred, thick with alcohol. "It's the middle of the fucking night."

"None of your business," I snap, yanking the door open.

"Don't you take that tone with me, boy!" Dad roars, his chair scraping against the floor as he stands. "You live under my roof, you answer to me!"

I whirl around, rage boiling in my veins. "Answer to you? Like you answered to the fucking bottle all these years?"

That's something that Gráinne and I have in common. Both of our dads are drunken assholes who get violent whenever the wind blows. Thankfully for me, as I've gotten older, stronger, and bigger, his violent outbursts aren't as frequent. As for Grá, she's small—barely five-two. She's also timid and fragile. That motherfucker of a dad of hers is going to do some serious damage one of these days if he doesn't lay off hurting her.

Dad's face contorts with fury. He lurches forward, but his drunken state makes him clumsy, and I easily sidestep his grab.

"I'm going out," I repeat, my voice low and dangerous. "And when I get back, you'd better not have laid a finger on Grá. You understand me?"

Before he can respond, I'm out the door, slamming it behind me. The cool night air hits my face, but it does nothing to calm the fire in my chest. My mind races as I stalk down the street, fists clenched at my sides.

Anthony. That piece of shit. I can still see Grá's terrified face when I found them. I can still hear her slurred protests as he tried to lead her away. If I hadn't shown up when I did...

I shake my head, pushing the thought away. It doesn't matter now. What matters is making sure he never tries anything like that again. With anyone.

I know where he lives. It's not far from here, just a few blocks over. As I walk, I try to plan what I'll do when I get there. Part of me wants to burst in, fists flying. But I know that's not smart. I need to be careful, calculated. Like when I count cards for Dad.

The thought of those nights at the casino makes my stomach churn. How many times did I sit there, helping him cheat, while Mam worried at home? How many times did I let myself believe it was okay because we needed the money?

No more. After tonight, things are going to

change. I'll find a way to make money that doesn't involve breaking the law or putting Grá in danger. But first, I have to deal with Anthony.

I reach his street and slow my pace, scanning the houses. There's his, second from the end. A light is on in an upstairs window. Good. He's home.

As I approach the house, I force myself to take a deep breath. I need to be smart about this. No evidence, no witnesses. Just a clear message that he'll never forget.

I step onto his porch, my hand raised to knock. Whatever happens next, there's no going back. But for Grá, for her safety and peace of mind, I'll do whatever it takes.

My knuckles connect with the door, the sound echoing in the quiet night. I wait, my heart pounding, muscles tense. After what feels like an eternity, I hear footsteps approaching.

The door creaks open, and there he is. Anthony's eyes widen in surprise then narrow with suspicion. He's home alone. He'd been bragging all night about having the house to himself. His parents are gone for the week, away on vacation.

"What the fuck do you want?" he slurs, clearly still drunk from earlier.

I don't answer. Instead, I shove past him into the

house, slamming the door behind me. Before he can react, I've got him by the collar, pinning him against the wall.

"Listen carefully, you piece of shit," I growl, my face inches from his. "If you ever, EVER come near Gráinne again, I will end you. You understand?"

Anthony tries to struggle, but I'm stronger, fueled by rage and adrenaline. "Get off me, you psycho!" he spits.

I slam him against the wall again, harder this time. "Do. You. Understand?"

Fear flickers in his eyes. Good. That's what I want to see.

"Yeah, yeah, I get it," he mumbles. "Just let me go, man."

But I'm not done. I throw a punch, the sound crunching against his nose confirms that I've broken it. Anthony crumples to the floor, blood gushing from his nose. I stand over him, fists still clenched, breathing heavily.

"That's for drugging her," I snarl.

He tries to scramble away, but I grab him by the shirt and haul him up. My next punch lands squarely on his jaw, snapping his head back.

"And that's for trying to take advantage of her."

Anthony slumps against the wall, dazed and

bleeding. Part of me wants to keep going, to make him feel every ounce of fear and helplessness that Grá must have felt. But I force myself to stop. I've made my point. I know if I go further, I'll be the one who lands himself in trouble, and I've got Grá to think about right now.

I lean in close, my voice low and menacing. "If I ever hear about you trying anything like this again—with Grá or any other girl—I'll make sure you regret it for the rest of your life. Got it?"

He nods weakly, unable to speak through the blood and pain.

I step back, my hands shaking with adrenaline. "Clean yourself up," I mutter. "And remember—I'm watching you."

As I turn to leave, he calls out, "You're fucking crazy. You know that?"

I pause at the door, looking back at him. "Maybe," I say. "But I'm not the one who tries to rape unconscious girls."

The cool night air hits me as I start the walk home. My knuckles throb, and I know they'll be bruised tomorrow. How will I explain that to Grá? To Mam?

I shake my head, trying to clear my thoughts. One problem at a time. Right now, I need to get home, make sure Grá is okay, and figure out our next move. Because one thing's for certain—we can't keep living like this. Something has to change. She can't live in that house with her dad any longer. He's going to do something he'll regret and I'll end up killing the fucker.

As I approach my house, I see the living room light is still on. Dad's probably passed out in his chair by now. I take a deep breath, steeling myself for whatever comes next. No matter what, I'll protect Grá. And somehow, some way, we'll find a way out of this mess. We have to.

I quietly let myself in, relieved to find the living room empty. As I pass the kitchen, I hear a soft voice.

"Connor?"

I freeze. It's Gráinne. She's sitting at the kitchen table with a cup of tea in front of her. Her eyes are red-rimmed, her face pale.

"Hey," I say softly, moving to sit beside her. "You okay?"

She nods then shakes her head, tears welling up in her eyes. "I was so scared when I woke up and you were gone," she whispers.

Guilt washes over me. In my anger, I hadn't thought about how she'd feel waking up alone. "I'm sorry," I say, taking her hand. "I just... I had to take care of something."

She looks at me, her eyes searching my face. "Anthony?" she asks quietly.

I nod, not trusting myself to speak.

Gráinne squeezes my hand and gives me a soft smile. "Thank you."

I give her hand a gentle squeeze. "Always, Grá. I'll always protect you."

"I CAN'T BELIEVE THIS SHIT," I snap, glaring at my dad who's standing across the kitchen from me.

"Watch your mouth," he grunts. "Don't forget who the fuck you're talking to."

"Of course you sent her back," I growl, my anger paramount. I'm beyond angry. I woke up this morning to no Gráinne and Dad smirking. Grá's dad was here first thing this morning demanding that his daughter be returned home. Of course, my dad loved it and sent her packing.

"You'd better watch yourself, Connor. You wouldn't want anything to happen to your precious Gráinne now, would you?"

My blood runs cold at his words. I take a step

toward him, fists clenched. "What the hell is that supposed to mean?"

Dad smirks, leaning back in his chair. "Just that her old man seemed pretty upset this morning. Who knows what he might do if he gets it in his head that you're a bad influence on his little girl?"

"You bastard," I snarl. "You know what he does to her. How could you send her back there?"

"It's not our problem," Dad says dismissively. "Besides, we've got our own issues to deal with. Speaking of which, when are we hitting the casino again?"

I stare at him in disbelief. "Are you fucking kidding me? After everything that's happened, that's what you're worried about?"

"Watch your tone, boy," Dad warns, his eyes narrowing. "Don't forget who puts food on the table around here."

"Food on the table?" I laugh bitterly. "You mean the money I help you cheat for? The money that's tearing this family apart?"

Dad stands up suddenly, his chair scraping against the floor. "You ungrateful little shit," he growls. "After everything I've done for you—"

"Done for me?" I interrupt, my voice rising. "You mean dragging me into your illegal schemes? Using me to fuel your gambling addiction? Yeah, thanks a lot, Dad."

His face contorts with rage, and for a moment, I think he might hit me. But then he just shakes his head, disgust clear in his eyes. "Unless you want Lorcan to come after us. After all, we owe him twenty grand."

I bite back a curse. Fucking Dad. He's so fucking useless. He's leveled up from Blackjack to playing poker. Something he knows I'm good at. I learned by watching the games while he was gambling our money away. I actually watched good players play, learning their tells and how to play the game the right way.

The games are run by an organization called Na Cártaí Dubha, which means The Black Cards in English. Lorcan Black runs the organization and does so with an iron fist. No one messes with his games. If they do, they'll pay the price.

"The fuck have you done?" I hiss. "Seriously? What the fuck are you playing at?"

Dad's face twists into a sneer. "Watch your mouth, boy. I did what I had to do to keep us afloat. You think it's easy to provide for this family?"

"Providing?" I scoff. "You mean gambling away every cent we have and then some? Christ, Dad, twenty grand to Lorcan Black? Do you have a death wish? And you didn't provide jack shit for this family. That's me. I'm the one who's ensuring that we have a roof over our heads. I'm the one who's earning the money. Not you."

"Semantics," Dad mutters, not meeting my eyes. "I know what the fuck I'm doing. I just hit a bit of bad luck."

I run my hands through my hair, fighting the urge to scream. "Bad luck? Dad, there's no fucking way you've lost twenty grand playing just poker." He's stupid, fucking useless, but he's not that fucking bad. "What else?"

"Blackjack," he grunts. "We'll get that money back."

"*We?*" I hiss. "I'm not doing shit. You're the idiot who got us into this mess."

"You fucking are!" Dad roars, slamming his fist on the table. "I'm not an idiot!"

"Could've fooled me," I mutter.

Dad's eyes flash dangerously. "You watch yourself, boy. I'm still your father."

"Yeah? Then start acting like it!" I shout back. "A real father wouldn't put his family in danger like this. A real father wouldn't send an abused girl back to her tormentor. A real father—"

The punch comes out of nowhere, the sound echoing in the small kitchen. My cheek stings, and I taste blood where my teeth cut into my lip.

"That's enough," Dad growls, his voice low and dangerous. "You don't know the first thing about being a man, let alone a father. Now, you're going to help me get this money, or so help me God, I'll tell Lorcan exactly who's been helping me count cards all these years. How do you think he'd feel about that, huh? You've taken a good bit from his casino."

I stare at him, my blood running cold. He wouldn't. He couldn't. But the look in his eyes tells me he absolutely would. If he spills to Lorcan, there's no fucking way either of us would survive the night.

"You're bluffing," I say, but my voice wavers.

Dad smirks, knowing he's got me. "Want to test that theory? Go ahead, call my bluff. See what happens to you. To your precious Gráinne."

At the mention of Grá's name, something inside me snaps. Before I know what I'm doing, I've got Dad by the collar, slamming him against the wall.

"You leave her out of this," I snarl. "You hear me? You so much as breathe her name again, and I'll—"

"You'll what?" Dad challenges, his breath hot on my face. "Kill me? Go ahead. See how far that gets you with Lorcan."

I release him, stepping back. My hands are shaking. I clench them into fists to stop the trembling.

"Fine," I say through gritted teeth. "I'll help you, but fuck, you're no longer blood."

He grins, and it's triumphant and sadistic. "Never thought of you as such anyway," he grunts. "Fucking freak."

I'll kill him. If he dares touch Gráinne, or even set into motion something happening to her, I'm going to kill him.

FIVE
BOZO

Nine Years Ago
Aged 16

"I need you to be on your best behavior," Dad snarls as he grips my shirt in his fist, pushing me against the sitting room wall. "We need this money. I need this money. If I lose this, we're all dead," he spits, his eyes wild and filled with fear and hate.

That hatred is directed at me. He hates that I'm able to fight back now. I haven't always, but I learned that I needed to be able to protect myself. Not just for me but for Grá too.

I grab hold of his wrist and use all my power to

rip his hand from me. "What the fuck do you need?" I grunt, pushing him away from me.

He forgets that I'm no longer the small nine-year-old he could bully around to get his own way. No, I'm a lot bigger and smarter than that.

"Do the fucking job I tell ya, freak," he snaps. "You don't, and we're all fucked."

I laugh. He's a useless bastard. Always has been. He's a drunk, and a violent one at that. Not to mention, he loves to gamble, and most of the time he uses money that he doesn't have.

"You mean you are fucked, right?" I ask with a raised brow.

"Connor," Mam sighs. "Please, son, no arguing. Just one night."

She's getting worse. The cancer has ravaged her body, and over the past few months she's deteriorated a lot more than any of us had expected. She doesn't have much longer left.

"Fuck," I hiss as I turn back to my dad. "What do you need?"

The triumphant smirk on his face is enough to make me want to snap my fist into his jaw. But I refrain—barely. Mam doesn't need this shit. "You're playing a no-limit stake poker game in Palmerstown."

I raise a brow. "Oh? With what money? You're broke."

That motherfucking smirk of his grows wider. "That, my son, is where you come in. I know you've got money hidden. I finally found it." He reaches behind the sofa and pulls out the duffle bag that I know has about three-hundred-thousand Euro inside. That fucker, he's been searching through my room.

"Connor," Mam says quietly. "I'm sorry," she whispers. "But we need the money for the treatment."

I swallow hard. Christ, he's even got Mam in on his bullshit. We all know what the doctor said. The cancer is too far advanced. They doubt any treatment will work. And yet my dad is adamant on trying to push Mam into every fucking drug trial going, despite the fact that it's making her worse.

I clench my fists, feeling the rage boiling inside me. But I can't lose it, not now. Not with Mam watching, her eyes pleading. I fucking hate that look in her eyes; the sorrow, the pain, the hurt. She's been dealing with Dad for too fucking long.

"Fine," I growl through gritted teeth. "I'll play, but you're not coming."

Dad's face contorts with anger. "Now listen here, boy—"

"No, you listen," I cut him off, stepping closer. "We both know you'll piss all the money away before the first hand is even dealt."

He looks ready to explode, but Mam's weak voice stops him. "Let him do it, Craig. Connor's good with numbers. You know that."

Yeah, and that's what's gotten me into this shit. Dad's been using my brain since I was a young boy and he learned that I was good with numbers. When the doctors later told us that I have an eidetic memory, my father nearly jumped for joy. Dad's used me as much as he could. He's made millions off me and pissed it all away.

Dad's nostrils flare as he glares at me, but he knows he's beat. "Fine," he spits. "But you'd better not fuck this up."

I snatch the duffle bag from him. "I won't. Unlike you."

As I turn to leave, Mam catches my hand. Her skin is paper-thin, her bones jutting out. "Be careful, love," she whispers.

I squeeze her hand gently. "I will, Mam. Don't worry."

The drive to Palmerstown takes almost an hour. I

can't believe I'm doing this shit yet again. I thought as I got older, this shit would stop. But then again, I should have realized that my dad would never fix himself up. He's always going to be a bastard.

As I pull up to the address, I take a deep breath, steeling myself for what's to come. The building is a rundown warehouse on the outskirts of town. Perfect for an illegal high-stakes poker game.

I grab the duffle bag and make my way inside, nodding to the big, muscular bouncer at the door. The smell of smoke and whiskey hits me as I enter, along with the low murmur of voices and the clinking of chips.

I spot the table immediately—five men, all older, all with the look of seasoned gamblers. One chair sits empty, waiting for me. Damn, my dad sure knows how to set it up to take the money off the high rollers. All of them are watching me with narrowed eyes and barely concealed eagerness. They want to take my money and leave me broke. They're sorely mistaken if they think that's how tonight is going to end.

"Ah, you must be Connor," a man with slicked-back gray hair says as I approach. "Craig's boy, right? We've been expecting you."

I force a smile, taking my seat. "That's right. Hope I didn't keep you gentlemen waiting."

"Not at all," another man chimes in, eyeing me. "Though we were surprised when Craig said he was sending his son in his place. You sure you're up for this, kid?"

I don't respond to the condescending tone. Instead, I pull out a stack of cash from the duffle bag and set it on the table. "I'm here to play, not chat," I say coolly, meeting each of their gazes in turn. "Shall we begin?"

The dealer, a young woman with a stern face, nods and begins to shuffle the cards with practiced ease. She deals us all two cards each. Once done, she holds the deck in her hand and stares ahead, waiting for the guy with the slicked-back gray hair to act.

I watch each of them for the first few hands, analyzing their play, learning their tells, and once I've settled into the game, I know that I've got these guys on the ropes. I'll have the money Mam needs by the end of the night.

It doesn't take long before I start raking in the money. It's easy. These men are old school. They play their own way and don't like to change it up. It's really easy to find out when they have a good hand and when they don't. They're shit at bluffing, which means I'm able to make a fuck ton of money.

"Lucky bastard," one player mutters under his

breath as I rake in the biggest pot of the night. Almost six hundred thousand euro in one hand alone. I know that I'm close to a million for the evening.

I just smile, knowing it has nothing to do with luck. It's all about the numbers, the patterns, the tells. And I've been reading them all night.

"Last hand, gentlemen," the dealer announces and begins to deal the cards.

Once play comes around to me, I look down at my cards: a pair of kings. A strong hand but not unbeatable. I keep my face neutral as I glance around the table. The tension is palpable. Everyone knows this is their last chance to recoup their losses.

The first round of betting is conservative. No one wants to show their hand too early. I call, watching carefully as the flop is revealed: seven of hearts, jack of spades, three of clubs. Nothing that helps me, but nothing too threatening either. This flop is the perfect one for me, unless someone's sitting with a pair in their hand.

The man to my left, a balding man in his late fifties, bets aggressively. The next two players push their cards away, folding, leaving me, Baldy Guy, and Slick Hair left in the game. I call Baldy Guy's bet as my mind whirls with the possibilities that could happen when the turn is uncovered.

The turn card is revealed, showing the king of diamonds. I have three of a kind. It's a great hand. There's nothing right now that can beat me. Of course, that could change once the river hits. Baldy Guy bets again, even higher this time, causing Slick Hair to fold with a muttered curse. I reach for my chips, taking a few seconds to hesitate before raising his bet.

I can see the sweat beading on his forehead; the slight tremor in his hand as he reaches for his chips. He's bluffing. He's the type of man who doesn't like to lose, especially not to someone young. He's got nothing and he's trying to bully me out of the pot.

His eyes narrow on me as he re-raises me. I instantly call and watch as his eyes twitch at the move. He's nervous. Good.

The river card is dealt: ace of hearts. It doesn't change anything for me, but I see the man's shoulders relax just a fraction. I now know that he has an ace in his hand, meaning he's just paired the ace. He'll think he's got this in the bag.

Baldy Guy leans back in his chair, a smug smile playing at the corners of his mouth. He's confident now, thinking his pair of aces has saved him. He pushes a large stack of chips into the middle, his eyes challenging me.

"All in," he declares, his voice steady. Okay, so maybe he's got a little more than just a pair. Glancing down at the cards on the table, I look over them. He's got at best, two pairs.

The other players at the table lean forward, all of them eager to watch this play out. I can feel their eyes on me, waiting to see what I'll do. I take a deep breath, keeping my face impassive as I consider my options.

I know I have him beat. My three kings are stronger than his two pairs. But there's more at stake here than just this hand. I need to maximize my winnings, to ensure I have enough for Mam's treatment and to finally get the fuck away from Dad when the time comes.

I meet the man's gaze, letting a flicker of uncertainty cross my face. "That's a hefty bet," I say, my voice purposefully hesitant. I've sat at card tables since I was seven years old. I've played some of the best players in the world. I know what it takes to make people think I'm hesitant about the hand.

He grins, thinking he's got me on the ropes. "Too rich for your blood, kid?"

I pretend to wrestle with the decision, then slowly push my chips forward. "I call."

The man's grin widens as he flips over his cards, revealing the ace of spades to go with the ace on the board. "Two pairs, aces and jacks," he announces triumphantly.

I nod, keeping my expression neutral. "Nice hand," I say, then I slowly turn over my kings.

The man's triumphant grin falters, then crumbles entirely as he sees my cards.

"Three kings," I announce, watching as the realization of his defeat washes over him.

The table erupts in a cacophony of groans and low whistles.

"Three of a kind, kings. Pot goes to the young gentleman," the dealer announces as she pushes the chips toward me.

As I start to rake in the massive pile of chips, Baldy Guy slams his fist on the table. "You little shit!" he snarls. "You set me up!"

I meet his gaze coolly. "I played the hand I was dealt, same as you." I'm more than used to assholes getting rowdy because they lost. Don't put it on me because you couldn't fold when you should have. You should never bet money you're not able to lose.

Slick Hair puts a hand on Baldy Guy's shoulder. "Easy, Tom. The kid played fair and square."

Tom shrugs off the hand, his face red with anger and humiliation. "Bullshit! No one's that lucky!"

I start packing up my winnings, keeping one eye on Tom. "It's not about luck," I say, zipping up the duffle bag now heavy with cash. "It's about knowing when to fold." I'm being antagonizing on purpose. The man's been a fucking prick since the moment I sat down.

Tom lunges across the table, his hand reaching for my collar. But before he can grab me, two burly security guards materialize, restraining him.

"That's enough." The new voice cuts through the commotion. The room falls silent as a tall, imposing man steps out of the shadows. I recognize him instantly—Lorcan Black, the man behind Na Cártaí Dubha.

Black's cold eyes sweep over the scene, lingering on Tom, who's still being restrained by the guards. "You know the rules, gentlemen. No fighting, no accusations. What happens at the table stays at the table."

He turns to me, his gaze appraising. "Impressive play, young man. Your father said you were good, but I didn't expect this."

I nod respectfully but say nothing. The less said to a man like Black, the better.

"Tom," Black continues, his voice deceptively soft, "I suggest you leave now. Your debt will be settled by the end of the week, or we'll have a problem. Understood?"

Tom's face pales, the fight draining out of him. He nods jerkily, and the guards release him. He stumbles out without another word, leaving a tense silence in his wake.

Black turns back to me. "Connor, isn't it? A word, if you please."

It's not a request. I follow him to a quiet corner of the room, my grip tightening on the duffle bag.

"Your old man's in deep," Black says without preamble. "Deeper than you know. This win tonight? It's barely scratched the surface of what he owes."

I feel my stomach drop. Of course. Of fucking course. "How much?" I ask, my voice tight.

Black's eyes are cold, calculating. "Let's just say, even if you emptied that bag right now, it wouldn't cover half of it."

I clench my jaw, fury bubbling up inside me. That bastard. That lying, gambling bastard. "I'm not responsible for my father's debts," I say, fighting to keep my voice steady.

Black's eyes narrow, but there's a hint of amusement in his voice when he says, "No, you're not. But you are responsible for your own choices. And right now, you have a choice to make."

I tense, ready for whatever threat is coming. But Black surprises me.

He leans in closer, his voice low. "You've got talent, kid. Real talent. The kind that could make a man very rich or very dead, depending on how he uses it."

I don't like where this is going. "What are you suggesting?"

"Work for me," Black says bluntly. "Use that brain of yours to help run my games. In return, I'll wipe your father's debt clean. You'll be free of him, and your mother will get the care she needs."

I blink, caught off guard. "How do you know my mam?"

He smirks. "I know everything about every single person who comes to my tables, Connor."

I clench my teeth. Off course he does. I should have realized. "What kind of job?"

"Nothing illegal, if that's what you're worried about," Black says with a wry smile. "I run high-stake games all over Europe. I need someone who can play, who can spot cheaters, who understands the numbers. Someone like you."

My mind races. It's a way out, a chance to pay off Dad's debts and maybe even save enough for Mam's treatments. But it's dangerous. Getting involved with men like Black rarely ends well.

"I need time to think," I say carefully.

Black nods. "You have forty-eight hours. After that, your father's debt becomes due in full." He hands me a business card. "Call this number when you've decided."

As I leave the warehouse, my head spinning, I realize I'm at a crossroads. I can walk away and leave Dad to face the consequences of his actions, or I can dive deeper into this world, hoping to swim rather than sink.

Fuck, I already know the answer to that question. I'm going to dive as deep as I can get. I have to, for Mam and for Gráinne. If I make the money needed, I can ensure that she can escape her life too.

SIX
GRÁINNE

Six Years Ago
Age Seventeen

My ribs are smarting. They have been for the past two weeks. God, my dad really is a bastard. The sooner I turn eighteen the better. I can't wait to get out of the house. Go somewhere where he can get to me.

"Get me a drink, bitch," Dad snarls, his words slurred. He's been drunk as a skunk for the past ten years. Hell, even longer. He's a sorry bastard who gets drunk to block the pain and the memories. It's a way to mask his guilt. Ten years ago, Dad was driving home from my aunt's wedding, and Mam was in the front passenger's seat. I've only come to find out that Dad crashed the car into a wall. He'd had too much to drink. Mam never survived the crash. She died on impact. He admitted it to me whilst drunk a week ago and I'm still struggling to come to terms with it.

That's something he hasn't been able to live with, and he has been a drunken asshole ever since.

I shuffle to the kitchen, wincing with each step. The fridge light flickers as I grab a can of beer. I realize that he's forgotten to order food shopping. There's nothing in here, not even a beer. This is his last one, which means he's going to get even angrier.

"Hurry up!" he bellows from the living room.

My hands shake as I pop the tab, foam spilling over onto my fingers.

I take a deep breath, steeling myself. As I round the corner, I see him sprawled on the couch, eyes focused on the TV, which is blaring as he watches some game show. His eyes are bloodshot. I can barely see any white.

"Here," I mutter, thrusting the can at him.

He snatches it, sloshing beer onto the already-stained carpet. "Took you long enough," he grumbles.

I turn to leave, but his meaty hand clamps onto my wrist. "Where do you think you're going?"

My heart races. "I-I have homework," I stammer.

He yanks me closer, his boozy breath hot on my face. "Sit down and watch TV with your old man."

I sink onto the edge of the couch, as far from him as possible. Just a few more months, I remind myself. Just a few more months, and I'll be free.

I'm going to become a doctor. I want to help people, like no one has been able to help me.

Dad grunts and curses at the contestants whenever they get a question wrong, not that he's gotten any right. I sit rigid, barely breathing, hoping he'll forget I'm here.

My mind wanders to the college applications hidden under my mattress. I've been working on them in secret, staying late at the library to use their computers. Ms. Johnson, my guidance counselor, has been helping me look for scholarships. She has no idea how bad things are at home. Hell, no one does, not even Connor.

My best friend is the best man I know. His mam died last year, and he did what he always wanted to do. He escaped his father—something I want to do too, but until I hit eighteen, I can't, especially as I have no money and nowhere to go. Connor's been gone for months, working for Lorcan Black. He's paid off his dad's debt and is currently earning money as he plays for Lorcan. I don't begrudge him his happiness. He's finally got what he wanted, and I'm so proud that he's done it. But I miss him.

I'm pulled from my thoughts as Dad's empty can clatters to the floor. "Get me another," he demands, not even looking at me.

I hesitate, knowing what's coming. "That was the last one," I say softly.

His bloodshot eyes snap to me, narrowing dangerously. "What did you say?"

"There's no more beer," I repeat, my voice trembling. "You forgot to buy more."

He lurches to his feet, swaying slightly. "You useless piece of shit," he snarls. "You should've reminded me!"

I scramble backwards, but I'm not fast enough. His fist connects with my jaw, sending me sprawling. Pain explodes through my face as I taste blood.

"I'm sorry," I whimper, curling into a ball as he looms over me. "I'm sorry. I'll go get some now."

He kicks me in the ribs, right where they're already bruised. I gasp, tears springing to my eyes as white-hot pain lances through me.

"Damn right you will," he growls. "And don't you dare come back without my beer, or you'll really be sorry."

I struggle to my feet, clutching my side. The room spins as I stumble to the door, fumbling for my shoes. I can feel his eyes boring into my back as I slip out into the chilly night air.

This late at night, the nearest convenience store is almost a mile away. I start walking, each step sending jolts of pain through my body.

As I trudge along the dimly lit footpath, I imagine what it would be like to just keep walking; to never go back to that house; to disappear into the night and start a new life somewhere else. But I know it's just a fantasy. I have nowhere to go, no money, no one to turn to. It would be useless for me to run. I'd only end up on the streets. So right now, it's better the devil you know.

The neon lights of the store come into view. I pause outside, taking a deep breath to compose myself. The bell jingles as I push open the door. The bored-looking cashier barely glances up from his phone.

I make my way to the fridges at the back, grabbing a six-pack of the cheap beer Dad likes. As I head to the register, I pray that the cashier doesn't ask for ID. I'm not old enough to buy this, but I need to purchase it. If I don't... I swallow hard.

God, no, don't think about what could happen. Not now, I tell myself.

Thankfully, the cashier doesn't even glance at me as he rings up the beer. I quickly pay and get the hell out of there.

My cell rings and I answer it as I begin to walk back home. "Hello?" I answer.

"Guess where I am?" My spirits are instantly lifted when I hear Connor's voice.

"Where?" I ask, unable to keep the smile off my face. God, it's so good to hear his voice.

"Home," he replies simply, and my heart speeds up. "Where are you?"

I sigh. "Dad needed beer. I'm walking home. I'm glad you're home though. It's been too long."

"Wait, what? You're out getting beer at this time of night?" Connor's voice is laced with anger and concern. "Are you okay?"

I hesitate, not wanting to worry him. If he finds out what's really happening, he'll lose his mind. "Yeah, I'm fine. You know how he gets."

There's a long pause. "I'm coming to get you. Where are you exactly?"

"No, Con, it's okay. I'm almost home anyway," I lie, my pace quickening despite the pain in my side.

"Bullshit," he says flatly. "I know you, and I know

that tone. Something's wrong. Just tell me where you are."

I sigh, knowing he won't let this go. I quickly give him the address.

"Stay there. I'm on my way."

Before I can protest, he hangs up. I slow my pace, torn between relief at seeing my best friend and dread at what Dad will do if I'm not back soon.

Ten minutes later, headlights appear in the distance. Connor's brand new SUV pulls up beside me, and he leans across to open the passenger door.

"Get in," he says, his eyes scanning me with worry.

I slide into the seat, wincing as the movement jars my ribs. Connor notices, his jaw tightening. I pull on my seatbelt and breathe a sigh of relief that he's here.

"What happened?" he asks quietly as he pulls away from the curb.

"Nothing," I mutter, staring out the window. "Just tripped."

Connor scoffs, his knuckles white on the steering wheel. "Don't lie to me, Grá. I know you better than that."

I remain silent, unsure what to say. Part of me wants to tell him everything, to finally let someone know the hell I've been living in since he's been gone. But another part of me is terrified of what might happen if I do.

"Look," Connor says softly, "I know things have been rough since your ma died. Why haven't you told me that he's gotten worse? You should have told me, Grá. You could have stayed at my place."

I turn to look at him, really look at him for the first time. He's changed in the months he's been gone. There's a hardness to his eyes that wasn't there before, a confidence in the set of his shoulders. But underneath it all, I can still see my best friend.

"It's not that simple," I whisper, my voice cracking. "I'm not eighteen yet. I can't just leave."

Connor's eyes flash with anger. "Like hell you can't. We'll figure something out. I'm not letting you go back there."

As we approach my street, panic rises in my chest. "Con, you have to take me home. If I don't bring him the beer—"

He cuts me off. "No way. You're coming with me. We'll deal with your dad later."

I shake my head, my entire body trembling. "Please," I whimper. "God, Con, please. I need to go home."

He watches me. "Fuck," he snarls. "Fine, but I'm

coming in too. I'm not leaving you alone with that piece of shit."

Connor pulls up in front of my house, his jaw clenched tight. I can see the tension radiating off him as he kills the engine.

"You don't have to do this," I say softly, clutching the six-pack to my chest like a shield.

He turns to me, his eyes blazing with determination. "Yes, I do. I'm not leaving you alone with him again."

We get out of the car, Connor staying close to my side as we approach the front door. My hand shakes as I reach for the knob, dreading what awaits us inside.

The living room is dark except for the flickering light of the TV. Dad is sprawled on the couch, snoring loudly. Empty cans litter the floor around him.

I breathe a sigh of relief. Maybe we can just slip past him...

But as I take a step forward, my foot catches on an empty can. It skitters across the floor with a loud clatter.

Dad's eyes snap open. He lurches to his feet, swaying dangerously. "Where the hell have you been?" he slurs, stumbling toward us.

I shrink back instinctively, but Connor steps in front of me. "Back off," he growls, his voice low and dangerous.

Dad's bloodshot eyes narrow as he focuses on Connor. "What the fuck are you doing back?" he slurs.

"You're lucky your daughter hasn't called me before now. You touch her again, Joe, and we're going to have a bigger problem than we already do. I'm not letting you hurt Grá again," Connor says, his fists clenched at his sides. He's geared up for a fight, but I don't want anything to happen to him, and stupidly, I don't want my dad to get hurt either.

Dad's face contorts with rage. "You little shit," he snarls, lunging forward. But his drunken state makes him clumsy, and Connor easily sidesteps him.

"Grá, go pack a bag," Connor says, his eyes never leaving my father. "You're not staying here tonight."

I hesitate, torn between fear of my father's wrath and the desperate desire to escape. Dad turns his furious gaze on me. "You're not going anywhere," he growls.

Connor steps between us again. "Yes, she is. And if you try to stop her, I'll call the cops. How do you think they'll react to seeing those bruises?"

Dad's face pales slightly, but his anger doesn't

subside. "You can't take her," he spits. "She's my daughter."

"Some dad you are," Connor retorts, his voice dripping with disgust. "Grá, go. Now."

I don't wait for another word. I dart past them, racing up the stairs to my room, ignoring the pain that radiates throughout my body. With shaking hands, I grab a duffel bag and start shoving clothes into it. I can hear muffled shouting from downstairs, but I try to block it out.

As I'm zipping up the bag, I hear a crash followed by a pained grunt. My heart leaps into my throat. I rush back downstairs to find Connor standing over my father, who's sprawled on the floor, clutching his jaw.

"Let's go," Connor says firmly, grabbing my arm and steering me toward the door. I cast one last glance at my father, a mixture of fear and pity churning in my stomach.

As we step out into the darkness, I hear my dad's slurred voice behind us. "You'll be back," he calls out. "You've got nowhere else to go."

Connor's grip on my arm tightens as he leads me to his car. "Don't listen to him," he mutters. "You're never going back there."

We drive in silence for a while, the streetlights

casting intermittent shadows across Connor's face. I can see the tension in his jaw; his white-knuckled grip on the steering wheel.

"Where are we going?" I finally ask, my voice barely above a whisper.

Connor glances at me, his expression softening slightly. "My place. It's safe there."

I nod, not trusting myself to speak. The adrenaline is starting to wear off, and the pain in my ribs is becoming more pronounced. I shift in my seat, trying to find a comfortable position.

Connor notices my pain. "We should get you checked out," he says, concern evident in his voice. "Those ribs could be broken."

I shake my head vehemently. "No hospitals," I insist. "They'll ask questions."

He sighs but doesn't argue. "I know someone who'll help you be seen without questions."

I close my eyes, knowing there's no point in arguing.

"Hey, Grá," Connor says softly, gently pushing me awake. "We're here."

I blink awake. "Where are we?"

"Jerry Houlihan's home," he says nonchalantly.

My eyes widen at his words. "You're not serious?" I hiss. "Jerry Houlihan?"

"I know what you think, Grá. Trust me, I know. But Jer's not the man you think he is. Trust me."

I grit my teeth and nod. There's nothing I can do right now. We're here.

Jerry Houlihan is the head of the Houlihan Gang here in Ireland. The man is a cold-blooded killer, not to mention one of the biggest drug dealers in the country.

Connor helps me out of the car, his arm gentle around my waist as we approach the imposing mansion. My heart races as we reach the huge red front door. Connor knocks, and moments later it swings open to reveal a burly man with a shaved head.

He nods at Connor. "Boss is expecting you," he grunts, stepping aside to let us in.

The opulent interior takes my breath away. It's huge. There's glass everywhere, paintings hanging on the walls, and sculptures dotted around the place. It's a far cry from the dingy house I've been calling home.

We're led to a study where a man sits behind an enormous mahogany desk. Jerry Houlihan looks every bit the crime boss—expensive suit, gold rings on his fingers, an air of danger about him. But when he sees us, his face breaks into a warm smile.

"Connor," he says, rising to clasp Connor's hand. "And this must be the famous Grá I've heard so much about."

I'm too stunned to speak. Connor squeezes my shoulder reassuringly. "Jer, we need your help. Grá's been hurt. Can you get Doc Murphy to take a look at her?"

Jerry's expression darkens as he takes in my bruised face. "Of course. I'll call him right away." He picks up a phone on his desk. "Murphy? Get over here now. And bring your medical bag."

As we wait for the doctor, Jerry insists I sit in a plush armchair. Connor hovers nearby, his eyes constantly darting to me with concern.

"Can I get you anything, loveen?" Jerry asks, his voice surprisingly gentle. "Water? Tea?"

I shake my head, still too overwhelmed to speak. The reality of the situation is starting to hit me. I'm sitting in the home of one of Ireland's most notorious gangsters, waiting for a doctor to treat injuries inflicted by my own father.

How did my life come to this?

A few minutes later, there's a knock at the door. An older man with salt-and-pepper hair enters, carrying a black medical bag.

"This is Doc Murphy," Jerry introduces. "He'll take good care of you, Grá."

The doctor's eyes are kind as he approaches me. "Let's have a look at you, shall we?"

Connor moves to leave the room, but I grab his hand. "Stay," I whisper. He nods, squeezing my hand gently.

Dr. Murphy's examination is thorough but gentle. He frowns as he probes my ribs, causing me to wince.

"Two cracked ribs," he announces. "And some nasty bruising. Nothing life-threatening, but you'll need to take it easy for a few weeks."

He turns to Jerry. "She needs rest and pain management. I'll leave some medication, but she should be monitored for the next twenty-four hours."

Jerry nods solemnly. "She can stay here as long as she needs. I'll have a room prepared."

I open my mouth to protest, but Connor squeezes my hand, silencing me. "Thanks, Jer," he says. "We really appreciate it."

Dr. Murphy hands Jerry a bottle of pills. "For the pain," he explains. "Two every four hours. And make sure she gets plenty of rest."

As the doctor packs up his bag, I take two of the

pain pills as Jerry turns to me. "You're safe here, Gráinne. No one will hurt you under my roof."

I nod, unable to find words. The events of the night are catching up with me, and exhaustion is setting in.

Connor helps me to my feet. "Let's get you to bed," he says softly.

Jerry leads us upstairs to a guest room that's bigger than my entire house. The bed looks so soft, and I sink into it gratefully.

"I'll be right next door if you need anything," Connor says, tucking the blankets around me.

As he turns to leave, I grab his wrist. "Con," I whisper. "Thank you. For everything."

He gives me a sad, gentle smile. "Get some rest, Grá. We'll figure everything out in the morning."

As the door closes behind him, I'm left alone with my thoughts. The pain medication is starting to kick in, dulling the ache in my ribs and making my eyelids heavy. I drift off to sleep, my mind swirling with questions about what the future holds.

I AWAKE to sunlight streaming through the curtains. For a moment, I'm disoriented, not recognizing my surroundings. Then everything that happened last night comes rushing back.

I sit up gingerly, wincing at the pain in my ribs. There's a soft knock at the door.

"Come in," I call out.

Connor enters, carrying a tray laden with food. "Morning," he says softly. "How are you feeling?"

"Like I've been hit by a truck," I admit, managing a weak smile.

He sets the tray on the bedside table and sits on the edge of the bed. "Jer sent up some breakfast. You should try to eat something."

I nod, suddenly realizing how hungry I am. As I pick at the toast and eggs, Connor watches me intently.

"We need to talk about what happens next," he says finally.

I swallow hard, setting down my fork. "I can't go back there, Con. I just can't."

He nods. "You won't have to. But we need to figure out a plan. You're still underage, and your dad could cause trouble if he wanted to."

"What are my options?" I ask, fear creeping into my voice.

Connor runs a hand through his hair. "Well, Jer's offered to let you stay here as long as you need.

He's got connections, so your dad won't go against him."

I stare at him, hardly believing my ears. "And what does he want in return?" I ask. I'm not stupid; people like Jerry Houlihan don't do anything for free.

He grins. "Always so trusting," he quips. "Jerry has a proposition for you," he says. "He wants to pay for your school, for you to become a doctor, and in return, whenever he calls you, you'll come help him. No questions asked."

I blink, trying to process Connor's words. "He wants to pay for my education? And all I have to do is help him sometimes?"

Connor nods, his expression serious. "Look, I know it sounds too good to be true. But Jer's not what you think. He takes care of his own."

I chew my lip, considering. The offer is tempting; a chance to escape my father and to pursue my dream of becoming a doctor. But at what cost?

"What kind of help would I be expected to provide?" I ask cautiously.

Connor sighs. "Honestly? Probably patching up his men when they can't go to a hospital. Maybe some discreet house calls like Dr. Murphy did last night with you. Nothing illegal, Grá. He knows you want to be a doctor to help people. He won't ask you to compromise that."

I nod slowly, still processing. "And what about you, Con? How did you get mixed up in all this?"

He grins. "Nothing nefarious, Grá. I've met Jer a few times at poker tables. I helped him out a time or two, and I knew that he'd help me if the time came, which it did last night.

I reach out and take his hand, giving it a grateful squeeze. "Thank you," I whisper, so fucking grateful that he came home and came back to me.

"So, what do you say to Jer's offer?"

I take a deep breath. I'm unsure if I'm making the right choice or not, but it's the one that feels right to me. "Yes," I say, my voice a little hesitant. "I'm saying yes."

I really hope I've made the right decision.

SEVEN
BOZO

Five and a Half Years Ago

As I step out of the shower, I hear my cell ring. I wrap a towel around my waist and move toward the bedroom, where my phone is lying on the bed. I'm hoping it's Grá calling. Tomorrow is her eighteenth birthday. Instead, I see it's Lorcan Black calling.

What the hell? Why is he calling? "Hello?"

"Connor," he says. There's anger in his voice, which makes my blood run cold. "We've got a problem."

I raise a brow. The fuck? "We?" I ask, wondering when anything I did became a 'we' with him.

"Yes, we. Your dad's a fucking menace and today he's pushed me too fucking far."

I close my eyes. "What the fuck has he done?" I knew this day was coming. It was only going to be a matter of time before my dad pushed someone too far and ended up getting himself killed.

Lorcan's voice is cold and menacing. He's just as done with Dad's shit as I am. "Your old man tried to pull a fast one on me. Thought he could cheat at my tables and get away with it. He's sitting in my office right now, bleeding all over my fucking carpet."

"Is he...?" Not that I'd give a fuck if he was or not.

"He's alive. For now." Lorcan pauses, letting the threat hang in the air. "But that depends on you, Connor."

I frown. What the hell is going on? "What do you mean?"

"Tonight, your father has made it clear that he's willing to put his debt on you and Gráinne."

"That's impossible," I hiss, my anger rising through my body. "Grá has nothing, not one fucking thing, to do with that prick."

Lorcan chuckles darkly. "Oh, I know that, but your father has been very vocal this evening while at the tables about Grá being someone who'll pay his debt off."

Fuck. That bastard. I'm going to fucking kill him.

"It just so happened that Jerry Houlihan was sitting at the tables tonight," Lorcan continues. "I can hazard a guess that you know how he feels about this shit."

"Oh yeah. Jer's probably about ready to lose his mind. Am I right?"

"Yep, he's beyond pissed. He let it be known that if anyone comes after Grá, they'll have to deal with him. Of course, your father wasn't happy about that and started yelling about how much of a whore she is."

My blood turns to ice. "I'm going to fucking kill him," I growl. No one calls Grá a whore. Fucking prick.

"Then I suggest you get your ass down here." The line goes dead.

I stand there, phone in hand, trying to breathe through my rage. I need to sort this shit out. My fucking dad... I should have known he wouldn't slink away quietly. It's been fucking years since I last saw him.

I dress quickly, my anger still coursing through my body. My mind is reeling. I have no doubt that Jer's about to lose his shit. I wonder who made my dad bleed, Jer or Lorcan?

It takes me forty minutes to get to the casino. As I pull into the casino parking lot, my mind is racing. What the hell am I walking into? How bad is this situation really? And most importantly, how the fuck am I going to get Grá out of this mess?

I take a deep breath, trying to calm my nerves. I can't go in there looking like I'm about to lose it. I need to be cool, collected. I need to think.

The casino is buzzing with its usual nighttime crowd, but there's an undercurrent of tension in the air. A few regulars give me wary looks as I make my way through the main floor. They know who I am, who my father is. Word travels fast in places like this.

I spot Lorcan's right-hand man, Declan, standing near the entrance to the private rooms. He nods at me, his face grim.

"He's waiting for you," Declan says, jerking his head toward the back. "It's not pretty in there, Connor. Brace yourself."

I nod, steeling myself as I follow him down the hallway. The sound of raised voices grows louder as we approach Lorcan's office. I recognize Jerry Houlihan's booming voice, thick with rage.

"I'll fucking kill him myself if he so much as looks at her again!" Jerry roars.

Declan pushes open the door, and the scene inside makes me freeze.

My father is slumped in a chair, his face a bloody mess. Jerry looms over him, fists clenched, looking ready to deliver another beating. Lorcan sits behind his desk, cool as ever, but I can see the anger simmering in his eyes.

"Ah, Connor," Lorcan says, his voice deceptively calm. "So good of you to join us."

Jerry whirls around, his eyes locking onto mine. "Did you know about this?" he demands. "Did you know what this piece of shit was planning?"

I glare at the fucker. "Jerry, do you think if I knew, he'd be alive?"

Jerry's eyes narrow on my dad, his look of disgust so clear to see. He steps back, giving me space to approach my father.

I look down at the pathetic figure before me. My father, once so intimidating, now looks small and broken. He raises his head, his swollen eyes meeting mine. "Connor," he slurs, blood trickling from his split lip. "You gotta help me, son. These guys, they're gonna kill me."

I feel nothing but disgust as I look at him. "You brought this on yourself," I say coldly. "And don't you dare call me son."

I turn to Lorcan, ignoring my father's whimpers. "What's next?"

Lorcan grins. "It's up to you. I thought you'd be the one who would want to end him. After all, he's the one who made your life fucking hell growing up."

It wasn't exactly a secret that my dad was an asshole, especially as he used me to get money. Something that everyone in the casino scene witnessed.

I turn to my father. "You tried to bring Gráinne into your shit?"

My father coughs, spitting blood onto the already stained carpet. "She's a rich bitch now that Jerry's taken her in," he slurs, and the insinuation in his voice pisses me the fuck off. There's no way that anyone genuinely believes that Jer and Grá are anything but platonic. Sick fucker. "I figured she could spare some cash for your old man."

The rage I've been trying to contain explodes. Before I know it, my fist connects with his jaw, sending him sprawling to the floor. "You don't ever get to talk about her," I snarl. "You don't even get to think about her."

Jerry steps forward, a hand on my shoulder. "Easy, Connor. You need to make sure this is what you want to do. It's not something you can ever come back from."

I'm more than certain about what I want to do. My dad dies tonight, and at my own hands. I've let his shit go on for too fucking long already. But him trying to make Grá's life hell is something I'll never allow.

"How much does he owe?" I ask.

Lorcan raises an eyebrow. "Are you planning on paying his debt, Connor?"

I shake my head. "No. I want to know how deep of a hole this bastard has dug himself into."

"Two hundred grand," Lorcan says casually, as if discussing the weather.

I whistle low. That's a hell of a lot more than I expected. "And how, exactly, did he think Grá was going to pay that?"

My father, still on the floor, starts to mumble something, but Jerry silences him with a swift kick to the ribs.

Lorcan leans forward, his eyes cold. "He seemed to think she'd be willing to work it off—in one of my establishments."

The implication hangs heavy in the air. I feel sick to my stomach. We all know that Lorcan's women are not only waitresses and dealers. It goes a fuck of a lot more sinister than that. Most nights, the women are being paid to do whatever the hell Lorcan's high-rollers want them to do, which most of the time includes being fucked. "You didn't seriously consider—"

"Of course not," Lorcan cuts me off. "I may be a lot of things, Connor, but I don't fuck with my guys' women. You have been one of my guys for years, one of my most loyal ones. I wouldn't do that. Not to mention, she's Jer's fucking family."

I nod, relieved but still seething with anger. "So, what now?"

Lorcan leans back in his chair, studying me. "That's up to you, Connor. Your father's debt is substantial, but it's not just about the money anymore. He's crossed a line, threatened one of our own. That can't go unanswered."

I look down at my father, pathetic and cowering on the floor. I've already made my decision.

"I'll take care of it," I say, my voice steady. "But not here. I don't want this mess on your hands, Lorcan."

Lorcan nods, a hint of respect in his eyes. "Fair enough. Declan will help you get him out of here discreetly. What happens after that is your business."

Jerry steps forward, his face grim. "I'm coming

with you, Connor. This involves Grá, and that makes it my business too."

I don't argue. Having Jerry there might actually make this easier.

Declan and another of Lorcan's men help us get my father into the back of my car. He's barely conscious now, mumbling incoherently.

We drive out of the city, toward the docks, where Jer has a portacabin.

"You sure about this, Connor? There's no going back," Jer asks.

I grip the steering wheel tighter. "He threatened Grá, Jer. He was willing to sell her to pay off his debts. There's no forgiving that."

Jerry nods, his expression hardening. "You're right. Bastard deserves what's coming to him."

We pull up to the docks, and Jer directs me toward the portacabin. Once parked up, I drag my father out of the car, forcing him to his knees at the edge of the dock.

"Connor, please," he whimpers, finally seeming to understand the gravity of his situation. "I'm your father."

I look down at him, feeling nothing but cold contempt. "You stopped being my father a long time ago. And you sealed your fate when you threatened Grá."

Jer hands me a gun. I don't hesitate in taking it, the weight of it heavy in my hand. Jerry stands beside me, a silent witness.

"Any last words?" I ask, not really giving a fuck what he says.

My father opens his mouth, but before he can speak, I pull the trigger. The sound echoes across the docks, and his body slumps forward.

Jerry moves quickly, grabbing two cinder blocks from nearby and tying them to my father's limbs. Once it's done, he uses his foot and kicks my dad over the edge and into the water. Water splashes as he sinks down into the river.

"It's done," Jerry says quietly. "Let's get out of here."

As we drive back to the city, I feel a weight lift off my shoulders. My father is gone, and with him, the constant bullshit he put me through is finished. I'm relieved, so fucking relieved that he's gone and I won't ever have to listen to his fucking bullshit ever again.

I WATCH as she stumbles slightly toward me, a big, goofy grin on her face. She's unbelievably happy and I know it's because she's free. I don't think I've ever seen Gráinne so carefree and at ease.

She's eighteen and looks drop dead gorgeous. She's wearing a tight-fitted light pink dress and matching heels. I catch Grá as she stumbles into my arms, her laughter infectious. The party around us is in full swing, music pulsing through the air. Jer really went all out for her eighteenth birthday.

"Connor!" she exclaims, her eyes bright with joy and maybe a bit too much champagne. "You made it!"

I can't help but smile back at her. "Wouldn't miss it for the world, Sunshine."

She beams at the endearment, wrapping her arms around my neck. "Dance with me?"

How could I refuse? I let her pull me onto the makeshift dance floor, where other party goers are swaying to the music. Grá moves with ease, her body close to mine, and I'm hyper-aware of every point of contact between us.

There's no doubt in my mind—never has been—that Grá is the only woman I have ever loved and will ever love. But what I did last night is something that can't be brushed over. Jer was right, killing a man will change you. It'll shape you into someone you don't recognize, and that's me right now. Grá deserves everything in life. She deserves pure love and happiness. I'd taint that. She's had enough violence in her life. I won't ever bring that to her again.

"You okay?" Grá asks, noticing my distraction. "You seem a million miles away."

I pull her closer, breathing in her scent. "I'm right here," I assure her. "Just thinking about how far you've come."

She blushes, ducking her head. "I have you to thank for that," she whispers. "I don't know what I'd do without you."

"You're smart as hell, Grá. You'd have made your way, no matter what."

"I hate your dad, Con. I hate that he's made you into this man who doesn't believe his worth. I hate that he doesn't understand just how truly amazing, handsome, and brilliant you are."

Christ, she's fucking killing me. I know that she wants me. I've known for a while. But I'd never go there. I can't. She's too precious, too damn good for me.

I swallow hard, trying to keep my emotions in check. "Grá, you don't know what you're saying. I'm not—"

"Don't," she interrupts, her eyes flashing with determination. "Don't you dare try to brush this off, Connor. I know exactly what I'm saying."

She pulls back slightly, her hands moving to cup my face. The touch sends electricity through my body.

"I've known you for years," she continues, her voice low and intense. "I've seen you at your best and your worst. And I'm telling you, Connor, that you are the best man I know."

I close my eyes, overwhelmed by her words and the feelings they stir in me. "Grá, there are things about me... things I've done..."

"I don't care," she says fiercely. "Whatever it is, whatever you've done, it doesn't change what I know."

My eyes snap open, meeting hers. "You're too damn trusting. Too damn sweet."

She shrugs. "That may be so, but it doesn't change the fact that you're an amazing man, Connor. The very best there is."

"Grá," I start, my voice rough with emotion. "You don't know what that is. I'm not the man you think I am."

She shakes her head, a small smile playing on her lips. "You're exactly the man I think you are. Strong, loyal, protective. And yes, sometimes dangerous. But I'm not some delicate flower, Connor. I can handle it."

I'm torn between the overwhelming desire to pull her close and kiss her senseless, and the equally strong urge to push her away, to protect her from the darkness that surrounds me.

Grá steps closer. "You are my Connor."

Fuck. I drag her closer to me, my lips slanting against hers. The moment our lips meet, it's like a spark ignites between us. Grá melts into me, her body molding against mine. I can taste the champagne on her lips, sweet and intoxicating.

My hands slide down to her waist, pulling her even closer as the kiss deepens. Grá lets out a soft moan, her fingers tangling in my hair. The world around us fades away—the music, the party, everything disappears until it's just us.

But reality comes crashing back all too soon. I break the kiss, breathing heavily as I rest my forehead against hers. "Grá," I whisper, my voice rough. "We can't do this."

She pulls back slightly, her eyes searching mine. "Why not?" she demands. "I want this, Connor. I want you."

I close my eyes, trying to gather my thoughts.

"You deserve better than me, Sunshine. You deserve someone who isn't... tainted."

Grá's hand comes up to cup my cheek, forcing me to look at her. "Don't you get it, Connor? I don't want anyone else. I want you, with all your flaws and rough edges. That's what makes you real."

I shake my head, even as my resolve weakens. "You don't know what you're asking for, Grá. The things I've done..."

"Then tell me," she says firmly. "Whatever it is, we'll face it together."

I step back and shake my head. Never, not fucking ever, will I let her into this fucked up world.

"Happy birthday, Grá," I say, brushing my fingers along her cheek. "Enjoy your evening."

I turn on my heel and walk out of the club. I need to get the fuck out of here, away from her, before I lose my restraint and go back. I want Gráinne, more than I care to admit, but I won't be the reason that she's hurt or brought into this fucked up world I'm in.

She's my best friend and that's how it'll stay.

EIGHT
GRÁINNE

"Gráinne," Jer greets me as I'm brought to his table by the server. I lean across the table and press a kiss to his cheek. "How are you?"

I smile at him, my heart full of love for the man who has given me everything that my own father couldn't. Jerry hasn't been in my life for very long, but he's made such an impact that I could never repay him for everything he's done. "I'm good, thank you. How are you?"

He waves for me to take a seat opposite him. "I'm good. How was your party last night?"

I roll my eyes. "Jer, you were there with me." He watched everything, including Connor and I kissing, but of course Connor pulled away and left.

"How are you really, Grá? You've been in love with that man for longer than I've known you."

I sigh, fiddling with the napkin on the table. "I don't know, Jer. It's complicated."

"Love always is," he says with a knowing smile. "But that doesn't mean it's not worth pursuing."

I shake my head, memories of last night flooding back. "You saw what happened. He kissed me and then just... left."

Jer leans forward, his eyes kind. "Did you ever think that maybe he's just as scared as you are?"

"Connor? Scared?" I scoff. "He's not afraid of anything."

"Everyone's afraid of something, Gráinne. Especially when it comes to matters of the heart."

I bite my lip, considering his words. Could Connor really be scared? The same Connor who's always been my protector, my rock?

"But what if..." I start, my voice barely above a whisper. "What if I'm reading too much into it? What if he doesn't feel the same way?"

Jer reaches across the table, patting my hand gently. "You're not, but right now, Connor isn't ready for what he truly wants. He's dealing with a lot of shit, Grá. I know you love him, but sometimes, love isn't always the answer."

My heart aches at his words, but I understand what he means. Connor's dealt with so much shit in his life. Maybe a relationship is the last thing he needs right now.

"So, what do I do?" I ask, feeling lost. Connor has always been a constant in my life. He's my best friend, someone I have always known that I can rely on.

Jer gives me a sympathetic smile. "You be there for him, just as you've always been. As a friend. Give him time and space to sort through his own feelings. And in the meantime, focus on yourself."

"Focus on myself?" I repeat, the concept feeling foreign. I don't know how to do that.

"Yes, Gráinne. You've spent so much of your life taking care of others—your father, Connor. It's time you started thinking about what you want, what makes you happy."

I sit back in my chair, considering his words. What do I want? For so long, my wants and needs have been secondary to everyone else's. The idea of putting myself first is both exciting and terrifying.

"I... I don't even know where to start," I admit.

Jer chuckles softly. "That's okay. Start small. You're in college now. You've always dreamed of being a doctor—again, taking care of others—but I want you to really focus on that."

My heart warms even more at his words. "You're an amazing man, Jerry. You know that?" I can feel my cheeks heating. I'm not usually so emotional. "Thank you, Jer. For everything."

He waves off my gratitude. "That's what family does, Gráinne. Now, let's order some food. I'm starving."

Family... God, that's not something I've truly had. Connor was the only person I could ever rely on, who I could ever count on, and now I have Jerry.

"Now, I've brought you here to have a nice dinner to celebrate your birthday. Browse the menu and see what you'd like."

As I peruse the menu, I can't help but feel a glimmer of hope. Maybe Jer is right. Maybe it's time I started living for myself. And who knows? Perhaps in time, Connor will sort through his own feelings and be ready for something more.

But for now, I'll focus on being the best friend I can be to him, and on discovering who I truly am. It's a scary thought, but also an exhilarating one. For the first time in a long time, I feel like I'm on the brink of something new and exciting.

As I look up from the menu, catching Jer's warm,

fatherly smile, I realize that no matter what happens with Connor, I'm not alone. I have people who care about me, who want to see me thrive. And maybe, just maybe, that's enough for now.

"Jer," I ask a few minutes later as I take a sip of wine. "Why did you take me in? You didn't have to. You'd have been better off if you hadn't. I mean—" I fumble over my words. It's a question that's been on my mind for a while now. I don't understand why he'd want to become my guardian.

Jer sets down his glass, his eyes softening as he looks at me. For a moment, he's quiet, as if he's choosing his words carefully.

"Gráinne," he begins, his voice gentle, "when I first met you, I saw a young girl who'd been hurt and abused, but I also saw a girl with so much potential, so much fire in her eyes. But you also carried so much pain in your eyes that it hurt to look at."

He pauses, bringing his glass to his mouth once more and taking a sip. "I don't know if you know this, but I have a son. One that I love with everything that I am. But to him, I am not his father. I am a man who screwed his mam while she was married to his father. I'll never have that place that I should have. I've always wanted to have children. I just never found the right person to settle down with." He gives me a sad smile. I hate that he had to go through that. "Then you came into my life, and I saw an opportunity to be the father I've always wanted to be. To give you the love and support you deserved but never received."

His words hit me like a tidal wave, and I feel tears pricking at the corners of my eyes. I blink rapidly, trying to hold them back.

"But I'm not... I'm not an easy person to love, Jer," I whisper, my voice thick with emotion. "I'm broken. I have so much baggage." Losing my mam at such a young age and then having my father be an abusive asshole has taken its toll on me and I feel utterly broken.

Jer reaches across the table, taking my hand in his. His grip is warm, comforting. "Gráinne, you aren't broken, loveen; you're just bruised. Over time, the bruises will fade." He squeezes my hand. "And you, my dear, are more than worth it."

A tear escapes, rolling down my cheek. Jer pretends not to notice, giving me a moment to compose myself.

We fall into a comfortable silence as our food arrives. As I take my first bite, I realize how lucky I am. Not just for the food or the celebration, but for having someone like Jer in my life.

"Jer?" I say after a while.

"Hmm?" He looks up from his plate.

"Thank you. For everything. For being the father I never had."

His eyes soften, and for a moment, I see a flicker of something—pride, maybe?—in them. "It's my pleasure, Gráinne. Truly."

As we continue our meal, chatting about my studies and his work—the legitimate side of it—I feel a sense of peace settle over me. For the first time in a long time, I feel like I belong somewhere. Like I have a real family.

And even though my heart still aches for Connor, I know that with Jer's support, I can face whatever comes my way. Because now, I'm not just surviving. I'm learning to live.

One Week Later

"CHRIST, I'M STRUGGLING," Mike says with a low groan. "I knew it would be hard, but I didn't expect medical school to be this bloody hard."

Mike is one of the guys from my class. He's sweet and easy to get along with. I don't have many friends. I've never been one to make them easily.

I nod sympathetically, understanding all too well the challenges Mike is facing. "I know what you mean. The workload is intense."

I pull my bag onto my shoulder, glad another day is over. I can't wait to go home and crawl into bed and watch a movie. Jerry's supposed to be away this week in Spain with Malcolm—his son.

"How do you do it, Gráinne?" Mike asks, his eyes filled with frustration. "You always seem so... together. Like you've got it all figured out."

I can't help but let out a small, bitter laugh. If only he knew how far from 'together' I really am. "Trust me, Mike, I don't have it all figured out. I'm just... good at pretending, I guess."

Mike looks at me curiously, and I can see him debating whether to probe further. Finally, he says, "You don't have to pretend with me, you know. We're friends, right?"

The word 'friends' catches me off guard. It's been so long since I've had anyone other than Connor that I could call a friend. I feel a warmth spreading in my chest at the thought.

"Yeah," I say softly. "We're friends."

"Grá, loveen," I hear called out and turn, surprised to see Jerry waiting for me.

"I'll see you around, Mike," I tell him as I walk away smiling, happy to see Jerry. "Hey," I greet as I reach him. "What are you doing here? I thought you were in Spain?"

Jerry smiles warmly as I approach. "Change of plans, loveen. Malcolm had some work come up, so we postponed the trip."

I can't help but feel a twinge of disappointment on his behalf. "Oh, Jer, I'm sorry. I know you were looking forward to spending time with him."

He waves off my concern. "It's alright. These things happen. Besides, it means I get to spend more time with you." He smiles softly, but I know he's been excited to see Malcolm. "Now, how about we grab some dinner? I'm starving."

As we walk toward his car, I can't shake the feeling that there's more to this story than he's letting on. Jerry's protective of me, sometimes to a fault. "Jer," I start hesitantly, "you didn't cancel your trip because of me, did you?"

He looks at me, surprise evident in his eyes. "What makes you think that?"

I shrug, suddenly feeling self-conscious. "I don't know. It's just... You're always taking care of me. I don't want to be the reason you miss out on time with your son."

Jerry stops walking and turns to face me fully. His expression is serious, but his eyes are kind. "Gráinne, listen to me. You are not a burden. You're not keeping me from anything. I'm here because I want to be, because you're important to me."

His words wash over me, and I feel a lump forming in my throat. It's still hard for me to accept that someone could care about me this much; could put me first without expecting anything in return.

"Now," Jerry continues, his tone lightening, "how about that dinner? I was thinking Italian. What do you say?"

I nod, grateful for the change of subject. "Italian sounds perfect."

As we drive to the restaurant, Jerry asks about my classes, and I find myself opening up about the stress and pressure I've been feeling lately. It's a relief to share these thoughts with someone who understands, someone who doesn't judge.

We're seated at a cozy table in the corner of a small, family-owned Italian restaurant. The smell of garlic and fresh bread fills the air, making my stomach growl.

"So," Jerry says as we peruse the menus, "I

couldn't help but notice that young man you were talking to earlier. Mike, was it?"

I look up, surprised, wondering how he knows Mike's name. "Yeah, Mike. He's in my class. Why?"

Jerry shrugs, trying to appear nonchalant. "No reason. He seems nice."

I narrow my eyes suspiciously. "Jer, what are you getting at?"

He holds up his hands in surrender. "Nothing, nothing. I just thought... Well, it might be good for you to spend time with people your own age. Make some friends."

I sigh, setting down my menu. "Jer, I appreciate the concern, but I'm fine. I don't need—"

"I know you don't need anything," Jerry interrupts gently. "But it's not about need, loveen. It's about living, about experiencing life. You're young, Gráinne. You should be out there, making friends, having fun."

I feel a familiar tightness in my chest; the anxiety that always comes when I think about opening up to others. "I'm not good at that stuff, Jer. You know that."

Jerry reaches across the table and takes my hand. His touch is warm, comforting. "I know it's hard for you, but I've seen how you've grown. You're stronger than you give yourself credit for."

I look down at our joined hands, feeling a mixture of gratitude and fear. "What if... what if I mess it up? What if they don't like me?"

"Oh, loveen," Jerry says softly. "Anyone who truly gets to know you couldn't help but like you. You're kind, you're smart, and you have a heart of gold. Don't let your past keep you from your future."

His words hit me hard, and I feel tears pricking at the corners of my eyes. I blink them back, not wanting to cry in the middle of the restaurant.

"I'll try," I whisper, my voice barely audible over the chatter of other diners.

Jerry squeezes my hand. "Try, Gráinne. For yourself."

The waiter arrives then, breaking the moment. We order our meals, and Jerry starts to talk about a dinner that he's attending tomorrow evening with his family. He had two sisters; one died a few years ago, and from what I've heard about Nichola, she's not exactly the nicest sometimes. But they're Jer's family and he adores them. He has two nieces and a nephew.

The stress I've felt today ebbs away as we talk. Everything is different from when I was younger. I'm not afraid to walk around the house or to come and go as I please. I feel safe and protected. I know that if

I ever need anything, Jer will be there for me, as will Connor.

By the time we finish our dinner, it's dark out.

"Thank you," I say once we're leaving.

Jerry smiles as he clicks the button on his key fob to open the car. "Anytime, loveen. Now, let's get you home. You've got a big day tomorrow."

"A big day?" I ask, confused.

"Of course," he says with a wink. "You're going to meet the family."

I roll my eyes, but I can't help the small smile that tugs at my lips. "We'll see," I say, knowing I'm not really ready for that. I know he's trying to help, to get me to meet new people, but I'm not ready.

NINE
BOZO

One Year Ago

"You up for this?" Lorcan questions with a grin. The man has made millions—hell, probably even more than that. He takes a cut of my profit as he stakes me, not to mention the money he takes in from rake. Every cash game and tournament he puts on, he'll take a percentage. For tournaments, he'll have a buy-in, and part of that buy-in will include a handling fee that goes straight to Lorcan's business. Whereas the cash games are where he takes the most money, every pot played, a rake will be taken for the business. The higher the pot, the higher the rake.

"Always," I reply steadily. A poker game isn't ever going to shake me. I'm good at what I do and now everyone knows it.

Lorcan claps me on the shoulder, pride and greed etched on his face. "That's my boy. Remember, there are a lot of crime bosses here tonight. You don't need to worry about them. You're covered," he assures me.

One thing about Lorcan is he protects those he deems family, and for some fucked up reason, that includes me. We've been working together for years, and while I keep the hell out of the illegal side of his business and just play cards, I'm part of his family, and it's in a way that won't ever change no matter where my life takes me.

"Who's here?" I ask. Over the years, I've met a lot of the crime bosses. Some are decent, others are fucking assholes and hate to lose. It all depends on what type of mood tonight brings. If they're happy and joyous, they'll play looser and won't care about losing money, but if they're uptight and in no mood to play... well, that's when things can get dicey.

Over the years, I've changed a lot. I'm no longer the scrawny kid Lorcan met. I work out. I've gained about a hundred pounds, most of it pure muscle.

As we walk toward the private room, I see the

warehouse that Lorcan uses as a casino is full to the brim. He's holding a tournament tonight as well as a high-stakes cash game. The tournament is for those who can play fast and loose with a lot of money and love the thrill of playing poker.

I can feel the eyes of the players on me as we enter the back room where the cash game is taking place. Unlike the main floor, back here is decked out with plush leather seats for the players and waitresses ready to be at the beck and call of each player and get them drinks if they need.

Lorcan leans in close, his breath hot on my ear. "I've got a lot riding on this one, Connor."

I grin when I see my opponents. Jerry Houlihan and a couple of Americans are here, as are Lorenzo Mariano and Tempest, both here from Boston. Lorenzo is the son of Cesare Mariano, one of the heads of the Boston Syndicate Elite, and Tempest is the secretary for the Saint's Outlaws motorcycle club. There are also two other guys that I don't know. One is wearing a cut that says he's part of a motorcycle club here in Dublin called Fury Vipers. I've heard a little about them but haven't met any as of yet.

I nod to Lorcan, understanding what he means.

If we win tonight, we'll win big. If not, it could mean owing someone big, and that's not an option. This isn't just another game; it's a power play, a chance to solidify his position among these crime bosses.

As I take my seat at the table, I feel the familiar rush of adrenaline coursing through my veins. The green felt beneath my fingertips, the soft clink of chips being stacked, it's all part of the ritual I've come to love.

Jerry Houlihan catches my eye and gives me a nod of recognition. Over the years, we've grown closer. He's become almost a surrogate dad to Gráinne. He's kept to his word and helped her out, paying for her school tuition and anything else she needs. She's not seen her dad since the night I returned home. Instead, she stayed with Jer and became a member of the Houlihan family.

The Americans, Lorenzo and Tempest are eyeing me with curiosity. They've probably heard stories, but tonight they'll see for themselves what I can do.

The guy from the Fury Vipers is a wild card. His eyes are hard, constantly scanning the room as if expecting trouble. The other unknown player is older, in his late seventies, maybe older, with a full head of gray hair, and he's dressed in an expensive suit. He exudes an air of quiet confidence that tells me he's no amateur.

As the dealer begins to shuffle, I take a deep breath, centering myself. The first hand is dealt, and I glance at my cards—pocket kings. A strong start, but I'm not playing amateurs, that's for sure, so I'll take it easy and see how the play goes.

"Gentlemen," the dealer announces. "The game is No-Limit Texas Hold'em. Good luck."

The betting begins, and I can feel the tension in the room ratchet up a notch. The Fury Viper is first to act. He throws in a small bet; nothing too over the top, but enough to make a statement. The older gentleman smoothly calls, his face betraying nothing. He's old school; I know that by just looking at him. He won't be up to any bullshit tonight.

I consider my options carefully. With pocket kings, I'm sitting pretty, but I don't want to give away the strength of my hand too early. I match their bets, my chips sliding into the pot with a satisfying clink.

Lorenzo and Tempest fold quickly, clearly not willing to commit too much this early in the game. Jerry, however, surprises me by re-raising. His eyes meet mine briefly, a silent challenge dancing in them. Jerry knows me. He knows how good I am and what I'm capable of doing. He's testing to see how far I'll go in this first hand; how much I'm willing to show the other players at this early stage. The remaining players call Jer's raise and I follow suit.

The flop comes down: ace of hearts, seven of clubs, two of diamonds. Not ideal for my kings, but not terrible either. The Fury Viper leads out with the exact same bet as he did pre-flop. The gentleman calls again, his movements deliberate and unhurried.

I can feel Lorcan's eyes boring into me from across the room. He knows as well as I do that this hand could set the tone for the entire night. I take a moment, weighing my options, before calling, and I'm not surprised when Jerry does the exact same.

The turn brings the jack of spades. No help there. It's pretty much the same as the previous bet. It's annoying that the Fury Viper guy hasn't upped the ante, but I'm letting him lead, letting him set the pace, as we all are by the looks of things.

As the dealer prepares to reveal the river card, I can feel the tension in the room ratchet up another notch. The Fury Viper guy's fingers drum on the table, whereas the older gentleman remains perfectly still, his eyes fixed on the center of the table.

The river card slides into place: king of clubs.

I'd smile if I could. I've hit my set, and now I'm

sitting with the best hand there is. The Fury Viper hesitates for a moment before pushing forward a substantial bet, nearly half his stack. The gentleman considers for a long moment before folding with a resigned sigh.

Now it's my turn. I can feel Lorcan's gaze burning into me, silently urging me to make the most of this opportunity. I take a deep breath, not wanting to seem too eager, before pushing my entire stack into the middle.

"All in," I announce.

Jerry's eyebrows shoot up, a flicker of surprise crossing his face before he schools his features to remain impassive. He studies me intently, trying to read any tells, but I give him nothing. After what feels like an eternity, he shakes his head and folds.

All eyes turn to the Fury Viper guy. His eyes narrow on me as he watches me closely. He glances at his remaining chips, then back at the pot, clearly torn. His jaw clenches as he stares me down, his fingers tapping against the table. The tension in the room is palpable. Everyone is focused on his next move.

"Fuck it," he growls, shoving his remaining chips into the middle. "I call."

I keep my face impassive as I flip over my pocket

kings. The Fury Viper's eyes widen as he reveals his hand: ace-jack suited. He had the top two pair; a strong hand, but not strong enough.

"Fuck!" he snarls, running a hand over his head. He turns to me and smiles. "Heard a lot about you, kid," he says as he reaches across the table to shake my hand. "I'm Pyro."

I shake Pyro's hand, nodding respectfully. "Unlucky," I say, keeping my voice neutral. It's always a delicate balance in these high-stake games—you don't want to come across as arrogant.

Pyro leans back in his chair, a wry smile on his face. "Well, looks like I'm re-buyin'. Need to try and win some of my money back. It's goin' to be hard with this one," he says, jerking his thumb in my direction.

I can see Lorcan approaching from the corner of my eye. He claps Pyro on the shoulder, murmuring something I can't quite catch. Whatever it is, it makes Pyro laugh and nod. Lorcan clicks his fingers, and within seconds, Pyro's being re-stacked with chips.

The dealer begins shuffling for the next hand, and I take a moment to survey the players. Jerry's watching me with a mixture of pride and wariness—he knows better than anyone at this table what I'm capable of. The two Americans, Lorenzo and

Tempest are grinning. This isn't the first time I've played either man. They're close friends; something I found odd at first, not realizing that the motorcycle club and Italian mafia ran in the same circles, but I have since found out that their worlds are very closely entwined.

The older gentleman catches my eye and gives me a slight nod of respect. "Impressive play, young man," he says, his voice heavy with an Irish accent. "I'm afraid we haven't been properly introduced. I'm Henry Gallagher," he says, extending his hand.

Holy shit, it's the head of the Irish mafia. Henry Gallagher started the Gallagher crime family, otherwise known as the Gallagher Clann. He's the reason the family has spanned over two continents and is still getting stronger. He's a man many rarely see, but he's the most powerful man at the table.

I shake Henry's hand. "Connor O'Malley," I reply, my voice steady.

Henry's grip is firm, his eyes sharp as they assess me. "I've heard tales of your skills at the table. It seems they weren't exaggerating."

As Henry releases my hand, I can feel the weight of everyone's attention on us. This interaction hasn't gone unnoticed by anyone in the room.

The dealer announces the next hand, and we all

turn our focus back to the game. As the cards are dealt, I can't help but feel a mixture of wariness and excitement. I've just won a significant pot, and with it being the first hand, it means that the curse could be in effect.

The curse is that if you win the first hand, you'll lose every hand afterward. I've seen it happen to too many people. I've played against a hell of a lot of different poker players of different abilities, and it can still be the same for each of them. They win the first hand, and then they're not winning again. Of course, I put it down to superstition. They begin to think about the so called curse and set themselves off, getting in their own heads and trying to chase a pot rather than play it. It'll never work out that way.

I peek at my cards: Ace-Queen offsuit. A strong starting hand, but I know better than to get overconfident. In a game like this, with players of this caliber, anything can happen.

Lorenzo is first to act, and he comes out with a raise, three times the big blind. Tempest calls without hesitation, and I can see a silent communication pass between them. They might be friends, but they're not here to do each other any favors.

The action comes to me, and I take a moment to

consider. After my big win in the last hand, I decide to sit this one out and just watch it play out.

As the hand plays out, I observe my opponents carefully. Lorenzo and Tempest seem to be locked in their own private battle, raising and re-raising each other. The flop comes Ace-high, and I can't help but feel a twinge of regret for folding my Ace-Queen. Still, I remind myself that patience is key in a game like this.

Pyro, having just re-bought, is playing more cautiously now. He folds to a hefty bet from Lorenzo on the turn. Henry Gallagher, however, has been quietly calling along, his face an unreadable mask.

The river brings a queen, completing a possible straight draw. Lorenzo fires out a massive bet, nearly his entire stack. Tempest folds almost immediately, a look of frustration flashing across his face.

All eyes turn to Henry. The old man takes his time, his gaze on the center of the table and unmoving. Finally, with a slight smile, he pushes his chips forward. "Call," he says quietly.

Lorenzo's face falls as Henry reveals his hand. He has the straight. He is holding king and queen. Lorenzo mucks his cards without revealing them, but the slump of his shoulders tells the story. He was full of shit.

Henry has just won a pot nearly as large as the one I took down in the first hand. The smile the old man had is now gone and his poker face is back in full effect.

Five hours later and it's done. I've taken almost fifteen million. Tempest and Lorenzo both called it quits earlier on, having both been beaten, Lorenzo by me and Tempest by Pyro. They didn't take the option to re-buy. Instead, they stayed close by and watched the game play out.

Jerry Houlihan, on the other hand, did take his option to re-buy, and he did so by re-buying in for double his original amount. He lost that within the space of an hour thanks to both Pyro and I taking him out.

Henry, however, was smart. He kept his cards close to his chest and didn't let anyone know what his plan was. He cashed out when he lost a few million, but he left with some money.

Pyro cashed out with his buy-in—both of them—and called it quits, meaning I was the biggest winner of the night. Something that is a usual feat, but among the players I played tonight, it was a great night.

"You're smart. Too smart for this shit," Pyro tells me as we exit the casino. "You ever decide you want to make real money—not just poker winnings—you come find me."

I raise an eyebrow, intrigued by his words. "And what's real money to you?"

Pyro's smile widens. "The kind that doesn't rely on luck."

I can't help but laugh. "Alright, Py, let me know what you've got planned."

"I'm looking for prospects," he says simply.

I turn to face him, wondering what he's talking about.

"Prospects?" I ask, my interest piqued. "For the Fury Vipers?"

Pyro nods, his eyes gleaming in the dim light of the parking lot. "We're expanding and looking for smart, capable guys who can handle themselves. Someone like you could go far."

I consider his words carefully. It's not the first time I've been approached by one of these organizations. The money and power are tempting, but I've always kept myself at arm's length from the more illegal aspects of this world.

But this is the first time I've been offered something here at home in Dublin, where I'd be close to Gráinne.

"What does it entail? I don't want to be dragged

into illegal shit that'll land me in jail."

Pyro grins. "And what you're doing at the tables won't?" he asks, and I tilt my head to the side, conceding that he's got a point. It's illegal to play in an unsanctioned casino.

Pyro leans in closer, his voice low. "Look, we're not just some run-of-the-mill bike club. We've got our fingers in a lot of pies—some legit, some not so much. But we take care of our own. You'd start as a prospect and learn the ropes. After that, sky's the limit."

I run a hand through my hair, weighing my options. The poker world has been good to me, but I can't deny the allure of something more stable, more structured. And if I'm honest with myself, the thrill of the unknown is tempting.

"What about Lorcan?" I ask. "I can't just walk away from this." It's too damn lucrative.

Pyro shrugs. "Lorcan's a businessman. He'll understand. Hell, he might even see it as an opportunity to expand his own operations. Hell, you'd still be able to play games, just as I did tonight. But you'll do it wearing the colors of The Fury Vipers MC."

I nod slowly, my mind racing with possibilities. "I'll think about it," I say finally.

Pyro claps me on the shoulder. "That's all I ask.

Here's my number," he says, handing me a card. "Give me a call when you've made up your mind."

As Pyro walks away, I turn the card over in my hands, feeling the weight of the decision before me. The familiar rush of adrenaline courses through my veins, but this time it's not from the thrill of the cards.

Can I do it? Can I prospect for the Fury Vipers?

TEN
BOZO

I take a sip of the cheap whiskey. This pub isn't one of the greatest, but the booze is cheap and it's a little out of the town center so it's not busy and cramped like a lot of the other pubs.

"You doing okay, kid?" Donal asks. The old, frail man is the owner. This is the pub Dad would come to after I'd won him a lot of money. He'd want to celebrate.

I nod, not trusting myself to speak. Donal's seen people at their worst. He never judges them. He always has a sympathetic ear and a drink ready for everyone. He doesn't push, just tops off their glasses and moves down the bar.

The whiskey burns going down, but it's a welcome distraction from the constant thoughts that are running through my head. Since I spoke with Pyro, I've not been able to stop thinking about joining the Fury Vipers motorcycle club. From everything I've heard, they're supposed to be one of the best clubs there is. Anyone I've spoken to says they're fair but you don't want to cross them.

I take another sip, letting the warmth spread through my chest. The Fury Vipers have been around for decades. They're based mainly in the US, but Pyro met Chloe Gallagher and the Fury Viper MC started a chapter here in Ireland. Everyone says the same thing. The Fury Vipers MC are a brotherhood, a family.

That's not something I've ever had before. Gráinne is the only one who is even close to a family that I have.

The bell above the door chimes, and I glance over my shoulder. Two bikers saunter in, wearing the same cut Pyro had on the other night. They're part of the Fury Vipers club too.

They move to the pool table at the back of the pub. They're both American, their voices not loud, but also not quiet. They rack up the balls and start playing.

Donal shuffles over to take their order,

exchanging familiar greetings. It's clear they're regulars here too. I haven't seen them here before.

I turn back to my drink, my mind racing. Can I really do this? Join their world? What if they think just like my dad did, that I'm nothing more than a genius freak?

I signal Donal for another whiskey, and as he pours, I catch him eyeing the bikers, then me. There's a knowing look in his light brown eyes.

"Thinking of making some changes, lad?" he asks softly.

I hesitate then shrug slowly. "Maybe. I don't know yet."

He slides the fresh drink toward me. "Sometimes, the only way to know is to take the leap."

The thing is, I'm not sure if I'm wanting to take that leap. There's still a lot I don't know about them. I don't take uncalculated risks. Never have, never will.

"Christ," Donal grunts. "What the hell is Eamon doing here?"

I turn and see the man in question stumbling around. Christ, he's drunk as a skunk and slurring his words like a motherfucker. There's only one thing you can guarantee with Eamon: he'll be belligerent while drunk and start a fight. The man spends the majority of his time in the drunk tank. He also has a gambling addiction and owes Lorcan more money than he'll ever be able to repay.

Eamon staggers toward the bar, his bloodshot eyes scanning the room. His gaze lands on the bikers at the pool table, and a sneer twists his face.

"Well, well," he slurs, loud enough for everyone to hear. "If it ain't the Yankee boys playing dress-up."

The pub goes quiet. I tense, watching as the bikers slowly turn to face Eamon. The largest of them, a burly man with a thick beard, steps forward.

"You got a problem?" he asks, his voice low and dangerous.

Eamon laughs, a harsh, grating sound. "Yeah, I got a problem. You lot, thinking you can come over here and act like you own the place."

Donal moves from behind the bar, his weathered face creased with worry. "Now, Eamon, let's not start any trouble. Why don't you head on home?"

But Eamon's too far gone, too drunk and angry to listen to reason. He shoves past Donal, nearly knocking the old man over. I stand up, ready to intervene, but the bikers beat me to it.

"Hey!" one of them shouts, grabbing Eamon's arm. "Watch it, asshole!"

Eamon whirls around, his fist already swinging.

It connects with the biker's jaw with a sickening crack. In an instant, chaos erupts.

The bearded biker tackles Eamon, sending them both crashing into a nearby table. Glasses shatter, chairs topple, and patrons scramble to get out of the way.

I stand frozen, caught between the desire to help and the instinct to stay out of it. But when I see Donal trying to break up the fight, getting jostled and pushed in the process, I know I can't just stand by.

Taking a deep breath, I step into the melee. I grab Eamon's collar, yanking him back just as he's about to throw another punch. He stumbles, off-balance, and I use his momentum to spin him around.

"Eamon!" I shout, getting in his face. "That's enough! You need to leave, now!"

For a moment, his glazed eyes focus on me, confusion replacing the anger. Then recognition dawns, and he sneers.

"Well, if it ain't the little genius," he spits. "Daddy's golden goose. What are you gonna do, boy? Calculate me to death?"

I clench my jaw, fighting back the urge to punch him myself. Instead, I tighten my grip on his shirt and start pushing him toward the door.

"I said, leave," I growl.

Behind me, I hear the bikers regrouping, muttering to each other. I can feel their eyes on my back as I maneuver Eamon toward the exit. He's still struggling, but his drunken state makes him easy to control.

"Get your hands off me, you little shit!" he slurs, trying to twist out of my grip.

I ignore him, focusing on getting him out the door. Just as we reach the threshold, I feel a hand on my shoulder. I tense, expecting trouble, but when I turn, I see it's the bearded biker.

"Need a hand?" he asks, his voice gruff but not unkind.

I hesitate for a moment, then nod. Together, we half-drag, half-carry Eamon out onto the street. The cool night air hits us, and Eamon seems to deflate, the fight going out of him.

"Go home, Eamon," I say, releasing him. "Sleep it off."

He stumbles away, muttering curses under his breath. I watch him go, making sure he doesn't fall or try to come back in. When he's out of sight, I turn to the biker.

"Thanks," I say, suddenly feeling awkward.

He nods, eyeing me with curiosity. "That was

some quick thinking in there. You handled yourself well."

I shrug, not used to praise. "Just didn't want Donal's place getting trashed."

The biker grins. "Loyal. I like that." He extends his hand. "Name's Preacher."

I shake his hand, wanting to ask where he got the name Preacher from, but I refrain. Now ain't the time. "Connor," I reply.

Preacher's eyebrows rise slightly. "Connor? As in the poker player, Connor?"

I nod, surprised. "You know me?" I ask, wondering how he knows my name.

"Sure do. My prez, Pyro, mentioned meeting you the other night. He said you were a smart kid."

I feel a flush of pride at Pyro's words, quickly followed by a wave of uncertainty. What else has Pyro told them about me?

Preacher seems to sense my unease. He claps me on the shoulder, his touch surprisingly gentle for such a large man. "Hey, why don't you come back inside? I'm guessing if you're good at cards, you'll be good at pool, right?" There's no weirdness to his tone, just stating a fact.

I hesitate, glancing back at the pub. Through the window, I can see Donal and the other biker cleaning up the mess from the fight. I should go back to my spot at the bar and leave it be, but there's a part of me that wants to find out more about the bikers.

Maybe Donal was right. Maybe it is time to take a leap.

I take a deep breath and nod. "Yeah, alright. Thanks."

Preacher grins and leads me back into the pub. As we enter, I can feel the eyes of the other people on us. I follow Preacher to the pool table, wondering if I'm making the right decision.

As we approach the pool table, the other biker eyes me with a mixture of curiosity and respect. Preacher introduces me, "Wrath, this is Connor. He just helped us take out the trash."

The guy called Wrath is a little shorter than Preacher and has a full sleeve of tattoos. He nods appreciatively. "Nice work, kid. I'm Wrath."

Preacher turns to me. "What's your poison, Connor?"

"Whiskey," I reply, trying to keep my voice steady.

He nods approvingly and heads to the bar. I stand there awkwardly, not quite sure what to do with myself. I hate interacting with people I don't know. Wrath breaks the silence.

"So, Connor, Pyro tells us you're quite the card shark."

I shrug, uncomfortable with the attention. "I'm alright."

Wrath snorts. "Alright? From what we heard, you're a fucking savant."

Before I can respond, Preacher returns with our drinks. He hands me a glass of whiskey, noticeably better quality than what I was drinking earlier.

"To new friends," he says, raising his glass.

We clink glasses and drink. The whiskey is smooth, warming me from the inside out. As I lower my glass, I notice Donal watching us from behind the bar. He gives me a small nod of approval.

Preacher leans against the pool table. "So, Connor, Pyro mentioned you might be interested in learning more about the club."

My heart rate picks up and I take another sip of whiskey to calm my nerves.

"Yeah, I've been thinking about it," I admit.

Wrath grins. "Well, you've certainly got the balls for it. Not many people would jump into a fight like that."

"Especially not for a couple of strangers," Preacher adds.

I shrug again. "It was the right thing to do."

Preacher studies me for a moment, his eyes thoughtful. "You know, Connor, the Fury Vipers aren't just about riding bikes and looking tough. We're a family. We take care of our own."

The word 'family' strikes a chord in me. I think about my father, about the years of exploitation and neglect. Could this be the family I've always wanted?

"What would joining entail?" I ask, trying to keep my voice neutral. I'm truly interested. It's just a huge fucking decision.

Preacher exchanges glances with Wrath. "Well, first you'd start as a prospect. You'd have to prove yourself; show that you're loyal and willing to put the club first."

"And if I do?"

"Then you become a full member. A brother," Wrath says with a grin. "You'd have to be determined, and you'd need to have the balls to stick with it."

I nod, taking it all in. It's a lot to consider.

"That's all for another day. Right now, we're going to play pool. I want to see what the kid's got," Preacher says as he racks up the balls.

I smile. This is something I can do. It's angles and precision. I've been playing pool for as long as I can remember. I must admit that I'm a lot more at ease around these guys than I had thought I'd be. But Preacher's right, today isn't the day to decide. Right now, I'm focusing on the game. Tomorrow is a new day.

"CONNOR, THAT WAS A GOOD GAME." Lorcan grins as he hands me the money I won. "Gotta admit, taking you on was without a doubt the best decision I've ever made. You make me an extremely rich man."

I hear laughter behind me and turn to see Jerry Houlihan grinning as he steps up to us. "You got to him before anyone else could, Lorcan. Na Cártaí Dubha are lucky to have him."

The organization that Lorcan owns has grown a hell of a lot since I joined them. I technically don't work solely for them, but when I play poker, Na Cártaí Dubha take a percentage of the profit as they're the ones who are staking me in the game. It's a win-win for me as if I lose—which is extremely rare—then I don't lose money, Na Cártaí Dubha does. But I make them more money than any other revenue they have.

"You poached him when he was a boy, Lorcan," Jer continues. "No one stood a chance."

"That's because the boy is smart and knows what will make him the most money," Lorcan chuckles.

"That he is. Now, when's the next game? I'm wanting to win back some of my money. The boy fleeced me."

I chuckle. That's one thing I haven't done. Jer knows how to play and he's damn good at it. However, Eamon is beyond pissed. He borrowed a hundred thousand from Lorcan, more money than ever before, and he lost it within the first hour and has been seething quietly ever since.

I can feel Eamon's glare burning into my back as Jer and Lorcan chat. I try to focus on the conversation, but my instincts are screaming at me to watch my back.

"Next game's in two weeks," Lorcan says, clapping me on the shoulder. "Same place, same stakes. You in, Jer?"

Jerry nods eagerly. "Wouldn't miss it. Maybe I'll get lucky and the kid here will have an off night."

We all laugh, but I can feel the burn of Eamon's stare. It's starting to become unbearable. I glance over my shoulder, catching his bloodshot eyes for a moment before he looks away, muttering something under his breath.

"I'm going to head on home," I say, turning back to Lorcan and Jer. "I'll see you soon."

Lorcan nods, his smile still bright and filled with happiness. He's made a lot of money this evening. No doubt he'll spend it on expensive suits, much like the one he's wearing now. "Alright, Connor. We'll be in touch about the next game. Speak to you soon."

I nod my thanks and make my way to the door, purposely avoiding Eamon's corner of the room. I step outside, and I take a deep breath, trying to shake off the unease that's settled over me.

I've barely made it halfway down the block when I hear footsteps behind me. Heavy, stumbling footsteps. I don't need to turn around to know who it is.

"Hey, you little shit!" Eamon's slurred voice calls out. "Where do you think you're going?"

I keep walking, not giving him the satisfaction of turning. "Go home, Eamon. Sleep it off."

But Eamon's not backing down. I hear him getting closer, his breathing ragged and angry. "You think you're so smart, don't you? You think you can just waltz in and take everyone's money?"

I spin around, finally facing him. He's swaying on his feet, eyes unfocused but filled with rage. "I didn't take anything, Eamon. You lost fair and square."

He lunges forward, grabbing my shirt. His breath reeks of cheap whiskey. "Fair? Nothing's fair about you, you freak. You used that big brain of yours to cheat us all."

I try to push him off but he's got a death grip on my shirt. "I don't cheat, Eamon. You know that. Now let go before you do something you'll regret."

He laughs, and it's a harsh, bitter sound. "Regret? The only thing I regret is not putting you in your place sooner."

His fist comes flying toward my face, but his drunken state makes him slow and clumsy. I manage to duck, feeling the whoosh of air as his fist passes over my head.

"Fucking knew he'd start somethin'," I hear someone growl.

I spot a glint of silver as Eamon rights himself before getting ready to attack again. The fucker has a knife and there's an angry look in his eyes.

"I've lost everything," he growls, edging closer to me.

I square my shoulders and wait for him to attack. I may be a freak and a genius, but I know how to take care of myself.

"Touch him," I hear that voice say, "and you'll die."

I turn to my left, shocked to see Pyro still here, not to mention Wrath and Preacher alongside him.

"We knew he was up to no good," Pyro explains. "Fucker couldn't keep his eyes off you all night. Bastard."

Eamon's eyes dart between me and the bikers, his grip on the knife tightening. He doesn't heed the warning. Instead, he lunges forward, the blade of his knife coming toward me. He's drunk and sloppy, which means I'm able to move out of the way and grab hold of his wrist. I pull it back, loving the snap I hear as the knife in his hand drops to the ground.

"Fucking warned you," Pryo growls as he steps forward, his fist slamming into Eamon's face over and over again.

I watch in shock as Pyro unleashes a flurry of punches on Eamon. The drunk man crumples to the ground, his face a bloody mess. Pyro doesn't stop, his fists continuing to rain down on Eamon's now unconscious form.

"Pyro," Preacher says firmly, placing a hand on his president's shoulder. "That's enough. He's done."

Pyro stands, his breathing ragged as he stares down at the asshole on the ground. There's no mistaking that he's dead. His face is caved in from the beating he took.

"Fuck," Wrath growls low. "We need to sort this shit out." He walks away, his cell to his ear, and I hear him talking. He'll have someone here to clean up.

Pyro turns to me, his knuckles split and covered in blood, his eyes wild with rage. "You okay, kid?"

I nod, still processing what just happened. "Yeah, I'm fine. Thanks." I've never had someone step up for me before. Fuck, it feels fucking good.

Pyro spits on the ground next to Eamon's prone form. "Serves the bastard right. Nobody threatens one of ours."

His words hit me hard. One of ours. Is that what I am now?

"We should get out of here," Preacher says, glancing around. "Wrath is sorting everything."

Pyro nods then looks at me. "Meet us at the clubhouse, Connor."

I nod and watch as he and Preacher move toward their bikes. I hear their engines roar to life and know that it's time to go.

I stand there for a moment, staring at Eamon's lifeless body. The reality of what just happened starts to sink in. A man is dead because of me. Because he threatened me.

But there's no time to dwell on it. I need to get out of here before anyone else shows up. I turn toward my car, slide in, and start up the engine, my mind racing. Everything has changed in the span of a few minutes. The Fury Vipers just killed a man to protect me. They called me one of theirs. I hadn't known if I wanted to join, but I do now. They already think of me as one of their own. It's something I've always looked for: a family, a brotherhood, a sense of belonging, and with the Fury Vipers, I feel that's exactly what I'll have.

As I drive, I can't help but think about how this night has turned out. I went from winning a poker game to witnessing a murder in the span of a few hours. And now I'm heading to a biker clubhouse in the middle of the night.

I pull up to the clubhouse, seeing Pyro and Preacher's bikes already parked outside. Taking a deep breath, I step out of my car and walk toward the entrance. Before I can even knock, the door swings open.

Pyro stands there, his knuckles now cleaned of blood but still raw and red. "Come on in, kid," he says, his voice gruff but not unkind.

I step inside, immediately hit by the smell of leather, cigarette smoke, and beer. The main room is dimly lit, with a bar along one wall and various leather couches and chairs scattered around. A few other members are there, all eyeing me curiously.

Pyro leads me to a back room, closing the door behind us. Preacher is already there, along with another man I don't recognize.

"Connor, this is Raptor, our VP," Pyro introduces. The man nods at me, his face serious.

"Alright, kid," Pyro says, sitting down and gesturing for me to do the same. "We need to talk about what happened tonight."

I nod, sitting down across from him. "Thank you," I say. "I appreciate what you did."

Pyro's face hardens. "He deserved it. Nobody threatens one of ours and gets away with it."

There it is again. One of ours.

"So, what do you say, kid?" Raptor asks with a grin. "You ready to become a prospect?"

I don't even need to think. I've made up my mind.

"Yes," I say with a grin. "I am."

I know it's the right decision for me. I've been searching for something my entire life, and tonight I finally found it. This is what I want.

ELEVEN
GRÁINNE

My phone rings and my hands tremble, as they do every time that specific ringtone sounds. It's Jerry Houlihan. I owe the man everything. That's no lie. He took me under his wing and gave me a home. He helped me when I needed help the most, and he's been a great support system since the night I met him. But it comes at a cost, and that cost means stitching up his men or being unable to save his men who are close to death.

"Hey," I answer softly as I reach for my backpack. I'm supposed to be studying. I have exams in just under a month. If I pass them, I have one year left in University before I can start working in a hospital.

"Grá," Jer greets, his tone tight and hoarse. This is unlike the usual way he speaks to me. "I know you're busy, loveen, but I need you to come to my house. Can you do that?"

My brows knit together at the way he's speaking. "Is everything okay?"

"Everything's fine," he says, but I can hear the strain in his voice. "Just need you to come over. It's important."

I glance at my textbooks and notes spread across the table. The responsible part of me wants to refuse, to stay and study. But I know I can't. I owe Jerry too much.

"Okay," I sigh, packing the books up and zipping up my backpack. "I'll be there in twenty minutes."

The drive to Jerry's house feels longer than usual. My mind is racing as I imagine all the possible reasons he could need me. Is he in trouble? Hurt? Or one of his men? Do I need to stitch another one of them up?

It's hard seeing his men hurt. Over the past four years, I've come to know the majority of them, so stitching them up when they're hurt is never fun.

I pull into his driveway, noting the unfamiliar black SUV parked next to Jerry's silver one. As I approach the front door, I hear muffled voices from inside. Male voices, angry and urgent.

My hand hesitates on the doorknob. Something isn't right. But before I can decide whether to enter or flee, the door swings open. Jerry stands there, his jaw clenched, and his face etched with anger.

"Grá," he says thickly. "Come in, quickly."

As I step inside, I see a man I don't recognize seated in the living room. He's young, probably five or so years older than I am. Jerry closes the door behind me, and I feel a chill run down my spine.

"What's going on?" I ask, my voice barely above a whisper as my gaze darts between Jer and the mystery guy.

"Have you met Freddie Kinnock yet?" he asks me.

I breathe a sigh of relief. I know Freddie—well, I don't *know* him, but I've heard about him. He's one of Jerry's best men. He's known as the Thief, because he's good at thieving. He can get into the most secure places without being seen.

"Loveen," Jer says as he directs me to the sofa. "I know you've got a lot on with your studies and whatnot, and I have a feeling that this is going to throw everything up in the air, but the moment Freddie told me, I knew I had to let you know."

My brows furrow even more. "Let me know what?"

I watch as Jer's shoulders tighten and his lips purse.

"It's your dad, Gráinne," Freddie says, his voice gentle. "Since you came to live with Jer, we've been keeping an eye on him. Jer's orders. He means something to you, so Jer wanted to ensure he was kept on radar."

I turn to Jer, surprised he's done that. My heart warms. He really does have a soft heart behind the gangster facade.

"We hadn't seen him in a few days," Freddie continues. "We started to get worried."

My heart starts to race. "What do you mean? Is he okay?"

Freddie and Jerry exchange a look that makes my stomach drop.

"We found him, Grá," Jerry says softly. "But... it's not good news."

I feel the blood drain from my face. "What happened?" I whisper.

Jerry sits next to me on the sofa, placing a gentle hand on my shoulder. "Liver failure," he tells me. "Damn man drank himself to death."

The room starts to spin. My father, the man I left

behind years ago, the alcoholic who could never stay sober long enough to be a real parent—he's dead. I should feel relieved, maybe even happy that he'll never hurt me again. But instead, I feel a crushing weight of grief and regret. I should have been there to help him. Instead, I ran away and focused on myself.

I feel the tears welling up in my eyes, threatening to spill over. Jerry's arm wraps around my shoulders, pulling me close. Despite everything, despite the years of neglect and pain, he was still my father. And now he's gone.

"I'm so sorry, loveen," Jerry murmurs, his voice thick with emotion. "I know it's not easy."

Freddie clears his throat awkwardly. "There's more," he says quietly.

I look up, wiping my eyes. "What do you mean?"

Jerry and Freddie exchange another loaded glance. "Your dad," Jerry begins carefully. "He left something behind. For you."

My heart skips a beat. "For me?"

Freddie nods, reaching into his jacket pocket. He pulls out a small, worn envelope. "We found this in his apartment. It's addressed to you."

With trembling hands, I take the envelope. My name is scrawled across the front in my father's messy handwriting. I trace the letters with my finger, feeling a lump form in my throat.

"Do you want me to take you home?" Jer asks.

I stare at the envelope with my name on it in shock. Why did he write me a letter? I don't understand. He never cared about me, not after Mam died anyway. So why the letter?

"Grá." I hear the thick and gravelly voice of Connor and turn to look up at him. It's hard to make him out with tears in my eyes. "Come on, Sunshine, let's get you home."

I turn to find Jer watching me with a soft look, his eyes filled with concern, but he nods. "Go with Connor, Grá. I'll check in with you tomorrow."

I nod numbly, clutching the envelope to my chest as Connor gently guides me to my feet. The world feels hazy and distant as we walk out to his car. I barely register the drive home, lost in a fog of grief and guilt.

When we arrive at my small apartment, Connor helps me inside and settles me on the sofa. He disappears into the kitchen, returning moments later with a steaming cup of tea.

"Here," he says softly, pressing the warm cup into my hands. "Drink this. It'll help."

I take a sip, the hot liquid bringing me back to

reality. Connor sits beside me, and I'm so glad that he's here with me. We sit in silence for a while. The only sound is the ticking of the clock on the wall.

Finally, I look down at the envelope still clutched in my hand. With trembling fingers, I break the seal and pull out a single sheet of paper. My father's familiar scrawl covers the page, the ink smudged in places.

"Do you want me to leave?" Connor asks gently.

I shake my head, reaching out to grab his arm. I need him here with me. I'm not strong enough to do this alone. "No, please stay."

Taking a deep breath, I begin to read.

My dearest Gráinne,

If you're reading this, then I'm gone. I know I have no right to ask for your forgiveness after all I've put you through, but I hope that in my final moments, I can offer you some sort of explanation. Although truth be told, there is no justification for what I did to you.

When your mam died, a part of me died with her. I couldn't bear the pain, so I turned to the bottle. It was cowardly. I know that now. I should have been there for you, should have protected you and loved you the way a father should. Instead, I let my grief consume me, and I failed you in every way possible. You deserved so much better than what I gave you.

I've watched you from afar these past few years. I know about your studies, about your dream of becoming a doctor. I know that stems from my mistreatment of you. You want to help others because there was no one there to help you when you so desperately needed it.

I'm so proud of you, Gráinne. You've become the strong, compassionate woman your mam always knew you could be.

Never doubt just how much we loved you, because we did. I just wasn't strong enough to push through the guilt and pain of what I had caused your mam. I wish I had been a better man, a better dad. You deserved better.

But I do love you, Gráinne. I love you with every piece of me. I'm proud to call you my daughter.

Be happy, Gráinne. Never settle for anything less than you deserve, and my beautiful darling girl, you deserve the entire world.

You are loved. You are amazing, and you are beautiful.

Never forget that.

Love,

Dad

I stare at the letter, my vision blurring with tears. The words swim before my eyes as I read them over and over again, trying to make sense of it all.

Connor's arm wraps around my shoulders, pulling me close as I begin to sob. The letter falls from my hands, and I bury my face in his chest, letting out years of pent-up emotion. Connor holds me tight, letting me cry out my feelings as he comforts me.

As my tears begin to subside, I pull away slightly, wiping my eyes. "I don't know how to feel," I whisper, my voice hoarse. "He hurt me so much, Con. But reading this, I can't help but wonder what could have been if he'd just..."

"If he'd just gotten help," Connor finishes for me. I nod, fresh tears threatening to spill over. "It's okay to be confused," he says gently. "You can be angry and sad and hurt all at once. There's no right way to feel about this."

I take a shaky breath, picking up the letter again. My fingers trace over my father's words, feeling the indentations of the pen on the paper. It's the last tangible piece of him I have.

"He knew about my studies," I say softly. "He was proud of me."

"He was, and I know your mam would be too, just as I am."

I stare at the cup of tea that's no doubt ice-cold at this stage. "Do we have anything stronger?"

I hear his chuckle. "I'll find out. If you don't, I'll get on that."

I watch as he walks toward the kitchen, my mind racing as I notice his black cut with the word 'prospect' on the back with the Fury Vipers insignia.

He's prospecting for the Fury Vipers motorcycle club? Since when did he decide to do that? The last I heard, he was thinking about it but hadn't actually decided to do it.

"When did you start prospecting?" I call out, my voice still shaking from crying.

There's a pause, and I hear the clink of glasses. Connor returns, a bottle of whiskey in one hand and two tumblers in the other. He sets them down on the coffee table before answering.

"About a month ago," he admits, not quite meeting my eyes as he pours us each a generous measure. "I was going to tell you, but with your exams coming up, I didn't want to add to your stress."

I take the glass he offers me, swirling the amber liquid. "So you're joining a motorcycle club?" I ask, still trying to wrap my head around it. "Even though you've never wanted to do anything that would bring trouble to your door."

Connor sighs, running a hand through his hair. "I know it seems sudden," he says, taking a sip of his whiskey. "But things have changed. The club, they're not what you might think."

I raise an eyebrow, skeptical. I've heard a lot about them, some good, some not so much. "Oh? And what exactly are they?"

"They're a family, Grá," he says, his voice soft but serious. "They look out for each other, protect each other. And they do good in the community too, even if most people don't see it."

I take a long swig of my drink, wincing at the burn. "And what about the illegal stuff? The violence? Don't tell me that doesn't happen."

Connor's quiet for a moment, his eyes fixed on his glass. "I won't lie to you, Grá. There are aspects of club life that aren't exactly legal. But it's not like what you see in the movies. It's more complicated than that."

I shake my head, feeling a mixture of emotions I can't quite sort out. Today's been a shit show for my feelings. "Why now, Con? Why risk everything you've worked for?"

He looks at me, his eyes intense. "Because I want

that, Grá. I want that family. I want to belong to something, to have brothers at my back, to know that I'm more than a kid who is a fucking genius freak."

I feel my breath catch in my throat. "I've never thought that of you. You're so much more than your brain, Con. So much more."

Connor leans forward, his voice low and urgent. "I know that. You're the only one who's treated me like that, Gráinne, but I need more."

I grit my teeth, hating that I'll never be enough. "I understand," I whisper. "If this is what you want, I'm behind you a hundred percent."

He smiles at me, his piercing green eyes filled with relief. He was worried about telling me his decision. I'm glad that it's out in the open now and he can do what he needs to be happy. That's all I ever want for him. He's my best friend, the man who has always protected me since I was a child. He's the man that I love.

He settles onto the sofa beside me, his shoulders pressed close to mine. We continue drinking and I'm glad of the burn. I'm feeling emotionally wrecked, unsure of what to feel.

I'M drunk and I'm not the only one. Connor is too. The bottle of whiskey is gone. We spent the evening watching comedy movies and talking.

"You should go to bed," he tells me, his words slightly slurred. But even though he's telling me to go to bed, the hand that's around me is caressing the skin on my arm, causing goosebumps to break out.

"Hmm," I murmur, pressing closer to him. I look up at his beautiful green eyes and my heart soars. God, I'm so fucking happy to have him here. He's without a doubt the best man I've ever met. He's the best friend a girl could ever have. I don't know what I'd do if I didn't have him in my life.

I feel a warmth spreading through me that has nothing to do with the whiskey. Connor's fingers continue tracing patterns on my arm, sending tingles down my spine. Our faces are so close I can feel his breath on my cheek.

"Con," I whisper, my heart racing.

His eyes lock onto mine, dark, with an intensity I've never seen before. "Yeah?" he murmurs.

I'm not sure who moves first, but suddenly his lips are on mine. The kiss is gentle at first, hesitant, but quickly deepens as years of pent-up longing pour out. His hand cups my face as mine tangles in his hair, pulling him closer.

When we finally break apart, we're both breathing heavily. Connor rests his forehead against mine, his thumb caressing my cheek.

"Grá," he says softly, "I've wanted to do that for so long."

I smile, feeling a bubble of happiness rise in my chest. "Me too," I admit.

He pulls back slightly, his eyes searching mine. "Are you sure about this? With everything that's happened today—"

I nod, reaching up to trace the line of his jaw. "I'm sure. You're the one constant in my life, Con. The one person I can always count on. I don't want to waste any more time."

A slow smile spreads across his face. He stands, pulling me up with him. "Then let's not waste any more time," he says, his voice low and husky.

He leads me to the bedroom, our fingers intertwined. The moment we enter the room, a mixture of nervousness and excitement flutters in my stomach. This is Connor, my best friend, the man who's been by my side through everything. And now, he's about to become so much more.

He turns to face me, his hands coming to rest on my hips. "Are you sure?" he asks again, his eyes searching mine.

I don't say a word. Instead, I reach up and pull him down for another kiss. This one is deeper, more urgent.

I've never been surer about anything in my entire life.

TWELVE
BOZO

I slant my lips down on hers, needing to taste her once more. Our mouths fuse together, and I run my hands over her body, tracing every curve and dip. God, she's so fucking sexy.

Why the fuck haven't we been doing this before now?

She pulls me closer, her fingers tangling in my hair. With a gentle push, I guide her toward the bed. We tumble onto the soft mattress, a tangle of limbs and heated breaths. My lips trail down her neck, savoring the taste of her skin. She arches against me with a soft gasp.

I strip her clothes off piece by piece, revealing her smooth skin inch by inch. My hands caress every curve, loving how she shivers under my touch, her eyes dark with desire. I pause to drink in the sight of her, sprawled beneath me in all her naked glory.

"You're beautiful," I murmur against her collarbone.

She pulls me down for another searing kiss, her legs wrapping around my waist. I groan as she grinds against me, the friction driving me wild. My lips move lower, trailing kisses down her chest. I take one peaked nipple into my mouth, swirling my tongue around the sensitive bud. She cries out, her back arching off the bed.

"Please," she whimpers, "I need you."

I slide a hand between her thighs, finding her slick and ready. I stroke her clit slowly, teasingly, until she's writhing beneath me. But I need more. I want to taste her before I fuck her.

"Open up for me, baby," I growl, my voice low and rough as I lean over her. She obeys without hesitation, spreading her thighs wide. I glance down and my cock thickens at the sight of her puffy, wet pussy lips.

I trail kisses along her inner thigh, loving the way her breath catches. "Con," she whimpers.

I bury my face between her thighs, inhaling deeply and savoring the intoxicating scent of her arousal. I run my tongue along her folds, feeling her body tense and hearing a gasp escape from her lips. She arches off the bed, wrapping her legs around my shoulders as I continue to taste and tease her.

I don't hold back; I feast on her. There will never be anything as sweet as her pussy. She's utterly soaked. She's writhing in pleasure, grinding her pussy against my mouth. She wants more. I spear my tongue into her pussy and she releases a strangled moan. I do it over and over again, that husky hitch of her breath making my cock thicken. Christ, she's going to have me on the edge without even touching me.

"Please, Con," she says hoarsely. "Please make me come."

I swipe my finger along her folds, teasing her, and she releases a strangled groan. I bite back a curse as I push my finger into her tight, wet, warm channel. Christ, I need to fuck her. She grinds against my finger, my tongue laving at her clit. Her body is tense, and I know it's not going to take much longer until she detonates.

"So close," she whines. "Connor, please."

I add another finger, loving how her pussy ripples around them. Her body writhes with pleasure, her pussy grinding against my fingers. I roll my tongue around her clit, adding a bit more pressure than before. She moans long and hard. I switch it up, my fingers playing with her clit and my mouth at her pussy. I hear her breathing deepen and feel her legs tighten around my shoulders, and she detonates, her pussy flooding my mouth. Her words come out strangled as she orgasms. I lap up her juices, loving her taste.

I get to my feet and unsnap my button, freeing my cock. It's rock hard and in need of relief. I position myself at her entrance, and with one hand on her thigh and the other gripping my shaft, I slide into her wetness, groaning at the sensation. Her legs wrap around my waist, pulling me closer as I thrust deep into her. The sound of our moans fills the room as she spasms around me in the aftermath of her orgasm.

"Connor," she whimpers, urging me on.

My fingers dig into her soft flesh as I plunge back into her, feeling every inch of her tight walls clenching around me. She cries out at the sudden change in position, but it only spurs me on.

My thrusts are hard and fast now as I chase my own release. And she's meeting every one of them with equal force, driving us both closer to the edge. Her moans grow louder and wilder, matching my own grunts and curses.

I can feel it building inside me, that familiar tension coiling in my stomach.

"You're gonna come for me, baby," I snarl.

I slam into her with relentless force, my body slick with sweat as I thrust in and out of her. Every movement brings me closer to the edge, my cock throbbing with need. I can feel her walls clenching around me, and I know she's close too. Desperately, I reach down and find her clit, rubbing it hard and fast as my thrusts become more punishing. She cries out, her head falling forward, hair covering her face. Her body tenses beneath mine and I feel the telltale signs of her impending release.

"Fucking come," I demand.

Her body tightens and her pussy contracts around my cock. The feeling of her walls suffocating my cock is more than enough to pull the cum from my balls. I thrust harder and faster, chasing my own release. When it hits, it's like a freight train crashing through me, pleasure shooting through every nerve ending. I groan and bury myself deep inside of her, filling her with my cum.

"Shit," I hiss as I collapse on top of her, both of us panting and sweating.

I roll off her, staring up at the ceiling as I breathe heavily. For a moment, we just lie here in silence, the only sound our ragged breaths slowly returning to normal. I turn my head to look at her, taking in her flushed cheeks and tousled hair. She looks incredibly beautiful.

Guilt wells up in my stomach. She's perfect, pure, un-fucking-touchable, and I've just fucked her like a damn animal. What the hell is wrong with me?

"Well," she says finally, a small smile playing on her lips. "That was amazing."

"It was," I agree, knowing that it was beyond that. Gráinne has always been the person I've wanted but never let myself have. She deserves the best from life. She deserves to be loved and cherished. Neither are things I can give her.

"So," she says softly. "What happens now?"

Fuck. What the hell do I do now?

"Sunshine," I begin, turning to face her. I watch as her expression falls, and within seconds, it's completely closed off. "We've got so much shit going on—"

She nods. "I get it," she says, her voice a hell of a lot cooler than it had been. "We're friends. We don't want to fuck that up."

Fuck. Why the hell does it hurt having her say those words to me, even though it was what I wanted, what I had planned on saying?

I swallow hard, my throat suddenly dry. Fuck, how the hell have we fucked this up already? "Gráinne, I—"

"It's fine, Connor," she cuts me off, sitting up and pulling the sheet around her body. "Really. We got caught up in the moment. It happens."

But I can see the hurt in her eyes, no matter how hard she tries to hide it. And it kills me, knowing I put that pain there. I reach out to touch her arm, but she flinches away.

"Don't," she says softly. "Please don't make this harder than it needs to be." She sits up straighter, wrapping the sheet tighter around herself. "You should go."

I feel like I've been punched in the gut. Her words hang heavy in the air between us. I should go. I know I should. It's what she wants, what would be easiest. But something keeps me rooted to the spot. She's been my best friend since we were kids. When things got bad, she was my only constant. I can't fucking walk away and ruin everything.

My cell begins to ring from the pocket of my jeans. Gritting my teeth, I reach for it, pulling on my jeans as I answer it. "Yeah?"

"You're wanted back at the clubhouse," Preacher

says in a way of greeting. He doesn't wait for me to respond; he just ends the call.

I stare at Gráinne. She's watching me with a cold expression. She knows I have to leave. Hell, she's practically throwing me out. But I'm a prospect, and when the Fury Vipers MC calls me, I come running, as that's what a prospect does.

I run a hand through my hair, frustration coursing through me. "Gráinne, I have to go. Club business."

She nods, her face a mask of indifference. "Of course. The club always comes first, right?"

Her words sting, but I can't deny their truth. The club does come first. It has to. But that doesn't mean she doesn't matter to me.

"This isn't over," I say, my voice low and intense. "We need to talk about this."

She turns away, her shoulders hunched. "There's nothing to talk about, Connor. Just go."

I want to argue, to make her understand, but the clock is ticking. I can't keep the club waiting. With a growl of frustration, I finish dressing, shoving my feet into my boots.

At the door, I pause, looking back at her. She's still sitting on the bed, the sheet wrapped around her like a shield. "Gráinne," I say softly.

She looks up, and for a moment, I see the vulnerability in her eyes before she masks it. "What?"

"I'll be back," I promise. "We're not done here."

She doesn't respond, just turns her head away again. With a heavy heart, I leave, closing the door behind me. This is beyond fucked up. Everything is a fucking mess.

As I walk out of her apartment and into the frosty night, I feel like the biggest asshole in the world. I've just fucked up the best thing in my life, and for what? Because I'm too much of a coward to admit how I really feel?

I notice that my bike's sitting out front. I must thank Jer for sorting that out for me. When he called me earlier to say that Grá was at his house and she'd just found out her dad was dead, I knew I'd find her in a bad way. Reading that letter gutted her. She may have hated him at times, but he was her dad. He was a man that she loved deeply.

I climb onto my bike, the familiar rumble of the engine doing nothing to calm the storm in my head. As I ride toward the clubhouse, I can't shake the image of Gráinne's hurt expression. I've known her my whole life, been there for her through everything, and now I've gone and fucked it all up.

The road blurs before me as I push my bike

faster, trying to outrun my thoughts. Of course it's useless. Nothing will help me escape them.

I park my bike outside of the clubhouse and head inside, steeling myself for whatever awaits. I spot Preacher at the bar and make my way over.

"What's the situation?" I ask, sliding onto a stool beside him.

He gives me a small nod, his eyes bloodshot as he brings a glass of whiskey to his lips. I don't think I can recall a time when he was sober. The man's always got a drink in his hands. He's hiding a lot of pain. I don't know what happened, but it's fucked him up completely.

"Prez needs you to do a booze run," he says with a grin. "You and Cowboy are the lucky ones."

I grit my teeth. Fuck, it means there's going to be a party, and that means my ass is cleaning up the mess. Great. Fuck. The sooner I'm out of prospect probation and finally able to be a patched member, it will be a day to celebrate.

"Where is Cowboy?" I ask.

There are four of us prospecting at the same time. Cowboy is exactly as his name suggests. He got it due to the fact he's got his hands in everything. The mafia, the Fury Vipers MC, drugs, guns; anything he can, he's involved in. He's a cowboy, hence his moniker. Then there's Tank—the man's built like one—and Hustler—not much explanation needed for that one. I've played poker against him a few times. He's a cheat and he's not allowed to play at any table that Lorcan runs. So far, I'm the only prospect without a moniker. But I know that'll come when it's time.

Two Weeks Later

I'M BARTENDING in the club today, and I'm shocked as shit when Preacher shakes his head, not wanting the beer I push his way. Damn, the man's not drinking. Fuck, it must be a damn miracle.

It's been two weeks since I last saw Gráinne. She's hiding from me and I'm losing my shit. She'll text me—hell, she'll even answer my calls—but whenever I turn up to her apartment, she won't open the door and pretends that she's not home. I'm getting fucking sick of it. She'd better be ready, because once I'm finished here today, my ass is going to be at her house, and I'll be damned if I'm going to let her ignore me once again.

"Who's the Bozo that's parked their bike against the fucking gate, meaning no one can get in?" I hear a deep, familiar voice say. I turn to see Danny Gallagher standing in the doorway, Raptor, the vice president of the Fury Vipers, beside him, along with Wrath. Danny is the son of Denis Gallagher and grandson to Henry. I've met Danny a few times in the past. He's now in London as he runs the Irish mafia in the UK. "Gotta say, the club turned out a lot better than I expected. You've done a great job." His gaze moves to Preacher. "Good to see you, Preacher. Man, it's been a while. I swear I did a double take when I saw you. I thought it was Jesus Christ himself sitting there."

My lips twitch at what he's said, but then I realize what he's talking about and inwardly groan. Fuck, that's my bike.

"Oh shit," I groan. "That's my bike. Sorry, Danny, I'll move it."

Danny grins. "You may want to check you've not damaged it."

I quickly check on my bike. Thankfully, it's not damaged, but I move it to a better spot. I wasn't thinking when I parked it there this morning as I was trying to get Gráinne to talk to me over the phone. She's acting as though everything's fine but I call bullshit. If everything was as hunky dory as she's making out, why the fuck is she ignoring me whenever I come to her house?

As I get closer to the clubhouse door, I hear voices.

"Connor just got his road name, babe," Pyro says, and I can tell he's speaking to his old lady, Chloe, who happens to be Danny's younger sister and the daughter of Denis Gallagher.

I shake my head when I realize what my name's going to be. Fuck. Bozo.

"That's ironic, don't you think?" Callie asks. She's Chloe's step-mam and she's married to Denis Gallagher.

"Yep," Pyro says, and I can hear the amusement in his voice. "But the man's goin' to be made a club member in the next few weeks and he needs a road name."

My steps falter at his words. I'm going to be a patched member in just a few weeks? Fuck. Warmth spreads through my chest at the thought. This is what I've been working toward. This is what I've wanted.

"Do we all have to call him Bozo?" Callie asks.

"Would it not be mean? Like, the guy's the smartest man in the room. Calling him a word that means stupid or significant seems a little..." she pauses, as if she's trying to find the right word.

"Love that you think that, Mrs. Gallagher," I say, stepping back inside the clubhouse. "But being called Bozo isn't mean and isn't meant in that way."

Chloe nods as she reaches for her ma's hand. "It means that he's part of the family."

Fuck yeah, I'm going to be a part of this family. It may be fucked up, but Christ, it's the best family I've ever met.

I turn to Danny, who's watching me warily. "But that doesn't mean I won't give Danny shit every time I see him for me having this road name."

Danny chuckles, as do the rest of the guys. I glance at the clock and see I've got another three hours before Grá will be home. I'm going to make sure that I'm waiting for her when she is. I'm not letting her shut me out again. Not fucking happening.

This bullshit ends today.

THIRTEEN
GRÁINNE

I'm tired. God, I'm so fucking tired. It's been two weeks and I haven't recovered from the loss of my dad. I went to his funeral, something I did without having Connor at my side. That's not something I had ever imagined would happen, but I couldn't—can't—bring myself to see him right now. I'm hurt. Christ, I'm heartbroken.

Having sex with Connor was never supposed to happen. He's my best friend, and we were drunk, but we both knew better. Nothing good would ever come from us fucking, but we were stupid—ironic, given the fact that Connor's a damn genius. Now, I'm trying to find a way to overcome the heartache so we can get back to being friends.

As I unlock the door to my apartment, I'm

already fantasizing about a hot shower and crawling into bed. But as soon as I step inside, I freeze. Connor is sitting on my couch, his elbows resting on his knees as he looks up at me.

"Jaysus!" I cry, my hand flying to my chest. "You scared the shite out of me, Con. How did you get in here?"

He holds up a key. "You gave me this, remember? For emergencies."

I bite my lip, cursing myself for forgetting about that. "This isn't an emergency," I say coldly, dropping my bag and keys on the side table.

"The hell it isn't," he growls, standing up. "You've been avoiding me for two weeks, Gráinne. Two fucking weeks. That's not like you."

"I've spoken to you," I remind him. "We've talked almost every day."

He scowls at me. "Talked yeah, but you've not let me see you."

I cross my arms over my chest, trying to keep my emotions in check. "I've been busy. And grieving. In case you forgot, I just buried my father."

His expression softens slightly. "I know, Sunshine. And I'm sorry I couldn't be there for you. But you wouldn't let me."

"Because I needed space," I snap. "I needed time to process everything without complications."

"Complications?" he repeats, his voice low and dangerous. "Is that what I am to you now? A complication?"

I close my eyes, willing the tears not to fall. "Con, please. Can we not do this right now? I'm exhausted."

He takes a step closer, his eyes burning with intensity. "No, we need to talk about this. I'm tired of you shutting me out."

I feel my resolve weakening. God, I've missed him. Even with all the hurt and confusion, he's still my best friend. The one person I want to turn to when everything falls apart.

"I'm sorry," I whisper, my voice cracking. "I just... I didn't know how to face you after what happened."

His expression softens. "Grá, you don't ever have to hide from me. No matter what." He reaches out, gently cupping my face in his hands. I lean into his touch instinctively, feeling the warmth of his skin against mine. "I fucked up," he says softly. "I shouldn't have left like that. I shouldn't have made you feel like it didn't mean anything."

My heart races at his words. "Didn't it?" I ask, hating how vulnerable I sound.

He leans in, resting his forehead against mine. "It

meant fucking everything, but what we have, it's too fucking good to ruin by dating."

I swallow hard. He's right. As much as it hurts to admit. Dating would be one huge fucking complication, and if things went wrong, we'd end up hating one another, and that's not something I want happening.

I feel my heart clench at his words. He's right, but it still hurts. I take a shaky breath, trying to steady myself.

"So what do we do now?" I ask softly, my eyes searching his.

Connor's thumbs gently stroke my cheeks. "We go back to how things were."

"Friends," I say with a nod.

His eyes brighten, and the smirk that forms on his face has butterflies forming in my stomach. "Friends with benefits?" he asks with a raised brow.

Can I do that? Can I push aside my feelings and have sex with him time and time again and watch him walk away?

"I don't know, Con," I say softly, biting my lip. "That could get complicated real fast."

His eyes darken as they focus on my mouth. "Only if we let it," he murmurs, his thumb gently tracing my bottom lip. "We're both adults. We can handle it."

I shiver at his touch, desire coiling low in my belly. God, I want him. But I'm scared of getting hurt again.

"What if one of us catches feelings?" I ask, voicing my biggest fear.

Connor's hand slides to the back of my neck, pulling me closer. "Then we deal with it," he says, his breath hot against my lips. "Together. Like we always do."

I'm wavering, my resolve crumbling under the heat of his gaze. "Con..."

"Just say yes, Sunshine," he whispers, his lips barely brushing mine. "Let me make you feel good."

With a soft whimper, I give in. "Yes," I breathe against his mouth.

In an instant, his lips crash against mine, hot and demanding. I melt into him, my arms wrapping around his neck as he lifts me off my feet. My legs instinctively wrap around his waist as he carries me to the bedroom, his lips never leaving mine. He kicks the door shut behind us and lays me down on the bed, his body covering mine.

"God, I've missed you," he growls, trailing kisses down my neck.

I arch into him, my fingers tangling in his hair. "I've missed you too," I gasp as he nips at my collarbone.

His hands slide under my shirt, pushing it up and over my head. I help him remove it then reach for the hem of his T-shirt, desperate to feel his skin against mine. He sits up briefly to pull it off, and I take a moment to admire his muscular chest and abs.

"Like what you see?" He smirks, catching me staring.

I roll my eyes but can't help smiling. "Shut up and kiss me," I demand, pulling him back down.

He obliges, his mouth hot and insistent on mine as his hands roam my body. I moan as he cups my breast through my bra, his thumb brushing over my nipple.

"Off," I pant, reaching behind to unhook my bra. He helps me slide it off then lowers his head to take one peaked nipple into his mouth.

I cry out, arching off the bed as he sucks and licks, his other hand kneading my neglected breast. My hands scrabble at his back, nails digging into his skin as pleasure courses through me.

Connor's mouth trails lower, planting hot kisses down my stomach as his hands work to unbutton my jeans. I lift my hips, helping him slide them off along with my panties. He sits back on his heels, his eyes roaming over my naked body with hungry appreciation.

"Fucking beautiful," he growls, his hands sliding up my thighs.

I reach for him, tugging at his belt. "You're overdressed," I complain.

He chuckles, standing to quickly shed the rest of his clothes. My breath catches as I take in the sight of him, all hard muscle and tanned skin. His cock stands thick and hard against his stomach.

"Better?" he asks with a smirk.

"Much," I breathe, reaching for him.

He crawls back onto the bed, settling between my spread thighs. His cock brushes against my wet folds and we both groan at the contact. He captures my lips in a searing kiss as he slowly pushes inside me, stretching and filling me perfectly.

"Fuck," he hisses against my mouth. "So tight, Sunshine."

I wrap my legs around his waist, urging him deeper. "Move," I plead.

He doesn't need to be told twice. He starts to thrust, slow and deep at first then picking up speed as our bodies find their rhythm. I meet him thrust for thrust, my nails digging into his shoulders as pleasure builds inside me.

Connor's thrusts grow more urgent, his hips snapping against mine with increasing force. I can feel the tension building in his body, mirroring my own rising pleasure. His hand snakes between us, fingers finding my clit and rubbing tight circles.

"Come for me, Grá," he growls, his voice rough, causing me to shiver in delight. "I want to feel you come around my cock."

His words and touch send me over the edge. I cry out, my back arching as waves of pleasure crash over me. My inner walls clench around him, pulsing with my release.

"Fuck," Connor groans, his rhythm faltering. With a final deep thrust, he buries himself inside me, his cock pulsing as he comes.

We lay there for a moment, tangled together and panting. Connor's weight is comforting on top of me. I want him to stay here, but I know it's not going to stay like this forever. Eventually, he lifts his head to look at me, a soft smile on his lips.

"You okay?" he asks, brushing a strand of hair from my face.

I nod, returning his smile. "More than okay."

He rolls off me, pulling me into his side. I rest my

head on his chest, listening to his heartbeat slowly return to normal. His fingers trail lazily up and down my spine, sending pleasant shivers through me.

"So," I say after a while. "Friends with benefits, huh?"

I feel him chuckle beneath me. "Yeah," he says, his fingers still tracing patterns on my skin. "Are you okay with that?"

I take a deep breath, considering. Part of me wants more, wants to explore the deeper feelings I have for him. But I know that could jeopardize everything we have. And I'm not willing to risk losing him completely.

"I think I can handle it," I say finally. "As long as we're honest with each other. No secrets, no jealousy."

He nods, pressing a kiss to the top of my head. "Agreed. And if either of us starts to feel like it's too much, we stop. No hard feelings."

"Sounds good," I murmur, my heart pounding as I take a deep breath. "But that brings me to my next point. I'm on the pill, but you've gone ungloved twice. Are you with anyone else?"

Connor tenses slightly beneath me. "No, I'm not with anyone else," he says after a moment. "You're the only one, Grá."

I lift my head to look at him, searching his eyes. "Really? I mean, I know you hook up at parties sometimes..."

He shakes his head. "Not lately. And definitely not since... this," he gestures between us. "What about you?"

"No one else," I confirm. "But if that changes for either of us, we tell each other, right? And use protection?"

I watch as his jaw clenches. He's silent for a few moments. "Absolutely," he says thickly, his voice rough. "I don't want to risk your health, Sunshine. Or complicate things more than necessary."

I nod, settling back against his chest. We lie in comfortable silence for a while, his fingers continuing their gentle exploration of my skin.

"Con?" I say softly.

"Hmm?"

"I'm glad you came over tonight. I've missed you."

He tightens his arm around me. "Me too, Grá. Don't shut me out again, okay? No matter what happens between us, you're still my friend."

I swallow the lump in my throat. "I won't. I promise."

As I lie there in Connor's arms, I can't help but wonder if we're making a mistake. If this friends with benefits arrangement will end up destroying the friendship we both cherish so much. But for now, I push those thoughts aside, choosing instead to savor this moment. It's not going to last forever.

"I should probably go," Connor says reluctantly a while later. "I've got an early start at the clubhouse tomorrow."

I try to ignore the pang in my chest at his words. This is what I agreed to, after all. "Yeah, of course," I say, sitting up and wrapping the sheet around myself.

Connor gets up and starts gathering his clothes. I watch him dress, admiring the play of muscles under his skin. When he's fully clothed, he turns back to me with a soft smile.

"Are we good?" he asks, a hint of uncertainty in his voice.

I nod, forcing a smile. "We're good."

He leans down and kisses me softly, his hand cupping my cheek. "Get some sleep, Sunshine. I'll call you tomorrow."

I nod, not trusting myself to speak. He gives me one last lingering look before heading out of the bedroom. A moment later, I hear the front door open and close, and then the sound of his bike rumbling.

I flop back onto the bed, staring up at the ceiling. What have I gotten myself into? Friends with benefits sounds good in theory, but I know myself. I know how I feel about Connor. Can I really keep my emotions in check?

But the alternative—not having him in my life at all—is unthinkable. So I'll take what I can get, even if it means my heart might end up broken in the process.

With a sigh, I get up and head to the shower. As the hot water cascades over me, I try to wash away my doubts and fears. This arrangement with Connor might be complicated, but it's better than nothing. And who knows? Maybe it will be enough.

As I dry off and get ready for bed, my phone chimes with a text. It's from Connor.

Connor: Sweet dreams, Sunshine.

I can't help but smile, even as my heart clenches. God, I think I'm in trouble. I'm so in love with him that I don't think I could say no to him. This is going to end in heartache. I can feel it. I just pray that it doesn't leave me broken.

FOURTEEN
GRÁINNE

Present Day

"Gráinne," I hear Mike say as I exit the hospital. I turn and see him striding toward me, a sexy smile on his face.

He's still my friend and is now a doctor at the same hospital I am. I'm not blind; Mike is hot, and his smile would make anyone weak at the knees.

It's eight in the morning and the emergency room is already busy. Last night was crazy and I was rushed off my feet. Right now, I can't wait to crawl into bed and fall asleep. Thankfully, I have the next two days off before I do it all again.

"Hey, Mike," I respond, trying to keep my voice steady. "Heading home?"

He nods, falling into step beside me. "Long shift. I could use a coffee. Care to join me?"

I give him a soft smile. "If I have coffee right now, I won't be able to sleep. Can we have a rain check?"

His gaze heats as he grins wider. "Tell you what, Grá," he says thickly. "How about we change the coffee to dinner?"

My heart races. Holy crap, I hadn't expected him to ask me out. Shit. What do I say?

Things between Connor and I are still up in the air. We have sex—frequently—but he keeps me at arm's length. He's a fully patched member of the Fury Vipers MC and he's hell bent on ensuring that I'm not in any way, shape or form a part of it. I get it to some extent, but I work for Jerry Houlihan, for Christ's sake. That man has more enemies than anyone else I know.

But I love Connor. I have since I was a kid and had no idea what the feelings actually were, and I have no doubt that I'll love him until I die. But something's got to give. I can't keep coasting through life being his fuck buddy. I want more. I deserve more.

I give Mike a sad, small smile. "I appreciate the offer," I begin, hoping I don't hurt him by rejecting him, "but I'm kind of involved with someone." It's not a lie, but not exactly the complete truth either.

Mike's smile falters for a moment, but he recovers quickly. "Ah, I see. Lucky guy."

I nod, not trusting myself to speak. Lucky? Maybe. Complicated? Definitely.

"Well, the offer stands if things change," Mike says, his tone light and filled with a little hope. "You're a beautiful woman, Grá, and you're a good friend."

Heat rises to my cheeks. "Thank you, Mike. That means a lot."

We reach the parking lot, Mike close to me, matching me step for step. I fumble for my keys, suddenly eager to escape and get home.

"Take care of yourself, okay?" he says softly. "You work too hard."

I manage a small laugh. "Look who's talking. But I will. You too, Mike. I'll see you in a few days."

As I drive home, my mind races. Mike's invitation lingers in my thoughts, a tantalizing what-if. But as I pull into my driveway, I see a familiar motorcycle parked there. My heart leaps at the sight.

Connor.

I take a deep breath, knowing that he'll be here for a few hours before he'll leave again. I can't remember the last time he actually spent the entire night with me. I'm nothing more than a booty call, and I'm so deeply in love with him that I'll let it continue.

I step out of my car, my exhaustion momentarily forgotten as anticipation thrums through me. Connor's here, waiting for me.

As I approach my front door, it swings open. Connor stands there, all six feet of tattooed, muscular biker glory. He's gotten a lot more muscular in the past year. His dark eyes rake over me with a hungry look that sends shivers down my spine.

"Hey, Sunshine," he says, reaching out to pull me into his arms. "Missed you."

I melt into his embrace, inhaling his scent of leather. It's intoxicating, just like everything else about him. "I missed you too," I murmur against his chest.

He pulls back slightly, cupping my face in his rough hands. "Rough shift?"

I nod, suddenly aware of how bone-tired I am. "Yeah, it was crazy."

Connor's lips quirk into a smirk. "Well, let's get you to bed then."

My breath catches as he scoops me up, carrying

me effortlessly to my bedroom. He lays me down gently then starts to undress me with practiced ease.

"Connor," I whisper, my body responding to his touch despite my exhaustion. "I need to sleep…"

He chuckles, a low, rumbling sound that sends heat pooling in my belly. "Sleep, Sunshine. I'll be here when you wake up."

Surprise floods me. He will? That's new. He's never stayed before, always leaving right after we've had sex. This is different, and I'm not sure what to make of it.

He finishes undressing me, his touch gentle and sweet. Then he strips down to his boxers and climbs into bed beside me. I curl into him instinctively, relishing the warmth of his body against mine.

"Sleep," he murmurs, pressing a kiss to my forehead. "I've got you."

Despite my racing thoughts, exhaustion quickly overtakes me. I drift off to sleep, curled up in Connor's arms.

When I wake up, the room is bathed in late afternoon sunlight. I'm alone in bed, but I can hear movement in the kitchen. The smell of coffee wafts through the air.

I sit up, rubbing my eyes. Did Connor really stay? Is he actually making coffee in my kitchen?

I pull on a robe and pad out to investigate. Sure enough, there he is; his back to me as he stands at the counter. He's wearing just his jeans, his muscular back on full display.

"Connor?" I say, my voice still rough from sleep.

He turns, a mug in each hand. "Hey, Sunshine. Sleep well?"

I nod, still trying to process the situation. "Yeah, I did. You... you're still here."

He hands me one of the mugs, his expression unreadable. "Yeah, I am. Is that okay?"

I take a sip of the coffee, buying myself a moment to gather my thoughts. It's perfect– he remembers exactly how I like it. "Of course it's okay," I say finally. "It's just... different."

Connor leans against the counter, his dark eyes studying me intently. "Different good or different bad?"

"Good," I reply without hesitation. "Definitely good."

He nods, a small smile playing at the corners of his mouth. "Good."

We stand in comfortable silence for a few moments, sipping our coffee. I can't help but drink in the sight of him–his tousled hair, the sight of his bare skin and tattoos. He's gorgeous, and for once, he's not rushing out the door.

"So," I venture, breaking the silence. "What brought this on?"

Connor sets his mug down, his expression turning serious. "I've got a card game. I'll be gone for about a week," he tells me, his gaze no longer on me.

My heart starts to race. He's still working for Lorcan? I thought that stopped when he joined the Fury Vipers?

"For Lorcan?" I ask, trying to keep my voice steady.

He takes a deep breath, running a hand through his hair. "Yeah," he says thickly. "Na Cártaí Dubha is hosting one of the biggest cash games in Spain. Lorcan wants me there."

"I hadn't realized you were still working for Na Cártaí Dubha," I say, unable to keep the bite from my tone.

Connor's jaw tightens. "It's complicated, Grá. I can't just cut ties completely."

I set my mug down, frustration bubbling up inside me. "Can't or won't?"

He sighs heavily. "Both. Look, I know you don't like it, but this is who I am. The club, Na Cártaí Dubha—it's all part of my life."

"And where do I fit into that life?" I ask, the words escaping before I can stop them.

Connor's eyes snap to mine, intense and unreadable. "You know where you fit, Sunshine."

I shake my head, feeling tears prick at my eyes. "No, Connor, I don't. I don't know what we are anymore." I look up at him. "I don't know you anymore." The words slip from my lips before I'm able to stop them.

He takes a step toward me, his eyes wide and his face slack. "Grá..."

"No," I say, holding up a hand to stop him. "I'm too tired, Con. I'm so fucking tired." I pick up the mug once again. "I'm going to have a shower. I'll see you later."

I turn and walk away, my heart heavy in my chest. I hear Connor call my name, but I don't stop. I need space, time to think.

The hot water of the shower does little to ease the tension in my muscles or the ache in my heart. I lean my forehead against the cool tiles, letting the water cascade over me as I try to sort through my jumbled thoughts.

When I finally emerge from the bathroom, wrapped in a towel, I listen, my heart breaking when I realize he's actually gone. I thought he'd stay, want to talk, but I was wrong. I should have known better than to get my hopes up, to think that he'd want more. He's made it perfectly clear that we're just friends with benefits.

I quickly dry and get dressed. Once I'm done, I strip the bed sheets, needing to have fresh ones on. I don't want to smell him, not tonight, not when I'm so exhausted that I can hardly think straight.

After putting the sheets in the washing machine, I settle down on the sofa and put on a movie. I know that no matter how exhausted I am, I won't be able to sleep right now. My mind is whirling with thoughts of Connor and me. I have no idea what the hell I should do.

I hear a knock at the door as I'm about to put on another movie. I've remade the bed with fresh sheets and my house is clean. I couldn't sit down and watch the movie. I needed to do something and cleaning needed to be done.

My heart leaps as I make my way toward the door, thinking it might be Connor, but I quickly squash that hope. He's never come back after leaving before.

I open the door to find Mike standing there, a paper bag in his hand and a concerned look on his face.

"Hey," he says softly. "I hope I'm not intruding. I just... I couldn't shake the feeling that you needed a friend tonight."

I'm taken aback by his thoughtfulness. "Mike, I... Thank you. Come in."

He steps inside, holding up the bag. "I brought some food. Figured you probably haven't eaten yet."

The smell of Chinese food wafts from the bag and my stomach growls in response. I realize I haven't eaten since my shift at the hospital.

"That's really sweet of you," I say, leading him to the kitchen. "I appreciate it."

We settle at the kitchen table, and Mike starts unpacking the food. There's an awkward silence between us, and I can feel his eyes on me.

"Grá," he says finally, "I hope I'm not overstepping, but are you okay? You seemed off earlier."

I consider brushing off his concern, but something in his kind eyes makes me pause. "I'm... it's complicated," I admit.

Mike nods, passing me a container of lo mein. "Complicated relationships usually are," he says with a wry grin.

I sigh, picking at my food. "You could say that. It's just... I don't know where I stand with him. One minute he's here, making me feel like I'm the only woman in the world, and the next..."

Mike listens attentively, his brow furrowed in concern. "And the next?"

"The next, he's gone. Like he was never here at all." I push my food around with chopsticks, my appetite suddenly gone. "I know he cares about me, but sometimes I wonder if it's enough."

Mike reaches across the table, gently touching my hand. "Grá, you deserve someone who makes you feel valued all the time, not just when it's convenient for them."

His words hit me hard, and I feel tears welling up in my eyes. "I know," I whisper. "I just... I've loved him for so long. It's hard to imagine my life without him."

Mike squeezes my hand. "I understand. But sometimes, loving someone isn't enough. You have to love yourself too."

We sit in silence for a moment, his words sinking in. I know he's right, but the thought of letting go of Connor feels impossible.

"Thank you, Mike," I say finally, managing a small smile. "For the food and for listening. You're a good friend."

He smiles back, warm and genuine. "Anytime, Grá. That's what friends are for."

As we continue to eat, the conversation shifts to lighter topics. Mike tells me about his family and his brothers. He seems close to them, and from how he describes it, they have a great relationship. Mike's funny, and I can't help but laugh and smile. It feels good to do so, to forget about my complicated love life for a moment.

After we finish eating, Mike helps me clean up. Things between us are easy and I don't feel uncomfortable, which is surprising, but I'm grateful that he came over this evening.

As he's about to leave, he pauses at the door. "Grá," he says softly, "I know you're going through a lot right now, but I want you to know that I'm here for you, whatever you need."

My heart warms at his words. "Thank you, Mike. That means more than you know."

He nods then hesitates for a moment, before speaking again. "And Grá? Just remember, you deserve happiness. Real, lasting happiness. Don't settle for anything less."

With that, he leaves, and I'm left standing in my doorway, his words echoing in my mind.

I spend the rest of the evening trying to distract

myself with mindless TV shows, but my thoughts keep drifting back to Connor. And, surprisingly, to Mike. The contrast between them is like night and day. My mind is even more jumbled than before.

I'm halfway through the newest episode of Grey's Anatomy when my phone buzzes with a text. I glance down at the screen and see that it's from Connor.

Connor: Miss you already, Sunshine. See you when I get back.

I stare at the message, my heart aching. I didn't realize he was leaving today. God, no wonder he didn't leave me straight away.

Ugh, what the hell is wrong with me? I love Connor, I really do. He's one of the best men that I know. But he's made it more than clear that he doesn't want what I do, and maybe now is the time to start easing back from the arrangement we made. I want a lot more from life. I want to have a family, to have the chance to have a real family, one that's filled with love and happiness—everything that mine wasn't. I had always imagined it would be with Connor, but right now, I don't think that's ever going to happen, and I'm not sure I can wait any longer for him to decide if he wants me or not.

My mind turns to Mike and how sweet he was

for turning up this evening. But just as quickly as that thought hits me, my entire body seizes. A chill runs down my spine as the realization hits me. I never told Mike where I lived. How did he know? My mind races, trying to recall if I ever mentioned my address to him at work. No, I'm certain I didn't.

I jump up from the couch, suddenly alert and on edge. I double-check that all the doors and windows are locked, my heart pounding in my chest. Is Mike creepy? Or am I just being paranoid?

I grab my phone, my finger hovering over Connor's name in my contacts. But what would I say? That I'm freaked out because a coworker brought me dinner? It sounds ridiculous even in my head. Besides, Connor's probably already in Spain. What's he going to do for me over there?

Instead, I text Jerry, remembering the conversation we had at my graduation from university, where he met Mike, someone he already knew.

Me: Hey, quick question. Do you remember Mike from the hospital? You said he was the son of an associate. Did you give him my address?

Jerry's response comes almost immediately.

Jerry: No, I didn't. Why? Is everything okay?

My stomach drops. If Jerry didn't give Mike my address, how did he find out where I live?

Me: Just wondering. Everything's fine. No worries.

I lie, not wanting to worry Jerry unnecessarily. But my mind is whirling. Could Mike have accessed my personnel file at the hospital? That seems like a stretch, and a huge violation of privacy.

I pace my living room, trying to calm my racing thoughts. Maybe there's a logical explanation. Maybe I mentioned my address in passing and just don't remember.

I'm freaked out and have no idea what the hell to do about this. I need to keep Mike at arm's length until I can find out what the hell is going on.

I don't like it. I feel creeped the hell out. But he's not technically done anything wrong. In fact, it was sweet of him to check in on me and bring me dinner. I'd look like a crazy person if I went to HR with it.

Ugh, what the heck am I going to do?

FIFTEEN
BOZO

I keep a watchful eye on the men sitting at the table. Each of them are firmly on my radar. I received a call to fly out to Spain and participate in one of the biggest poker games in Europe. It wasn't the usual caller, Lorcan; this time, it was Pyro, my president.

Pyro had received a call from Denis Gallagher, whose son, Malcolm, runs the Irish mafia in Spain. Rumor has it that the notorious organization known as The Revenant has finally surfaced from the small time shit they had been at and are now making their way into central Europe with full force, and they want to know who and what is behind it all.

I've heard whispers about The Revenant, but no one dares speak too loudly about them anymore.

Anyone who had spoken about them is no longer alive to tell the tales. The Revenant is known for its cult-like loyalty. Once you're in, there's no way out except death.

Not much information is available about them; even their leader remains a mystery. That's why I'm here in Spain, trying to gather any intel possible while secretly observing a few members of The Revenant at the tables.

I take a sip of my whiskey, eyeing the players over the rim of my glass. There are five of them, all dressed sharp in tailored suits that scream money. Two I recognize from the underground circuit back home, but the other three are new faces. One of them, a tall blonde with a scar across his jaw, is surveying everyone just as I am.

There's a darkness about him, one that I've seen a lot of before. Many of the men I'm close to are the same. We've all got that darkness in us. We're all capable of the depravities I've seen committed. It just depends on how far you're willing to go. I've not crossed that line yet, but I know the line and what'll happen if it's crossed. The tall blonde, I've no doubt that he's crossed that line many times over.

The dealer shuffles the cards with practiced

precision, the soft sound barely audible over the low hum of conversation in the dimly lit room. I've been here three hours already, and so far, nothing's happened that screams 'new criminal organization'. But then again, that's how these things usually go. The real action happens between the lines, in the pauses between hands and the meaningful glances exchanged across the table.

I toss in my chips for the next hand, my mind racing. Pyro didn't give me much to go on, just that The Revenant was making waves across Europe, muscling in on established territories with a ruthlessness that had caught everyone off guard. And now here I am, trying to piece together a puzzle without knowing what the final picture looks like.

Lorcan heard I was looking for a game, and within the hour he had a location of where I needed to be. Lorcan decided that I wasn't coming here alone and joined me. It's been a while since he played a game, but he's good—not as good as me, but he can hold his own. Cowboy and Tank have also joined me. Our prez didn't want me coming alone. He wanted me to have backup in case shit hit the fan.

Malcolm Gallagher's also here, not to mention

his men that are casually playing, but they'll be paying attention. Jerry's also here. He's been spending more time in Spain the past few years. It would make sense for him to be here. Jer loves playing poker. It would be suspicious if he wasn't here.

"Étienne," I hear one of the men at the table say, his French accent thick and prominent as he stares at the blonde scarred guy.

Étienne glares at him. "Marcel," he growls, showcasing his own French accent. "Not here. I warned you."

The tension at the table goes wired, everyone watching the two of them with curiosity. I keep my face impassive but my mind is racing. Étienne and Marcel—these are names I haven't heard before. But I have a gut feeling that these two men are part of The Revenant.

I glance at Lorcan, who's sitting a few tables away. He's caught the exchange too, his eyes meeting mine for a split second before he turns back to his game. We've worked together long enough to communicate without words.

The tall blonde—Étienne—leans back in his chair, his posture relaxed but his eyes sharp. "Gentlemen," he says, his voice smooth, his accent even more defined. "Shall we focus on the game?"

The dealer nods and begins to deal the next hand. I pick up my cards, barely glancing at them. My attention is fixed on Étienne and Marcel, watching for any tells, any sign of them being part of The Revenant. I know they are. I can feel it in my gut.

As the night wears on, the stakes get higher. Étienne and Marcel are playing reckless, throwing as much money as they can at a pot in order to try to win it. They have sorely underestimated their opponents. We won't back down. Hell no. The other cash games have wound down and now the other players are watching our table with rapt interest.

Étienne's eyes glare at me as I raise the pot, pre-flop. I've watched him play, seen the way he likes to dominate the hands. Now it's time to switch it up. Let's see how he likes it.

I'm sitting with a pair of queens in my hand. Not the best starting pair, but also nowhere near the worst.

The flop comes down: ace of hearts, queen of spades, seven of clubs.

My heart rate quickens, but I keep my face neutral. Top set. I've got him.

Étienne's eyes narrow as he studies the board. He's first to act and he doesn't hesitate. "All in," he declares, pushing his stack of chips forward. The man's got close to five million in his stack. I've got a little more, meaning if I call and lose, I've a little behind to try to rebuild. But I'm confident in my hand.

The table collectively holds its breath. It's a massive overbet, way more than the pot. He's trying to bully everyone out of the hand.

Marcel folds quickly and the other players follow suit, until it's just me and Étienne.

I take a slow sip of my whiskey, letting the silence stretch. Étienne's jaw clenches, a flicker of irritation crossing his face.

"Call," I say finally, pushing my chips in to match his bet.

Étienne's eyes widen in surprise then narrow in suspicion. "Show your cards," he demands.

I shake my head. "You made the bet, you show first." It's the rules of the game. The person who calls the bet doesn't show their hand first. No, we bought the privilege of seeing his hand.

Étienne's face contorts in anger as he throws his cards face-up on the table. Ace-King of diamonds.

He has a pair of aces and that's it. Christ, it was beyond an overbet. It was reckless, stupid even.

I flip over my queens, revealing my set, and I conceal my smile as I watch the anger flash in his eyes. He knows he's beaten. There's no way in hell that he can win.

The turn and river come out blank, and just like that I know that I've made an enemy out of the Frenchman.

As the dealer pushes the massive pot toward me, I catch Étienne muttering under his breath in French. I'm not fluent in the language, but I know a little to get me by.

I can't make out all of what Étienne is saying, but I catch a few words. "Revenant" and "vengeance" stand out among the muttered French. My suspicions are confirmed—these men are definitely part of the organization I'm here to investigate.

As I stack my newly won chips, I feel the weight of Étienne's glare on me. The tension at the table has shifted. What was once a high-stakes game now feels like something far more dangerous. But Étienne would be stupid to try and start shit here. There are too many unknowns—for him at least. He'd never make it out of the building alive.

"Perhaps we should take a break," Marcel suggests, his voice tight. "Get some fresh air."

Étienne nods curtly, pushing back from the table. As he stands, I notice a flash of metal at his waist—a gun, concealed but not quite hidden enough.

"Good idea," I say casually, standing as well. "I could use a smoke."

As we file out onto the balcony overlooking the Spanish coastline, I catch Lorcan's eye. He nods almost imperceptibly, understanding the silent message. Things are about to get interesting.

The cool night air hits my face as I step outside; a welcome relief from the stuffy poker room. Étienne and Marcel huddle in a corner, speaking in rapid French. I light a cigarette, straining to hear their conversation while pretending to admire the view.

Suddenly, Étienne turns to me, his eyes cold. "You play well," he says, his voice laced with barely concealed anger.

I feel a hand land on my shoulder. "You should have done your homework," Jer says to Étienne. "You'd have known that the boy here is the best to have ever played the game."

Étienne's face contorts in disgust. "Lucky," he mutters. "Didn't realize that you know the..." he pauses, his gaze moving over me. "Kid. You didn't introduce us."

Jer nods. "I didn't. My mistake. Étienne, meet Bozo. He's a member of the Fury Vipers motorcycle club. Bozo, meet Étienne Moreau and his brother, Marcel Moreau, members of The Revenant."

I keep my face impassive at Jer's introduction, but inwardly, I'm reeling. He's just confirmed what I suspected about Étienne and Marcel's affiliation. Jer was quick to uncover everything this evening. Then again, I shouldn't be surprised. Jer always seems to know everything.

Étienne's eyes narrow, his hand twitching slightly toward his concealed weapon. "Fury Vipers," he spits out the words like they're poison. "I've heard of you. Causing trouble all over America and Ireland. Where next?"

I shrug, taking a long drag of my cigarette. "Wherever we like" I say coolly. "As for us causing trouble, I'd say that was you. From what I've heard, you're not exactly quiet about your business."

Marcel steps forward, his stance aggressive. "You have no idea what kind of business we're in," he growls.

Jer chuckles, the sound low and menacing. "Oh, I think we have a pretty good idea. The Revenant's been making quite a name for itself lately. Bit sloppy though, if you ask me."

Marcel's face flushes with anger. "Sloppy?" he hisses. "We've taken over half of central Europe in less than a year. Our leader—"

"Marcel," Étienne cuts him off sharply. "Enough."

But it's too late. Marcel's outburst has confirmed what we came here to find out. The Revenant is indeed behind the recent wave of violence and territory grabs, not to mention the new influx of trafficking.

"Mr. Moreau," I hear a woman say from behind me, "your car is waiting."

Étienne glares at me as he walks back inside. "I'm sure I'll be seeing you gentlemen again."

I watch as Étienne and Marcel disappear back into the casino, their backs rigid with tension. The woman who called for them follows close behind, her heels clicking on the marble floor.

"Well, that was interesting," Jer says, lighting up a cigar. "Seems our French friends are a bit touchy about their new enterprise."

I nod, my mind racing. "You and they confirmed what I had suspected, that they are part of the organization. The Revenant is behind the recent power grabs in Europe. But who's their leader? Marcel was about to say something before Étienne shut him up."

Jer takes a long drag on his cigar, his eyes scanning the coastline. "That is the million-dollar question. Whoever's running The Revenant is smart, keeping themselves hidden. But everyone slips up eventually."

I feel a presence behind me and turn to see Lorcan approaching, his face grim. "Cowboy and Tank are tailing the Moreau brothers," he says in a low voice. "We should head back inside, keep up appearances."

As we re-enter the casino, I can't shake the feeling that we've stumbled into something much bigger than we anticipated. The Revenant isn't just another criminal organization; they're a force to be reckoned with, and they're not afraid to show it.

I settle back at the poker table, but my mind isn't on the game anymore. I'm replaying every interaction, every word spoken by Étienne and Marcel. There has to be something we missed.

The dealer shuffles the cards, and I force myself to focus. I can't afford to lose too badly at the table. It would draw unwanted attention. Questions would arise as to how the hell Bozo would lose all the money he gained. That's not something I would do. Not ever.

It's around three a.m. when I call it a night. I've made more money than I had expected and now it's time to go to bed and regroup. We've got what we wanted. Now it's time to refocus on what's next.

Just as I exit the casino, my phone buzzes in my pocket, letting me know I have a new text message.

Cowboy: Lost them. Slippery bastards.

Fuck. There goes the lead we had.

SIXTEEN
BOZO

My grip tightens on the bottle of beer as I watch Gráinne smile brightly at the guy offering to buy her a drink. She looks stunning, utterly fucking beautiful, and that dress, it's like it was made to drive me wild. Not to mention those heels. Christ, I want to fuck her in nothing but the heels.

I take another swig, trying to drown the jealousy burning in my gut. The sound of Gráinne laughing has my teeth clenching. I watch as she laughs at something the guy says, tossing her dark hair over her shoulder. The movement draws my eyes to the curve of her neck, and I remember how it feels to trail kisses along that soft skin. My cock tightens against my pants as it does whenever I think about touching her.

Fuck, I shouldn't be here torturing myself like this. But I can't seem to tear my eyes away from her. Whenever she goes out and lets her hair down—which is rare—I'm always here, watching, waiting, making sure she's okay. I won't ever let anything happen to her. Grá is by far the most important person in my life and I will protect her with everything I have.

The bartender slides another beer in front of me without asking. He knows the routine by now. I nod my thanks, but my attention is drawn back to Gráinne as she accepts the drink from her admirer. Their fingers brush as she takes the glass, and I grip the edge of the bar so hard my knuckles turn white.

Gráinne glances in my direction, her eyes meeting mine for just a moment. I'm rooted to the spot as she gives me that soft as fuck smile, the one that's solely reserved for me. That smile, it's like a punch to the gut. If things were different, if I were different, I'd give her what she deserves, be the man she deserves. I want to go to her, to pull her away from that guy and claim her as mine. But I can't. That's not something I can do. Her life is untouched, the way it should be. After all the shit her dad put her through, I won't be the reason she's hurt again.

I take another long pull from my beer, trying to

cool the fire in my veins. The guy leans in closer to Gráinne, whispering something in her ear. My jaw clenches so hard I think I might crack a tooth. Fuck, I know that over the past few weeks, she's changed. She's cooler with me. She's not wanting to lose the friendship we have, but I won't be able to keep my cool if she wants to start dating other people. Fuck.

Gráinne laughs again, but this time it sounds forced, uncomfortable. I straighten up, every muscle in my body tensing. I know that laugh. It's the one she uses when she's trying to be polite but wants to escape. The guy doesn't seem to notice, or maybe he doesn't care. He puts his hand on her lower back, and I see Gráinne stiffen.

That's it. I'm off my barstool before I even realize I've moved. I weave through the crowd, my eyes never leaving Gráinne. As I get closer, I see that she's tense as a bow and there's a slight tremble that runs through her body.

"Thank you for the drink, but I should really be going," I hear her say, her voice tight and forced.

The guy's hand tightens on her waist. "Come on, the night's still young. How about we get out of here?"

I'm at Gráinne's side in an instant, my hand coming to rest on her shoulder. She jumps slightly at the contact, but then relaxes as she realizes it's me. I see the relief shining in her eyes.

"Everything alright here, Grá?" I ask, my voice low and dangerous. I turn to the asshole who's still got his arm around her waist. My eyes are locked on him, daring him to make a move.

"Con," she breathes, relief evident in her voice. "I was just leaving."

The guy looks between us, confusion and annoyance warring on his face. "Hey, man, we were in the middle of something here."

I feel Gráinne press closer to me, her warmth seeping into my side. It takes everything in me not to wrap my arm around her and pull her even closer.

"Doesn't look like it to me," I growl. "She said she's leaving. I suggest you let her."

He scoffs, puffing out his chest. "And who the fuck are you? Her boyfriend?"

"I'm leaving," Grá says, her voice soft, but I can hear the fear in it.

She moves to step away, but the guy grabs her arm. "Come on, don't be like that—"

In a flash, my hand is wrapped around his wrist, squeezing it tight. There's no doubt that I'm going to leave a bruise, but he shouldn't be fucking touching her.

"The lady said she's leaving," I growl, my voice low and dangerous. "I suggest you take your hand off her."

The guy's eyes widen, a flicker of fear crossing his face as he realizes he's out of his depth. He releases Gráinne's arm, and I let go of his wrist. He takes a step back, rubbing his wrist and glaring at me.

"Whatever, man. She's not worth the trouble anyway," he mutters, trying to save face as he slinks away into the crowd.

I turn to Gráinne, my eyes scanning her for any sign of harm. "You okay, Grá?"

She nods, still trembling slightly. "Yeah, I'm fine. Thanks, Con."

I want to pull her into my arms, to hold her and never let go. But I can't. Instead, I settle for placing my hand on the small of her back, guiding her toward the exit.

"Come on, let's get you out of here."

We step out into darkness, and I feel Gráinne take a deep breath beside me. She's still shaking, and I can't help but pull her closer to my side.

"Your place isn't far," I say, trying to keep my voice neutral when all I want to do is go back in there and kill that motherfucker for putting his hands on her. "We can grab a taxi if you want."

Gráinne looks up at me, her eyes shining in the streetlights. "Can we just walk for a bit? I need to clear my head."

We start walking in comfortable silence, my hand still on her back. I can feel the tension slowly ebb away from her.

"I'm sorry, Con. I shouldn't have gone out tonight. I just needed a distraction."

I glance down at her, a frown furrowed between my brows. "A distraction from what?"

She sighs, running a hand through her hair. "Everything. Work, life... you."

My steps falter for a moment. "Me?"

Gráinne stops walking and turns to face me. "Con, I can't keep doing this. I've been trying to protect our friendship, but the truth is I want more. But you—" she pauses, shaking her head.

My heart is racing as I watch her. The fuck is going on? "But me, what, Grá?"

She takes a shaky breath. "But you'll never want more. You're never going to want more. You'll never want me that way."

Is she for real? "Grá," I say thickly. "If there was anyone in this world that I'd want more with, it's you. You're the only one that I'd ever..." I pause, my heart hammering in my chest. The words are right there, on the tip of my tongue, but I can't seem to get them out. Gráinne's looking at me with those big, beautiful eyes, a mixture of hope and fear swirling in their depths.

"The only one you'd ever what, Con?" she whispers, her voice barely audible over the sound of passing cars and the distant thrum of the city.

I swallow hard, my throat suddenly dry. "The only one I'd ever want to be with," I finally manage to say. "But Grá, you deserve so much better than me. I'm not good for you."

She takes a step closer, her hand coming up to rest on my chest. I can feel the warmth of her palm through my shirt, and it takes everything in me not to pull her against me.

"Don't you think I should be the one to decide what's good for me?" she says, her voice stronger now. "Con, I've known you for years. I know who you are, what you do. And I still want you."

My hands move of their own accord, coming to rest on her hips. "Grá, you don't understand. The things I've done, the things I might have to do... I can't drag you into that world."

She shakes her head, a small, sad smile on her lips. "I'm already in that world, Con. I've been in it since you brought me to Jer." She gives me a sad smile and takes a step backward. "But I get it," she says, her voice soft and filled with sadness. "I need you to understand that you're amazing, Connor, that you're worthy of love." She takes yet another step backward, and the space she's putting between us is pissing me the fuck off. "I don't think I can wait around for you to find out if you'll ever be ready for more."

I grit my teeth. This is what I was dreading. I knew there'd come a time when she'd want more, when I wouldn't be able to give her what she needs.

Fuck, I can't speak. I can't do anything but watch her and pray that she doesn't walk away.

I hear her heavy sigh, watching the disappointment seep into her eyes. "I think," she says as she licks her lips, her gaze sliding to the left, away from me, "that it may be best to have some space."

My jaw clenches. "Not going to happen," I say. Not a fucking chance. "I get that you want a fuck of a lot more than I can give you, Sunshine, but I ain't going anywhere."

"What?" she splutters. "But you just said that you can't give me what I want."

I nod. "I can't, but that doesn't mean I'm going to give you space. Not done that in all the years I've known you. Why the fuck should I do that now?"

Gráinne stares at me, her eyes wide with confusion and frustration. "Because it hurts, Con," she says, her voice barely above a whisper. "It hurts to be around you, to want you, and know that I can't have you."

Her words hit me like a physical blow. The last thing I ever wanted was to cause her pain. I take a step toward her, closing the distance between us. "Grá," I say, my voice rough with emotion, "I never meant to hurt you."

She looks up at me, her eyes shining with unshed tears. "I know you didn't. But that doesn't change how I feel."

I reach out, cupping her face in my hands. Her skin is soft under my palms, and I can feel her pulse racing. "Tell me what to do, Sunshine. Tell me how to fix it." I can't fucking lose her. It's just not an option. "What can I do?"

Gráinne stares at me, her eyes wide with disbelief. "Connor, you can't have it both ways. You can't expect me to be okay with just friends right now. I'm not able to turn off my feelings like a fucking light switch. You may find it easy to push me away but I can't—"

I release her and run a hand through my hair,

frustration building inside me. "I'm not pushing you away, Grá. I'm trying to protect you."

"From what?" she demands, her voice rising. "From you? From your world? I told you, I'm already a part of it."

"You don't understand—"

"Then make me understand!" she shouts, her eyes flashing with anger and hurt. "Stop making decisions for me and just talk to me, Con!"

I take a deep breath, trying to find the right words. "Grá, my life is dangerous. The things I do, the people I deal with... it's not safe. And the thought of you getting caught up in that, of you getting hurt because of me..." I shake my head. The thought is too much to bear.

Her expression softens slightly, but the determination in her eyes doesn't waver. "Con, I'm not some fragile doll that needs to be protected. I'm stronger than you give me credit for."

"I know you're strong," I say, my voice low. "You're the strongest woman I know, but that doesn't change things."

She sighs, her arms hanging loosely by her sides. "So that's it then?" she asks, sounding defeated.

I don't know what the hell to say. There's nothing left to be said. We both know where we stand. I just wish that things were different. That I wasn't such a fucking coward. If I could, I'd be with her in a heartbeat.

"I want to go home," she whispers as she turns away from me and starts to walk toward her house.

I follow her, not willing to leave her alone, knowing the darkness that lurks in the shadows.

We walk in silence, the tension between us thick and heavy. This isn't something I'm used to. Things between Grá and I have always been easy, carefree, stress free.

As we near her apartment building, I notice her steps slowing. She turns to face me, her eyes shimmering with unshed tears.

"Con," she says, her voice barely above a whisper. "I don't want to lose you."

The vulnerability in her voice tears at my heart. I step closer, unable to resist the pull she has on me. "You won't lose me, Sunshine. Not ever."

She looks up at me, her gaze searching mine. "But things can't stay the same, can they?"

I swallow hard, knowing she's right. Things have shifted between us, and there's no going back. "No," I admit. "They can't."

Gráinne nods, a sad smile tugging at her lips. "So what do we do now?"

I reach out, tucking a strand of hair behind her ear. My fingers linger on her cheek, and I feel her lean in to my touch. "I don't know," I say honestly. "But we'll figure it out. Together."

She takes a shaky breath, her eyes never leaving mine. "Okay," she whispers, a tear falling from her eyes. "Goodnight, Connor."

I press a kiss to her forehead. "Night, Sunshine," I reply, my voice hoarse.

I watch as she enters her home and feel a heaviness settle over my chest. She closes the door behind her, not once looking backward.

Christ, what the fuck have I done?

SEVENTEEN
GRÁINNE

"Another one for you, Grá," Sandra tells me with a sigh. "It's busy tonight."

I take the file from her hands. "It's Friday night," I reply. It's always busy in the emergency room on a Friday night. Hell, every single night is busy.

I flip open the file and scan the patient details. Male, mid-forties, multiple lacerations and contusions. Possible concussion. Another bar fight, most likely.

"Cubicle three," Sandra says, already moving on to the next case.

I nod and make my way down the crowded hallway. Taking a deep breath, I pull back the curtain to cubicle three. The man on the bed looks up at me, his left eye swollen shut, dried blood caking his nose and split lip.

"Good evening," I say, keeping my voice steady and professional. "I'm Dr. Fallon. Can you tell me what happened?"

He winces as he tries to sit up straighter. "I do not recall," he tells me, his French accent thick and heavy. "I woke up like this."

I sigh. This isn't the first time I've heard a patient tell me they don't recall how they got their injuries. It's usually one of three reasons. One, they're a victim of domestic violence and are unable to speak up. Two, they're affiliated with a gang, mafia, or club. Then there's the third option: they get so drunk or high, they actually don't remember what the hell happened to them. "Let's take a look at those injuries, shall we?"

As I begin my examination, I can't help but wonder how many more patients like this I'll see before the night is through. It's going to be a long shift.

I gently probe the man's face, noting the extent of the bruising and swelling. His right cheekbone feels tender, possibly fractured. As I examine the lacerations on his scalp, he winces and pulls away.

"Sorry," I murmur. "I know it hurts. I'll try to be quick."

His one good eye watches me with rapt attention as I continue my assessment. There's something off about him, which has me on edge.

"Can you tell me your name?" I ask, shining a penlight in his eyes to check pupil response.

He hesitates a beat too long before answering. "Jean. Jean Dubois."

I make a noncommittal sound, jotting notes in his chart. The name doesn't match the one on his intake form.

"Well, Mr. Dubois, I'm going to order some x-rays and a CT scan to rule out any fractures or internal bleeding. In the meantime, I'll have a nurse come clean and dress these wounds."

As I turn to leave, his hand shoots out and grabs my wrist. His grip is surprisingly strong. "No one," he growls thickly. "No one is to know that I'm here."

"Mr. Dubois," I say, reaching for his fingers and prying them from my wrist. "This is a hospital. You cannot manhandle me." Once I get him to release his hold on me, I ease out of the cubicle.

My heart races as I pull the curtain closed behind me. Something is definitely not right with this patient. I make my way to the nurses' station, my mind whirling with possibilities.

"Sandra," I call out, spotting her behind the desk. "That patient in cubicle three, can you pull up his intake form again?"

She nods, tapping away at the computer. "Here you go," she says, turning the screen toward me.

I scan the information quickly. The name on the form reads Antoine Robert, not Jean Dubois. My stomach clenches as the unease grows. There's definitely something suspicious about this man.

"Everything okay?" Sandra asks, noticing my furrowed brow.

I hesitate, unsure how much to share. "Can you do me a favor? When you go in to clean his wounds, take note of any tattoos or identifying marks. And be careful. There's something off about him."

Sandra's eyes widen slightly, but she nods. "Will do, Dr. Fallon."

I'm about to head off to my next patient, when the emergency room doors burst open. Two men stride in, their faces grim. But my spine tingles as I look at them. One of them is blonde and has a scar on his jaw; the other has dark hair and even darker eyes. Both men look as though they don't belong.

"We're looking for a man," one of them

announces to Sandra, his accent just like my patient's. French. "Mid-forties, dark hair. He's injured."

My blood runs cold. Whoever these men are, they're after my patient. I catch Sandra's eye, and she nods imperceptibly. She feels it too.

I know that she has this under control. I continue on with my other patients, needing to ensure that they're cared for, but my mind races as I think of the patient with the fake name. He's been really worked over, and I can't help but think that he's in trouble. Serious trouble. The two men who came to look for him scream danger.

It takes me around thirty minutes before I'm able to check on the patient again. As I approach cubicle three, I hear hushed, angry voices. I sneak into the cubicle, making sure not to make a noise with the curtain, but I freeze when I see both the men have entered his cubicle. The blonde one has his back to me.

"You should have realized what would happen, Antoine. You should have known we'd come for you."

"I won't tell," Antoine pleads. "The moment I'm out of here, I'll be gone. No one will ever hear from me."

"That's not going to do," the dark-haired man

growls. "You've displeased Dragomir," he snarls. "There's no escaping for you. No leaving."

I watch as Antoine trembles. "You're going to kill me—here?"

I pull in a ragged breath. I have no idea what the hell is going on.

The air turns static as everyone turns to face me. I take a step backward, my heart pounding. "Sorry," I stumble. "I have to check Mr. Dubois' vitals."

The blonde man watches me carefully, his eyes narrowed, before he steps closer to me. "You like eavesdropping?" he accuses.

I swallow hard, plastering on a fake smile as I skirt around him. "I didn't eavesdrop," I assure him as I move toward my patient. "If you wouldn't mind giving us some privacy," I say, not looking at them, my gaze focused on Antoine. "I'll check on him and once I'm done, I'll call you back in."

"If it's all the same to you, Doc," the blonde growls, "we'll stay where we are."

I spin around and face the two dangerous men, my heart pounding, my hands trembling. "I'm sorry," I tell them. "But every patient has the right to privacy."

I'm so distracted by the two men that I forget that my patient is also dangerous. While my back is turned, he surges up from his bed. His hand wraps around my neck, and I still as I feel a sharpness at the base of my throat.

"I won't go with them," he stammers. "I won't."

"Antoine," the blonde man snaps, his eyes wild as he stares at us. "You can't escape what's about to happen." He edges closer to us.

"Stay back!" my captor hisses, his arm tightening around me. "I'll cut her if you come any closer!"

"Let her go, Antoine," the blonde one says, his voice cold. "You know how this ends."

"No!" Antoine grunts, pressing the blade harder against my throat. I feel a warm trickle of blood and try not to whimper. "I know too much. You'll kill me the moment I surrender."

My mind races, trying to find a way out of this nightmare.

I can hear sirens in the distance–the gardai are on their way. I wonder if someone knows that I'm here, that I'm trapped in this nightmare?

"Listen to me," I say, my voice barely above a whisper. "This isn't the way you're going to get out of this."

Antoine's breath is hot on my ear as he considers my words. For a moment, I think he might relent, but then the dark-haired man takes a step forward, and Antoine tenses.

"Back!" he snaps. "Back now, or I swear I'll kill her!"

The smirk on the blonde man's face is unlike anything I've ever seen. "I do not care," he states. "She's heard too much as it is. You did this. You know what the repercussions are, Antoine. You knew that but you still came here."

Antoine's grip on me releases slightly and I try to push away from him, but he's too strong. I feel Antoine's grip tighten again as he pulls me back against him. The blade digs deeper into the skin on my neck, and I can't help but let out a small gasp of pain.

"You're bluffing," Antoine says, but his voice wavers with uncertainty.

The dark-haired man steps forward once again, his hand reaching inside his jacket. "He's not bluffing, Antoine. We have orders. No loose ends."

Time seems to slow down as I realize that these men truly don't care if I live or die. I'm just collateral damage in whatever game they're playing.

I hear a commotion outside the cubicle, followed by Sandra's raised voice. I hear her tell someone that

I need help. My heart hammers against my chest. Oh God, I hope it's the gardai.

The men glance at one another before shooting Antoine with a dark, warning look. They quickly flee, no doubt realizing that the gardai are here. They leave me alone with Antoine, his blade still pressed tightly against my throat.

"We're going to get out of here," he growls, pressing the blade harder against my throat. More blood trickles down my neck.

The sound of heavy footsteps grow closer, and within seconds, the curtain is ripped open, revealing two uniformed gardai.

"Garda! Drop your weapon!" one of them shouts.

Everything happens at once. Antoine shoves me to the side, lunging for the window. I stumble, my head hitting the edge of the bed as I fall. Black dots fill my vision as I try to catch my bearings.

Footsteps sound as the gardai rush toward Antoine.

Pain shoots through my body, and I can't help but cry out in agony. Desperately, I curl up into a ball and cover my head with my arms, hoping to escape the chaos. But it's too much, and everything goes black as I lose consciousness, sinking into the darkness like I'm sinking into an abyss.

The chaos around me fades into silence.

EIGHTEEN
GRÁINNE

I groan as I move toward my front door. I'm still a little tender. It's been a week since I was attacked. After I fell unconscious at the hospital, I was kept overnight for observations. But doctors don't make the best of patients, and I needed to get out of there. Thankfully, other than a few scrapes and bruises, I was okay and didn't need any further treatment.

The knocking at the door gets louder, which causes the pounding in my head to intensify. I've got a raging headache and whoever is at the door isn't helping matters. I wrench the door open, ready to snap at the person on the other side, but the words die on my lips as I stare at the blonde man from the hospital, the one my patient was terrified of.

"Ms. Fallon, such a pleasure to see you again," he says with a sinister smile.

"How did you find out where I live?" I ask, my voice trembling. I know this man is dangerous. I'm not stupid. I know he's here to kill me. *"We have orders. No loose ends."* That's what the dark-haired man said to Antoine.

My heart races as I take an involuntary step back. The man's smile widens, his eyes gleaming with malice.

"Oh, come now, Dr. Fallon. Finding you was child's play. You should know better than to underestimate us."

He takes a step forward, forcing me further into my apartment. I frantically scan the room for a weapon, anything I can use to defend myself.

"What do you want?" I manage to croak out, trying to buy time.

"I think you know exactly what I want," he replies smoothly. "You've seen too much, heard too much. We can't have you running around with that kind of knowledge."

My back hits the wall. I'm cornered. The man reaches into his jacket, and I know this is it. I won't let him kill me. Hell no.

"You're crazy. You know that, right?" I hiss as my hands reach out to my left, where I know the lamp is. "I don't know what you think I overheard, but I didn't. I have hundreds of patients every week. I was busy. I entered Mr. Antoine's room and gasped as I hadn't expected visitors."

His eyes narrow on me as he steps forward. "You're a good liar, Dr. Fallon," he grunts, pulling a knife from his pocket. "But we both know that you're lying."

"I'm not," I tell him, my voice trembling.

He laughs, and it sounds manic, almost crazy. He brushes the tip of his knife along my cheek. "It's a shame," he says, his gaze raking over me. "You are pretty, but I have instructions."

In a flash, I grab the lamp and swing it with all my might. It connects with his head with a sickening crunch, sending shards of ceramic flying. The man staggers back, momentarily stunned. I hear the sound of his knife clattering against the floor. I don't waste a second. I bolt for the door, my heart pounding in my ears.

But he's quick to recover. His hand latches on to my arm, yanking me back with brutal force. I cry out as I'm slammed against the wall. "That wasn't very nice, Dr. Fallon," he snarls, blood trickling down his temple. "I was going to make this quick, but now... now I think I'll take my time."

Panic surges through me. I knee him in the groin, hard. He doubles over, cursing, and I make another dash for the door. Fingers grasp my hair and pull hard. I cry out as he tugs hard, causing my hair to be pulled at the root. I fall backward, needing him to release me.

I hit the floor with a thud, my head bouncing off the ground. "I do love a good fight," he growls, before raising his hand and punching me in the face.

Stars explode behind my eyes as his fist connects with my cheek. The pain is blinding, too much. I'm struggling to breathe, to form any kind of coherent thought.

Over and over again, he lets loose on me, punching me. Pain unlike anything I've ever experienced hits me as my vision starts to fade. No, I can't let this happen. I swallow the fear as adrenaline surges through me, dulling the pain just enough. I won't go down without a fight.

As he pulls back for another punch, I thrust my palm upward, catching him square in the nose. There's a satisfying crunch, and he reels back, blood gushing down his face.

"You bitch!" he roars, but his grip on me loosens.

I scramble to my feet, my vision blurry, my head spinning. The door. I need to get to the door. But my legs are wobbly, and I stumble, crashing into the side table.

The man is on me again, grabbing my shoulders and spinning me around. His face is a mask of rage, blood streaming from his nose. "I'm going to enjoy this," he snarls, the knife now pressed against my throat.

How the hell did he manage to get the knife again? Fuck. I don't know what I'm going to do. How the hell am I going to get out of this?

My fingers barely graze the doorknob, when I feel a sharp, burning pain in my side. I look down to see the knife buried in my flesh, the man's hand still gripping the handle.

"No loose ends," he whispers in my ear as he twists the blade.

I scream, the pain blinding. But through the pain, fear, and panic, I hear something else—sirens. They're getting closer. Did someone call for help? I really hope so.

The man hears them too. His eyes widen with alarm. "Damn it," he mutters, yanking the knife out.

I collapse to the floor, pressing my hand against the wound. The man hesitates, his eyes darting between me and the door. The sirens are getting louder, closer. He curses under his breath, clearly torn between finishing the job and saving his own skin.

"This isn't over," he snarls, wiping his bloody nose with the back of his hand. "We'll find you, wherever you go."

With that, he bolts for the door, wrenching it open and disappearing. I lie there, gasping, my hand pressed firmly against my side. Blood seeps through my fingers, warm and sticky. The room spins around me, and I fight to stay conscious.

The sirens stop abruptly, replaced by the sound of car doors slamming and hurried footsteps. "In here!" I try to shout, but it comes out as barely more than a whisper.

Suddenly, two gardai rush in, guns drawn. Their eyes widen as they take in the scene—the shattered lamp, the blood-stained floor, and me, crumpled against the wall.

"We need an ambulance, now!" one of them shouts into his radio as the other kneels beside me.

"Ma'am, can you hear me? Stay with us. Help is on the way," the garda says, pressing his hands over mine to stem the bleeding.

I try to speak, to warn them about the man, about

the danger, but my vision is fading. The last thing I see is the garda's concerned face before darkness claims me.

I drift in and out of consciousness, catching snippets of conversation and flashes of light. The wail of an ambulance siren. Paramedics shouting medical jargon. The rush of a hospital corridor. Then nothing.

I'M BEYOND SORE. I've got a broken nose, multiple contusions, and I feel like I've been hit by a damn truck. My entire body feels as though it's been through the wringer.

"Dr. Fallon? Are you awake?" I hear a familiar voice ask.

I turn my head slightly to see Detective Connolly—the garda who interviewed me after Antoine attacked me at the hospital—entering my room. His face is etched with concern.

"Yes, I'm awake. You found me?" I croak, my throat dry and scratchy.

Connolly leans forward, his voice low. "Someone tried to kill you, Dr. Fallon. We got a call about a disturbance at your address. When we arrived, we found you bleeding out on the floor. The attacker had fled."

I close my eyes, the memories flooding back. The blonde man, the knife, the pain. "He said... no loose ends," I whisper.

Connolly's expression darkens. "We believe this is connected to Antoine's murder. Dr. Fallon—"

Panic rushes through me. "Murder?" I ask. What the hell does he mean, murder? No. God no.

Connolly nods grimly. "Antoine was found dead days after he attacked you. We think whoever did it came for you next."

My heart races as the implications sink in. Antoine is dead. They killed him, just like they tried to kill me. And they won't stop until I'm silenced too.

I hear footsteps in the hall, close to my room, and my body tenses. Is it the man? Is he coming back to kill me?

"Grá." I hear the low, anguished tone of Jerry Houlihan as he steps into my room. "God, what the fuck happened? I swear to God, girlie, you've about put me into an early grave. This is the second time in a week, Gráinne," he growls. "What the fuck is going on?"

"Mr. Houlihan," Detective Connolly begins as

he rises to his feet. "I'm currently speaking with Dr. Fallon—"

Jer cuts his gaze to the detective. "Yeah?" he spits. "Tell me what the fuck you're doing about this shit? Hmm?"

Detective Connolly's jaw tightens as he faces Jerry. "Mr. Houlihan, I understand you're upset, but this is an ongoing investigation. I can't disclose—"

"My daughter is lying in a hospital bed, and you're giving me the runaround? I want answers, and I want them now!"

I wince at the volume of Jerry's voice, my head still pounding. "Jer," I croak, "please, not so loud." But my heart is beating rapidly. His daughter? God, he's the fucking best.

Jerry's gaze softens as he looks at me, concern replacing the anger. He moves to my bedside, taking my hand gently in his. "Christ, Grá. Look at you. I should've been there. I should've—"

"You couldn't have known," I whisper, squeezing his hand weakly.

Connolly clears his throat. "Mr. Houlihan, I assure you we're taking this very seriously. We have officers stationed outside Dr. Fallon's room, and we're working on identifying her attacker."

Jerry scoffs. "And what about when she leaves the hospital? What then?"

I feel a chill run down my spine at the thought. The blonde man's words echo in my mind. *"We'll find you, wherever you go."*

"Why don't you go and do your job," Jerry hisses, turning his back on Detective Connolly and facing me. "I've got her."

I hear the sound of the chair scraping against the floor, followed by footsteps. I take a deep breath when the door closes behind the detective. I have no idea what the hell I'm going to do. I thought I was safe, but today proved I'm far fucking from it.

"Grá, how are you feeling?" Jer asks softly.

"Like I've been hit by a truck." I manage a weak smile. "But I'm alive."

Jerry's eyes fill with tears. "Christ, Gráinne, when I got the call... I thought..." He trails off, unable to finish the sentence.

I swallow hard. "I know. Me too," I whisper. "Please don't tell Connor," I plead with him.

Things between the two of us have been awkward since our talk. I still love him but I need time. I need to adjust to everything. Having the craziness of the past week hasn't helped. I've wanted to call him so many times, but haven't.

Jerry's eyes narrow. "Don't tell Connor? Are you out of your mind, Grá? He needs to know."

I shake my head weakly. "No, please. Things are... complicated between us right now. I don't want him to worry."

Jerry sighs heavily. "Gráinne, I know you two are having issues, but this is bigger than that. You were nearly killed. Twice. He deserves to know, and you need all the support you can get right now."

I close my eyes, feeling tears well up. "I'm scared, Jer," I admit quietly. "I don't know what to do. These people, whoever they are, they're not going to stop."

Jerry squeezes my hand. "That's exactly why you need Connor. And me. And everyone else who cares about you. We'll figure this out together and keep you safe."

I know he's right, but the thought of dragging Connor into this mess makes my stomach churn. "What if they come after him too? I couldn't bear it if something happened to him because of me."

"Connor's a big boy, Grá. He can handle himself. And he'd want to be here for you, no matter what's going on between you two."

"He doesn't," I tell him honestly. "That's why things are so awkward between us. He doesn't want what I want and that's okay. But I need space."

Jerry's brow furrows as he processes my words. "What do you mean, he doesn't want what you want? Connor's crazy about you, Grá."

I sigh, wincing as the movement causes pain to flare in my side. "He doesn't want anything more than sex, Jer. He made that pretty clear."

Jerry's eyes widen in surprise. "He said that? To you?"

I nod, feeling the sting of tears again. "We've spoken about it. We're at an impasse. Jer, I'm ready to find someone who'll love me and settle down."

Jerry runs a hand through his hair, looking troubled. "Jesus, Grá, I had no idea. But still, this situation—"

"Is exactly why I can't drag him into it," I interrupt. "What's the point of putting him in danger?"

He shakes his head. "I don't agree, but if this is what you want, then I'll respect that. But Grá, anything else happens to you and I'll be calling Connor myself."

I sigh with relief. "Thank you," I whisper. "When can I go home?" I hate being in the hospital. I just want to be at home where I can be alone.

"Not yet," Jer tells me softly. "I've got someone currently installing extra security at your apartment.

By the time you're released, your apartment will be back to normal."

I feel like I could cry. God, what the hell did I do to deserve Jerry to love me like a child and protect me like one too? I reach out and take his hand. "Thank you."

"Never thank me for doing all I can to protect you Grá. I'll make sure that you're not alone. Not anymore."

I give him a smile. "You're the best. You know that, Jer?"

He chuckles. "Only sometimes. Now rest, Grá. You need to rest. It's the only way your body will heal."

A KNOCK SOUNDS on the door, and I watch as the door opens slightly and Mike pops his head in. "Hey, Grá," he says with a big smile.

Since he asked me out, he's backed off somewhat but has remained friendly. Which I'm thankful for.

"Hey," I reply. Thankfully, today's the day I get to leave here.

Mike steps into the room, his smile fading slightly as he takes in my appearance. "Wow, you look... well, you've looked better," he says, attempting humor.

I manage a weak laugh. "Thanks, Mike. Just what every girl wants to hear."

He approaches the bed, his expression growing serious. "How are you feeling? Really?"

I sigh, wincing as I shift in the bed. "Like I've been hit by a truck, stabbed, and then run over again for good measure. But hey, at least I'm alive, right?"

Mike nods solemnly. "That's the spirit. Listen, Grá, I heard about what happened. I can't believe someone would... I mean, it's just..." He trails off, clearly at a loss for words.

"Yeah, it's pretty messed up," I agree. "But I'm okay. Or I will be, anyway."

Mike hesitates for a moment before speaking again. "I know things have been a bit awkward between us since... well, you know. But I want you to know that I'm here for you. As a friend. If you need anything at all."

His sincerity touches me. "Thanks, Mike. That means a lot."

He gives me a soft smile. "The offer of a date still stands, Grá. Just say the word."

"I appreciate that," I tell him, but I'm not sure I'm ready for anything like that. Not now anyway.

Just then, Jerry returns with a nurse. "Alright, Grá," he says, his gaze on Mike, and I watch as his eyes narrow. "Time to get you out of here. Your chariot awaits."

I can't help but smile at the sight of the wheelchair. "Thank God," I sigh dramatically. I'm so glad I can get out of here. I just pray that the man doesn't return.

NINETEEN
BOZO

We've still not found out anything else about The Revenant. Everyone is fucking tight-lipped and it pisses me off. Someone out there has to know something and is willing to talk.

Pyro, Raptor, and I enter the clubhouse. I'm shocked to see Gráinne here. I haven't seen her in weeks. Things have been weird since she told me she wants more. I wish I could be the man to give it to her. I know she deserves better, but fuck, the thought of some other man with her makes me feel murderous.

"Darlin'," Raptor says to his old lady, Mallory. She's been through shit and is slowly recovering. "Everythin' okay?"

Mallory nods, a bright smile on her lips. "Yeah,

I'm good. Just catching up with Grá." Since everything went down with Mallory, Gráinne's been her doctor and has helped out, and the two women have grown closer.

Raptor turns to Gráinne. "Doc, everythin' okay with her?"

I watch as she clasps her hands together. "Yes, Raptor, her pregnancy is coming along perfectly."

The entire clubhouse descends into silence. "Wanna repeat that?" Raptor growls, and I tense. No one fucking speaks to her like that. He turns to Mallory. "You're pregnant?"

"Surprise," she says weakly. "Yeah, honey, we're having another baby."

He closes the distance between them and hauls her into his arms.

"And that's my cue to leave," Gra says, laughing. "Mallory, I'll speak to you later."

I watch as she gets closer, and my gut twists as I see the bruises that mar her face. "The fuck happened to your face?" I growl as I reach for her arm and pull her closer. Fuck, her face is fucked up. What the hell happened?

"I'm fine," she insists, wrenching her arm from my grip.

"Fine my ass. Fuck, Gra, what the hell?"

She shakes her head. "I've got to go."

"Gra, call me and let me know how the date goes," Mallory calls out.

Grá's eyes widen before she ducks her head and hurries from the room.

I turn to Mallory, anger pulsing through me as I glare at her. "What date?" I hear the sound of Grá's car starting up and peeling away from the clubhouse.

Mallory crosses her arms over her chest and glares right back at me. "She's not going to wait around for you to get your head out of your ass, Bozo. You don't want her, fine, but someone else does. Leave her alone and let her be happy."

I storm out of the clubhouse, my mind racing. The image of Gráinne's bruised face is seared into my brain, fueling my rage. Who the fuck touched her? And now she's going on a date? Over my dead body.

I hop on my bike, the engine roaring to life beneath me. I need answers, and I need them now.

The ride there is a blur as I'm filled with angry thoughts. No one touches Grá. Not one fucking person should ever put their hands on her. She's sweet and pure. She's already had her world rocked by pain and suffering. No more. No fucking more.

When I pull up to her apartment, I see her car in the driveway. She's home.

I pound on her door, not giving a shit about the neighbors. "Gráinne, open up!"

After a moment, I hear the click of the lock and the door swings open. She stands there, looking exhausted and weary. Her face is free of makeup, showcasing every fucking bruise on her face. Christ, it's a fucking lot worse than I had ever imagined. "What do you want?"

I push past her into the apartment, my eyes scanning for any signs of trouble. "Who hit you?"

She sighs, closing the door and crossing her arms over her chest. "It's nothing, just an accident at work. A patient got violent."

"Bullshit," I snarl, turning to face her. There's no way it was an accident. She's been worked over. No fucking way was it anything but intentional. "Don't lie to me, Gra. Who did this to you?"

Her eyes flash with anger. "Why do you care? You made it clear you don't want anything more than sex. I told you, Connor, I can't do this."

Her words hit me like a punch to the gut. I take a deep breath, trying to calm the rage burning inside me. "I care because it's you, Gráinne. I always care when it comes to you."

She lets out a bitter laugh. "That's rich, coming from you. You push me away at every turn, and now you're here acting like some knight in shining armor?"

I run a hand through my hair, frustration building. "Look, I know I've been an asshole. But seeing you hurt, it's killing me. Please, just tell me who did this."

Gráinne's eyes soften slightly, but she stands her ground. "It's not your problem to solve, Connor. I can handle my own issues."

"The hell you can," I growl, stepping closer. "You're walking around with a face full of bruises. I can see your fucking nose is broken. Now you're about to go on some date. What if this guy's dangerous?"

She rolls her eyes. "For your information, I hadn't decided about the date. And it's none of your business anyway."

I feel a wave of relief wash over me at her words, but I push it aside. "It is my business. You're important to me, Gra."

She looks at me, her eyes searching mine. "What does that even mean, Connor? Because I can't keep doing this dance with you. It hurts too much."

I swallow hard, knowing I'm at a crossroads. I can keep pushing her away, keep pretending I don't feel what I feel, or I can finally man up and admit the truth.

"It means I'm in love with you, Gráinne," I blurt out, the words tumbling from my lips before I can stop them. "I've been fighting it because I'm not good enough for you. You deserve better than a guy like me, with all my baggage and bullshit. But seeing you hurt and thinking about you with someone else... it's tearing me apart."

Gráinne's eyes widen, her mouth falling open in shock. For a moment, she just stares at me, and I feel my heart pounding in my chest.

"You... you love me?" she whispers, her voice barely audible.

I nod, taking a step closer to her. "I do. I think I always have. I've pushed you away because I know my family was fucked up. My dad was a cunt and my mam was too weak to stand up to him. But I can't stand the thought of losing you."

Tears well up in her eyes, and she shakes her head. "Connor, you can't just say that and expect everything to be okay. I was trying to get over you. You hurt me by always walking away."

"I know," I say, my voice rough with emotion. "And I'll spend the rest of my life making it up to you if you'll let me. Just please, give me a chance to prove it to you."

She takes a shaky breath, and I can see the conflict in her eyes. "What about the club? Your lifestyle? All the reasons you've given me. They haven't changed."

I step closer, gently cupping her face in my hands, careful of her bruises. "You're right, they haven't changed. But I have. I realize now that none of that matters if I don't have you. The club, the life—it's all meaningless without you by my side."

Gráinne's eyes search mine, hope and uncertainty warring in her gaze. "Are you sure? Because I can't go through this again, Connor. I won't survive it if you push me away again."

"I'm sure," I say firmly. "I love you, Gráinne. I want all of you. No more running, no more excuses."

She leans in to my touch, her eyes fluttering closed. "I love you, too," she whispers. "God help me, but I do."

I pull her closer, resting my forehead against hers. "Then let me in, Sunshine. Let me help you. Tell me who did this to you."

She tenses in my arms, and I can feel her starting to pull away. "Connor, I—"

"No more secrets," I say softly. "We're in this together now. Whatever it is, we'll face it together."

Gráinne takes a deep breath, then nods. "I had a patient show up at the hospital. He was injured. I knew he was dangerous, but I'm a doctor, Con. I had to help him. Two men showed up." She shakes her head, her voice trembling. "I've never been so scared in my life. They were threatening my patient. I overheard what they were saying, but I pretended I didn't."

I hold her close, my heart racing. "Carry on, Sunshine," I say, my anger barely concealed.

"My patient was frightened. He had no escape, so he used me as a shield. He had a blade against my throat." Tears tumble from her eyes.

"He did this?" I ask, my voice barely audible. I'm so fucking angry.

"Last week, one of the men from the hospital turned up here," she whispers.

My blood runs cold at her words. "What did he want? What did he do?"

Gráinne trembles in my arms. "He said they knew I'd overheard things I shouldn't have. He was here to tie up loose ends. He was going to..." She trails off, unable to finish.

"To what?" I growl, already knowing the answer.

She looks up at me, fear clear in her eyes. "Kill me. They think I know too much."

My mind races, so many thoughts rushing through it. I don't know anyone who'd want to hurt Grá. "Why didn't you come to me, Gra? To the club?"

She shakes her head. "I was scared. He hurt me, Con. I was so terrified that he'd hurt you or come back for me."

I cup her face gently, mindful of her bruises. "Listen to me. He won't get to you again," I vow, "No one is going to hurt you again, Grá."

Gráinne nods, leaning in to my touch. "What are we going to do?"

I press a soft kiss to her forehead. "First, we're going to get you somewhere safe. Then, I'm calling a club meeting. We need to find out who the fuck is behind this."

She looks up at me, worry etched on her face. "Will they help? Even though it's me?"

"You're family now, Sunshine," I say firmly. "And we protect our own."

"Jer has tightened security here," she tells me.

"That fucker knew and never told me?" I growl, my anger beyond fucking palpable at this stage.

"I begged him not to, Con. I didn't want you to be hurt. I didn't want you to know. I don't want you involved. I couldn't live with myself if something happened to you."

I clench my jaw, trying to contain my anger. Not at Gráinne, but at the whole fucked up situation. "I appreciate you wanting to protect me, Sunshine, but that's my job. I'm the one who's supposed to keep you safe."

She sighs, leaning her head against my chest. "I know. I just... I've been so scared, Con. I didn't know what to do."

I wrap my arms around her, holding her close. "You don't have to be scared anymore. I'm here now, and I'm not going anywhere."

We stand there for a moment, just holding each other. I can feel her trembling slightly, and I tighten my grip, wanting to shield her from everything.

"Pack a bag," I say finally, pulling back to look at her. "You're coming with me to the clubhouse. It's the safest place for you right now."

Gráinne nods, wiping at her eyes. "Okay. What about work?"

"Call in sick," I tell her. "Your safety comes first. We'll figure out the rest later."

As she moves to pack, I pull out my phone and dial Pyro. "We've got a situation," I say when he picks up. "I need your help."

"What's going on, brother?" Pyro asks, concern evident in his voice.

I glance at Gráinne, who's stuffing clothes into a suitcase.

"It's Gráinne," I say, keeping my voice low. "She's in danger. Someone attacked her. I haven't got the full details yet, but I need her somewhere safe."

There's a sharp intake of breath on the other end of the line. "Shit. How bad?"

"Bad enough. She's been attacked twice already. I'm bringing her to the clubhouse."

"Alright," Pyro says, his voice grim. "I'll call everyone in once you have the details. We'll figure this out, brother."

I end the call and turn back to Gráinne. She's zipping up her suitcase, her movements jerky and nervous.

"Ready?" I ask, moving to her side.

She nods, but I can see the fear in her eyes. "Con, are you sure about this? I don't want to put anyone else in danger."

I cup her face gently, mindful of her bruises. "Listen to me, Sunshine. You're not putting anyone in danger. We're choosing to help you because we care about you. Because I love you. Got it?"

Gráinne takes a shaky breath, then nods. "Okay. I trust you."

We make our way outside, and I wait until she's in her car before climbing onto my bike. I wish she was on my bike with me, where I know she'll be safe, but right now, she's injured and I'm not sure how fucking bad it is.

As we pull out of Gráinne's driveway, I keep a close eye on her car in my rearview mirror. My mind is racing, trying to piece together everything she's told me. Someone's after her, someone dangerous enough to make her fear for her life. The thought of her going through this alone, thinking she couldn't come to me, makes my chest ache.

The ride to the clubhouse is tense. I'm on fucking edge. I've never felt this kind of fear before, this overwhelming need to protect someone. It's new, and it's terrifying, but I know I'd do anything to keep Gráinne safe.

As we pull into the lot, I see Pyro and Raptor waiting outside. Their faces are grim, and I know they understand the severity of the situation. I park my bike and hurry over to Gráinne's car, opening her door before she can even reach for the handle.

"You okay?" I ask, helping her out.

She nods, but I can see the exhaustion in her eyes. "Just tired," she murmurs.

I wrap an arm around her waist, supporting her as we walk toward the others. Pyro's eyes widen as he takes in Gráinne's bruised face.

"Jesus Christ," he mutters. "What the fuck happened?"

"Let's get inside," I say, not wanting to discuss this out in the open. We enter the clubhouse and I'm surprised to see only Preacher and Wrath sitting down. Everyone else is gone.

"Jesus, Grá," Preacher says thickly. "The fuck didn't you say anything?"

"She hasn't told anyone," I grunt and see that she's glaring at me. "But she's going to tell us what she knows."

Gráinne sighs but takes a seat. "I don't know the men. There were three of them. Antoine was a patient. He was beaten really badly. The other two men were looking for him."

"What did they look like?" Raptor questions, standing against the bar with his arms crossed.

"One of them is blonde and has a scar that runs along his jaw, the other has dark hair and dark eyes. Both men are French." She pauses, her eyes squinting. "They mentioned the name Dragomir and said that

Antoine had displeased him. That was all that I had heard. He never did mention the two men's names."

I glance at Pyro, my gut tightening at the description she gave of the two men. They sound very much like the two assholes who were at the poker table in Spain. The two men who are very much a part of The Revenant.

Pyro's eyes meet mine, and I can see he's thinking the same thing. This can't be a coincidence.

"Gráinne," I say, keeping my voice calm despite the storm brewing inside me, "Did you hear anything else? Any other names or places?"

She shakes her head, wincing slightly at the movement. "No, that was all. They were just telling Antoine that he'd fucked up and wouldn't survive. They ended up killing him. He was found dead a few days after the incident at the hospital."

Raptor pushes off from the bar, his face set in a grim line. "This Dragomir character, he's gotta be connected to The Revenant. It's too much of a coincidence."

"Agreed." Pyro nods, running a hand through his hair. "But why go after Gráinne? She's not involved in any of this shit."

"Wrong place, wrong time," Wrath speaks up, his

voice low and dangerous. "She overheard something she shouldn't have and now they're tying up loose ends."

The thought makes my blood boil. Gráinne, my Gráinne, caught in the crosshairs of some fucked up gang war. I pull her closer to me, feeling her tremble slightly.

"What do we do now?" Preacher asks, looking around the room.

I take a deep breath, trying to think clearly through the rage and fear clouding my mind. "Who hurt you?" I ask, needing to know who the fuck turned up at her apartment and hurt her.

"The blonde man. He told me it was easy to find out where I lived. If one of my neighbors hadn't called the police when they did..." She shakes her head, her hand clutching her side. "He told me he was tying up loose ends."

"Fuck," I growl, my fists clenching at my sides. The thought of that bastard laying his hands on Gráinne makes me see red. I can't wait to fucking find him. When I do, he's in for a world of fucking hurt. "We need to find these fuckers and end this. Now."

Pyro nods, his face set in grim determination.

"Agreed. But we need to be smart about this. We don't know how deep this Revenant shit goes."

"First things first," Raptor says his voice steady despite the anger I can see in his eyes. "We need to make sure Gráinne's safe. She can't go back to her place. It's not secure enough."

"She'll stay here," I say firmly, leaving no room for argument. "She'll stay in my room."

Gráinne looks up at me, her eyes wide. "Con, I can't just leave my life behind. What about my job? My patients?"

I cup her face gently, mindful of her bruises. "Sunshine, your safety comes first. We'll figure out the rest later, I promise. But right now, I need you safe."

She hesitates for a moment, then nods, leaning in to my touch. "Okay," she whispers.

"Alright," Pyro says, taking charge. "Wrath, I want you to dig into this Dragomir character. See what you can find out about him and his connection to The Revenant."

"I need to make a call to Jerry Houlihan. That fucker knew she was injured and never called me."

Pyro nods. "You do that, and get him to come here. We're going to need him to help us uncover this shit."

I rise to my feet and help Grá up. "Let's get you in bed, Sunshine."

She nods, her eyes filled with pain and tiredness. "Yeah," she whispers as she shuffles toward me.

I lift her into my arms, careful not to jostle her. I don't know where else that fucker has hurt her. Once she's asleep, I'll find out what that cunt did to her.

She's safe here. This is the only place I know she'll be completely protected. I need that. I can't fucking lose her.

TWENTY

BOZO

"Is Gráinne okay?" Jerry asks as I enter Pyro's office.

I glare at Jerry, my anger barely contained. "No, she's not fucking okay. She's been beaten, threatened, and is terrified. And you knew about it."

Jerry has the decency to look ashamed. "I wanted to tell you, Bozo. But she begged me not to. Said she didn't want to put you in danger."

"That wasn't your call to make," I growl, stepping closer to him. "She's my woman. It's my job to protect her."

"Your woman?" Jerry raises an eyebrow. "Last I heard, you two weren't together."

I clench my fists, fighting the urge to punch him. "Things change. Now, tell me everything you know about what happened to her."

Jerry sighs, running a hand through his hair. "I don't know much more than what she's probably told you. She called me after the first incident at the hospital, scared out of her mind. I increased security at her place, but..."

"But it wasn't enough," I finish for him, my voice hard.

He nods, looking defeated. "I'm sorry, Bozo. I should have pushed harder, should have made her tell you."

I take a deep breath, trying to calm myself. Getting angry at Jerry won't help Gráinne. "What have you found out about The Revenant since the card game?"

Jerry's eyes widen slightly. "The Revenant? What do they have to do with this?"

"Everything, apparently," I say. "Those two fuckers at the card game?" I say and watch him nod, his eyes narrowed. "Yeah, those fucks were at the hospital and it was the blonde one who hurt Grá."

Jerry's face pales at my words. "Jesus Christ," he mutters. "This is worse than I thought."

"No shit," I growl. "Now, what do you know?"

He takes a deep breath, composing himself. "Not much, unfortunately. The Revenant keeps their operations tight. But I've heard whispers. They're expanding their territory, pushing into areas that were previously neutral ground."

I lean against Pyro's desk, my mind racing. "And what about this Dragomir character? Gráinne overheard them mention his name."

Jerry's eyes widen. "Dragomir? Are you sure?"

I nod, watching him carefully. "Yeah, why? You know something?"

He runs a hand over his face, looking suddenly exhausted. "Dragomir Popescu. He's a big player in the European underworld. Romanian, I think. If he's involved with The Revenant, this is fucking huge. It means that the Revenant spans the entirety of Europe and who fucking knows how much further."

"Fuck," I mutter, the gravity of the situation hitting me hard. "How the hell did Gráinne get caught up in this?"

Jerry shakes his head. "Wrong place, wrong time. But now that they know she overheard something, they won't stop until they're sure she can't talk."

My blood runs cold at his words. The thought of those bastards coming after Gráinne again makes me want to tear the world apart.

"That's not going to happen," I growl, my voice low and dangerous. "I'll die before I let them touch her again."

Jerry nods, his face grim. "I believe you. But, Bozo, this isn't as easy as finding these two fucking bastards. We're talking about an international criminal organization. We need to be smart about this."

I push off from the desk, pacing the small office. "What do you suggest?"

Jerry takes a deep breath. "We need more information. About The Revenant, about Dragomir, about their operations here. Without that, we're flying blind."

"And how do you propose we get that information?" I ask, my patience wearing thin. "No one fucking talks about them."

"Then it's time to make them," Jerry says. "We have a whole fucking lot of power behind us. It's time to use it."

"Time is something we don't have," I interrupt. "Every minute we wait is another minute those bastards could be planning their next move."

Jerry holds up his hands. "I know, I know. But rushing in half-cocked is only going to get us all killed. And then where will Gráinne be?"

I hate to admit it, but he's right. As much as I want to hunt down every last member of The Revenant and make them pay for what they've done to Gráinne, I know we need to be smart about this.

"Fine," I say finally. "But I want updates every day. And if anything, and I mean anything, happens to her, I won't be held responsible for my actions."

Jerry nods solemnly. "Understood. I'll put all my resources on this, Bozo. We'll find out what's going on and put an end to it."

I run a hand through my hair, feeling the weight of everything pressing down on me. "Alright. What's our first move?"

"We need to start with what we know," Jerry says, pulling out his phone. "I'll reach out to some of my European contacts and see if they have any intel on Dragomir or The Revenant's operations there."

"Good." Pyro nods. "I'll have Wrath dig deeper into their local activities. Maybe we can find a weak link, someone who might be willing to talk."

Jerry looks at me, his expression serious. "Bozo, you need to be prepared. This might get ugly. The Revenant isn't known for playing nice."

I meet his gaze, my jaw set. "Neither am I. Not when it comes to protecting what's mine."

He nods, a hint of respect in his eyes. He's grown to love Gráinne as a daughter. I know that she loves and respects him as a father figure. He's feeling her being hurt just as much as I am. I know that he'll do whatever the hell it takes to get answers. This time, he won't be alone doing it. "Alright then. Let's get to work."

As Jerry leaves to make his calls, I head back to check on Gráinne. I find her asleep in my room, her face still marred by bruises but looking peaceful for the first time since I saw her earlier.

I sit on the edge of the bed, gently brushing a strand of hair from her face. "I'm going to fix this, Sunshine," I vow. I won't let anyone hurt her again.

I watch Gráinne sleep for a few moments, my heart aching at the sight of her bruised face. The anger I've been barely containing threatens to explode again, but I force it down. I can't afford to lose control now. Gráinne needs me to be smart.

As I'm about to leave the room, her eyes flutter open. "Connor?" she murmurs, her voice thick with sleep.

"I'm here, Sunshine," I say softly, moving back to sit beside her. "How are you feeling?"

She tries to sit up, wincing as she does. I gently help her, propping her up against the pillows. "Like I've been hit by a truck," she admits with a weak attempt at a smile. "But better now that you're here."

I take her hand in mine and press a kiss to it. "I'm not going anywhere," I promise. "You're safe now."

Gráinne's eyes fill with tears. "I'm so sorry, Connor. I should have told you what was happening. I just... I was so scared. I didn't want you to get hurt because of me."

"Hey, hey," I soothe, gently wiping away a tear that escapes down her cheek. "You have nothing to be sorry for. This isn't your fault."

She shakes her head, her voice trembling. "But it is. If I had just stayed away from the room... I knew they were dangerous."

"Sunshine, you were doing your job. That's not something you should ever apologize for." My gaze roams over her face, my gut twisting at the sight of every bruise. "Okay, Grá, I know you don't want to tell me, but I need to know. Where else are you injured?"

I watch as her eyes close and a tear falls from them. "Please don't be mad," she whispers.

My heart clenches at her words. "Gráinne, I could never be mad at you for this. Please, tell me."

She takes a shaky breath, her eyes still closed. "My side hurts, my stomach, my nose, and my neck. He punched me a lot, but it was the stab wound that hurt the most. I was in the hospital for a few days. I'm doing okay."

My blood runs cold at her words. "Stab wound?"

I repeat, my voice barely above a whisper. "Gráinne, where?"

She hesitates, then slowly lifts her shirt. I inhale sharply at the sight of the bandage on her left side, just below her ribs. The white gauze is tinged with a faint pink, a reminder of how close I came to losing her.

"Jesus Christ," I mutter, gently touching the area around the bandage. "Why didn't you tell me sooner?"

Gráinne's eyes fill with fresh tears. "I didn't want you to worry. And I... I was ashamed. I should have been able to protect myself better."

I cup her face in my hands, forcing her to look at me. "Listen to me, Sunshine. You have nothing to be ashamed of. You survived. That's what matters."

She nods weakly, leaning into my touch. "I was so scared, Connor. I thought I was going to die."

The raw fear in her voice breaks something inside me. I carefully gather her into my arms, mindful of her injuries. "I've got you now," I murmur into her hair. "I won't let anyone hurt you again."

We stay like that for a long moment, her body shaking with silent sobs as I hold her. When she finally calms down, I gently lay her back against the pillows.

"Gráinne... Christ, Sunshine." I can hardly fucking breathe. "I could have lost you."

She grips my hand tight, and I know she's terrified. "I'm scared."

I close my eyes. The sound of the fear in her voice is like a fucking slice to my heart. She's always so fucking strong, always able to push through the pain. I've never seen or heard her so terrified.

"You're safe," I promise her. "No one is going to harm you again," I vow. I'll die before anyone even tries. "I'm right here with you, baby."

"Stay with me," she pleads, her eyes filled with tears.

"Always," I promise, carefully settling onto the bed beside her. I wrap my arm around her shoulders, letting her rest her head on my chest. "I'm not going anywhere."

We lay there in silence for a while, my hand gently stroking her hair. I can feel her trembling against me, and it takes everything in me not to go out and hunt down the bastards who did this to her right now.

"Connor," she says softly, breaking the silence. "What are we going to do?"

I take a deep breath, considering my words carefully. "We're going to keep you safe, Sunshine. Jerry and I are working on gathering information. We're going to find out everything we can about The Revenant and this Dragomir character."

She tenses at the mention of The Revenant. "Who are they?" she asks. "I've never heard of them, but I know they're dangerous."

"I know," I say, tightening my arm around her. "But so am I. Especially when it comes to protecting you."

Gráinne lifts her head to look at me, her eyes searching mine. "I don't want you to get hurt because of me."

I cup her face gently, mindful of her bruises. "Listen to me, Gráinne. You're worth any risk. I love you, and I'm not going to let these bastards take you away from me."

"I love you too," she cries. "I'm so happy."

I press a kiss to her forehead, wishing I could kiss her how I'd like, but she's too injured for that and I don't want to cause her any more pain than she's already in.

I hold Gráinne close, savoring the warmth of her body against mine. "I'm happy too, Sunshine," I murmur into her hair. "We're going to get through this together."

She nods against my chest, her breathing starting

to even out. I can tell she's exhausted, both physically and emotionally.

"Get some rest," I tell her softly. "I'll be right here when you wake up."

As Gráinne drifts off to sleep, I find myself on high alert, listening for any sound that might indicate danger. I know we're safe here, surrounded by my brothers, but I can't shake the feeling of unease.

My mind races, going over everything I know about The Revenant and the situation we're in. It's not much, and that fact gnaws at me. We need more information, and we need it fast.

I carefully reach for my phone, making sure not to disturb Gráinne. I send a quick text to Jerry.

Me: Any updates?

It doesn't take him long to respond.

Jer: Nothing concrete yet. My European contacts are digging. Wrath's working on local leads. Will keep you posted.

I sigh, frustration building. We're working as fast as we can, but it doesn't feel fast enough. Not when Gráinne's lying beside me, battered and bruised. Not when I can still hear the fear in her voice.

Jer: How's Gráinne?

I glance down at her sleeping form, my heart clenching at the sight of her injuries.

Me: Resting. She's in a lot of pain. Jer, they stabbed her. She could have died. You should have fucking told me.

I'm beyond pissed that he didn't inform me the moment he got word that she was hurt. I should have been there when she was in the hospital. Instead, I'm finding out when it's too late.

Jer: We'll find these bastards, I promise you that.

Me: We'd better. Because if we don't, I'm going to tear this city apart until I do.

I put my phone down, careful not to wake Gráinne. My mind is racing, trying to piece together everything we know. The Revenant, Dragomir, the two men from the card game. There has to be a connection, something we're missing.

As I'm lost in thought, I feel Gráinne stir beside me. She mumbles something in her sleep, her face contorting in distress. A nightmare.

"Shh, Sunshine," I whisper, gently stroking her hair. "You're safe. I'm here."

She settles at the sound of my voice, her body relaxing against mine once more. I press a soft kiss to her forehead. I won't let this lie. No fucking way. The moment I have a lead I'm running it down no matter what.

Grá is mine. She always has been. No one gets to harm her and get away with it. I'll not have her living in fear, constantly watching over her shoulder. She had enough of that shit when she was a teenager living with that motherfucking cunt of a father of hers. I won't allow it to happen again.

I've fucked around and fought against what I've been feeling for years. Now I'm finally giving in to what I want, what I've always wanted, I'm not going to lose the only person I've ever loved.

As I watch Gráinne sleep, I make a silent vow. No more running from my feelings. No more pushing her away to try to protect her. She's safest by my side, and that's where she'll stay.

I think back to all the times I've pushed her away, all the moments I've denied what I feel for her. It was all for nothing. She still ended up in danger, and I wasn't there to protect her. Never again.

My phone buzzes with another message from Jerry.

Jer: Got a lead. One of Wrath's contacts spotted one of the men from the card game. He's at a bar in Leopardstown.

My body tenses, every muscle coiled and ready for action. This is it. Our first real lead.

Me: I'm on it.

Jer: Bozo, wait. We need a plan.

But I'm already carefully extricating myself from Gráinne's embrace. I can't wait. Not when we finally have something concrete to go on.

I gently lay Gráinne back on the pillows, making sure she's comfortable. She stirs slightly but doesn't wake. I press a soft kiss to her forehead.

"I'll be back soon, Sunshine," I whisper. "I promise."

I grab my cut and pull it on, then I reach for my gun, checking to make sure it's loaded. As I head for the door, I take one last look at Gráinne. The sight of her bruised face hardens my resolve. These bastards are going to pay for what they've done.

I quietly slip out of the room, careful not to wake Gráinne. As I make my way down the hallway, I run into Pyro.

"Where are you going?" he asks, eyeing my gun.

"Got a lead on one of the fuckers who hurt Gráinne," I growl. "He's at a bar in Leopardstown."

Pyro's eyes narrow. "You're not going alone," he says, his tone leaving no room for argument.

I want to protest, to tell him this is something I need to do myself, but I know he's right. Going in alone would be stupid, and I can't afford to be stupid right now. Not when Gráinne's safety is on the line.

"Fine," I concede, knowing there's no point in arguing. What the prez says goes. "Gear up. We leave in five."

Pyro nods and disappears down the hallway. I head to the clubhouse, finding Wrath, Preacher, Cowboy, and Tank gathered around the bar.

"Bozo," Wrath calls out. "Jerry filled me in. Are you going after that bastard?"

I nod grimly. "Yeah. Are you coming?"

Wrath stands, cracking his knuckles. "Wouldn't miss it for the world."

I grin as I step out of the clubhouse, my brothers at my back. Tonight, we're going to get answers. No more fucking around. Those motherfuckers went after the wrong woman. They'll die for what they've done to her.

TWENTY-ONE
BOZO

The ride to Leopardstown is tense, the roar of our bikes doing little to drown out the thoughts racing through my head. Images of Gráinne's bruised face, the bandage covering her stab wound, flash before my eyes. Each one fuels the rage burning inside me.

We pull up a block away from the bar, killing our engines. Pyro turns to face us, his expression grim.

"Alright, listen up," he says, his voice low. "We go in quiet. We're not here to start a war. We find this fucker, we get him out, and we make him talk. Understood?"

We all nod, the seriousness of the situation not lost on any of us. This isn't just about revenge. It's about protecting Gráinne and potentially uncovering a threat that could affect all of us.

"Bozo," Pyro continues, fixing me with a hard stare. "I know you're angry. We all are. But we need him alive and talking. Control yourself."

I clench my jaw but nod. As much as I want to tear this bastard apart with my bare hands, I know Pyro's right. We need information more than we need vengeance. At least for now.

We make our way to the bar, trying to look as inconspicuous as a group of bikers can. As we enter, the noise of the crowded pub hits us. It's a typical Friday night, the place packed with people unwinding after a long week.

My eyes scan the room, searching for the face I've committed to memory. The face of one of the men who were at the card game. It doesn't take long to spot him. He's sitting at the bar, nursing a drink, seemingly without a care in the world. Unfortunately, it's not the asshole who hurt Grá.

As we get closer, the man seems to sense something's off. He looks up from his drink, his eyes widening as he spots us. For a moment, he looks like he's considering making a run for it. But then his eyes land on me, and I see recognition flash across his face.

"Remember me, asshole?" I growl as I reach him, grabbing him by the collar of his shirt.

He tries to pull away, but I've got him in an iron grip. "I don't know what you're talking about," he stammers, his eyes darting around frantically.

"Wrong answer," I snarl, pulling him closer. "Your brother hurt someone I care about. And now you're going to tell me everything you know."

The man's eyes widen in fear as he realizes the gravity of his situation. "Please," he whimpers. "We're just following orders. He didn't know that she was yours."

His pathetic plea only fuels my rage. I tighten my grip on his shirt, my knuckles turning white. "Orders from who?" I demand, my voice low and dangerous. "Who's Dragomir?"

At the mention of Dragomir's name, the man's face pales even further. "How do you know about Dragomir?" he whispers, his voice trembling.

Before I can respond, Pyro steps in. "Let's take this somewhere more private," he says, his tone leaving no room for argument.

I nod, roughly pulling the man off his barstool. We make our way toward the back exit, my brothers forming a tight circle around us to prevent any escape attempts. We push through the door into the alley behind the bar.

"Talk," I growl, slamming the man against the

brick wall. "Who's Dragomir and what does he want with Gráinne?"

The man's eyes dart between us, clearly weighing his options. After a moment, he seems to deflate, realizing he has no way out. "Dragomir Popescu," he says, his voice barely above a whisper. "He's the head of The Revenant. We were just supposed to tie up loose ends. The girl... she wasn't supposed to be there. She heard things she shouldn't have."

"And that gives your brother the right to beat her? To stab her?" I snarl, my fist connecting with his jaw before I can stop myself.

Pyro puts a hand on my shoulder, pulling me back slightly. "Easy, Bozo," he warns. "We need him talking."

I take a deep breath, forcing myself to calm down. "What's The Revenant planning?" I ask, my voice cold and hard.

The man swallows hard, his eyes darting around nervously. "They're expanding," he says finally. "Moving into new territories. Dublin is just the beginning. Dragomir has big plans."

"What kind of plans?" Wrath asks, stepping forward.

The man shakes his head. "I don't know the

details. I'm not in the know. I'm not one of the leaders. But I know it's big. Bigger than anything we've done before."

I exchange a glance with Pyro. This is worse than we thought. If The Revenant is planning a major expansion, it could mean war. And Gráinne is caught right in the middle of it.

"Where can we find Dragomir?" I demand, turning back to the man.

He lets out a bitter laugh. "You can't be serious. No one finds Dragomir unless he wants to be found. He's like a ghost."

I slam him against the wall again, my patience wearing thin. "Wrong answer. Where. Is. He?"

The man winces, fear flashing in his eyes. "I swear, I don't know. He moves around and never stays in one place for long."

I step back, my fists clenched at my sides. Every fiber of my being wants to beat this man to a pulp, to make him feel even a fraction of the pain Gráinne felt. But I know we need to be smart about this.

"Now, where's your brother, Étienne?" Pyro asks, his voice cold. "That's someone you'll know the location of."

He shakes his head, his eyes wide and full of fear. "I do not know," he lies.

Pyro grins wickedly, stepping forward and pulling out his gun. He cocks it, pointing it at the fucker's head. "You have one chance. You tell me where Étienne is, or I pull this trigger."

The man's eyes widen in terror as he stares down the barrel of Pyro's gun. Sweat beads on his forehead, and his breath comes in short, panicked gasps. But he doesn't answer Pyro. He stares ahead, his breathing choppy and his eyes wide.

"So be it," Pyro growls and pulls the trigger.

The gun clicks, empty. The man flinches violently, a whimper escaping his lips. Pyro's face twists into a cruel smile.

"That was your free pass," he says, his voice dangerously low. "Next time, it won't be empty. Now, where's Étienne?"

Once again, he doesn't answer the question, but he does speak. "Would you give up your brother?" he asks, his voice trembling. "No," he answers himself. "Neither would I. So do it. End me. I do not care. You'll never find Étienne or Dragomir." The stupid grin on his face is enough to piss me off. "Don't worry, that whore of a doctor will get what's coming to her. No matter what you do, you won't be able to keep her safe. We'll find her, and when we do, they're going to enjoy raping and killing her."

The gun sounds off once again. This time, Pyro didn't give him a warning. The bullet sinks between his eyes. He's dead before he even realizes the bullet was fired.

The man's body crumples to the ground, a small trickle of blood running down his forehead. The alley falls silent, the echo of the gunshot fading away.

I stare at the corpse, a mixture of shock and anger coursing through me. Part of me is glad the bastard is dead, but another part knows this complicates things.

"Fuck, Pyro," Wrath hisses, glancing around nervously. "What happened to keeping him alive?"

Pyro's face is a mask of cold fury as he lowers his gun. "He crossed a line," he says simply, his voice devoid of emotion. "No one threatens one of ours like that and lives."

My anger is palpable. I want to find that motherfucking Étienne. He won't get a chance to hurt Gráinne. I'll kill that motherfucker before he even gets the chance. I'm going to hunt him the fuck down.

But killing this bastard means we've lost our only lead.

"What now?" I ask, looking at Pyro.

He holsters his gun, his expression grim. "Now we clean this up and regroup. We might not have gotten everything we wanted, but we know more than we did before."

"We need to find Étienne. It might be our only chance to get to Dragomir," I say, my anger coursing through me. Fucker died to protect that bastard Étienne.

Pyro nods, his face grim. "Agreed. But we need to be smart about this. We need more intel on the Revenant. We need to know where the fuck they're holed up."

"We'll need to find the location, then figure out our approach and scout it before we go in," Wrath says. "The last thing we need to be doing is going into a trap. But first, we need to find Étienne."

I nod, my mind already racing with possibilities. "And we need to keep the women safe. If they find out she's with us..."

"We'll increase security at the clubhouse," Pyro assures me. "No one gets in or out without us knowing."

As we make our way back to our bikes, I feel a mixture of emotions swirling inside me. Anger at what's been done to Gráinne, fear for her safety, and a grim determination to end this threat once and for all.

"You okay, brother?" Wrath asks as we mount our bikes.

I take a deep breath, my hands gripping the handlebars tightly. "I will be," I say, "once we put an end to this and Gráinne is safe."

Right now, I just want to get back to the clubhouse and make sure that my woman is okay. I need to see with my own eyes that she's alive and breathing.

AS WE ROAR BACK toward the clubhouse, my mind is a whirlwind of emotions and plans. The need to see Gráinne, to hold her and make sure she's safe, is overwhelming. But beneath that is a simmering rage, a burning desire for vengeance against Étienne and Dragomir.

The clubhouse comes into view, and I feel a relief that we're back, that I'll see Gráinne.

We park our bikes, and before I'm able to enter the clubhouse, Wrath and Pyro stop me. I raise a brow and Pyro grins manically. "You told her you love her, didn't you?"

I stare at him, wondering what the fuck this has

to do with anything and how the fuck he knew that. But I don't answer him, the nosey fucker.

"Christ," Wrath laughs. "You did? Christ, Bozo, what the fuck were you thinking? You have kept her at arm's length for years, then she gets hurt and you're all in?"

"Have you seen her?" I snarl. "Seen the bruises on her body? I tried to keep her from this shit, but she's so fucking deep now that I can't think straight. She's all I have ever wanted."

They both nod. "We see that. Trust me, brother," Pyro says. "We get it. If anyone does, it's us. But you have to realize that she doesn't. She loves you too, but she's not going to truly believe you love her all of a sudden."

I run a hand through my hair, frustration and worry mixing in my gut. "What the fuck am I supposed to do then? I can't take it back. I don't want to take it back."

Pyro puts a hand on my shoulder, his expression softening slightly. "No one's saying you should take it back, brother. But you need to show her you mean it. Words are easy. Actions are what matter."

Wrath nods in agreement. "You've kept her at arm's length for years. She's probably wondering why now, why after she got hurt. She might even think you're just saying it out of guilt or pity."

Their words hit me like a punch to the gut. They're right, and I know it. Gráinne's no fool. She's probably questioning everything right now.

"Fuck," I mutter, leaning against my bike. "How do I fix this?"

"You don't fix it," Pyro says firmly. "You prove it. Every day, with everything you do. You show her that this isn't just because she got hurt, that it's not temporary. You show her that you're in this for the long haul."

I nod slowly, absorbing his words. "And in the meantime? While we're dealing with this Revenant shit?"

Wrath grins, clapping me on the back. "You keep her close, keep her safe, and you don't let her doubt for a second that you mean what you said."

With a deep breath, I straighten up. They're right. I've wasted enough time keeping Gráinne at a distance. Now it's time to show her—and everyone else—exactly what she means to me.

"Thanks, brothers," I say as I turn toward the door. It's time to set Grá straight and show her just how fucking much she means to me.

I'm so fucking in love with her that I can't think straight.

TWENTY-TWO
GRÁINNE

"I'm so glad you're here," Mallory says as she slides onto the seat beside me. Ailbhe, Hayley, and Chloe also come and sit with us. "I was worried about you and rightly so. Damn, Grá, your face is a lot worse than I had thought. Why didn't you tell me what happened?"

I sigh. It's weird; I've never had women as friends before. I'm so introverted that I tend to stick to myself. But Mallory has snuck under the radar and is someone I really like. I hate that she was worried about me. Growing up, Connor was the only one who really ever cared about me. That was until I met Jerry, and then things changed. I had someone I could turn to if I needed help.

Now, I have all these people who are here and

want to help. It's overwhelming to say the least. Mallory is Raptor's old lady, Ailbhe is Preacher's, Hayley is Wrath's, and Chloe is Pyro's. I've known Chloe for a while, since her mam is Jerry's niece, but I haven't really interacted with her much.

"I was scared, Mal," I admit, something that I find hard to do even now. "I didn't want anyone else brought into it."

Mallory's eyes soften with understanding. "Oh, honey, I get it. But you don't have to face this alone. We're here for you, all of us."

Ailbhe nods in agreement. "That's right. The club protects its own, and you're family now, Grá."

"Exactly," Hayley chimes in, a soft smile on her face while nodding. "Plus, we've all been through some crazy shit. We know what it's like to feel scared and alone."

Chloe reaches across the table and squeezes my hand. "You can always count on us, no matter what."

Their words of support bring tears to my eyes. I blink them back, not wanting to cry in front of everyone. This is something I'm not used to, but I'm so grateful for. "Thanks, girls. I really appreciate it," I say, thickly.

Mallory wraps an arm around my shoulders. "Now, tell us everything that happened when Bozo followed you home. I'm guessing by the crazed look on his face when he left that he finally admitted that he loves you?"

I feel heat creeping up my cheeks. "Yes," I say, unable to keep the smile from my lips. They all stare at me, waiting for me to continue, but I hesitate, unsure of how much to reveal. I'm still getting used to having friends to confide in.

"He did," I admit softly. "But it's complicated."

Mallory raises an eyebrow. "Complicated how? The man's crazy about you, Grá. Anyone with eyes can see that."

I sigh, fiddling with the napkin in front of me. "I'm ready to settle down, start a family. Connor, I don't think he's there yet." Hell, it was only yesterday he decided that he wanted to be with me, to fully commit. "I've loved him for years. I can't remember a time when I haven't loved him. He's never once shown me that he loves me other than as his friend, until yesterday."

The women exchange glances. Ailbhe leans forward, her voice gentle. "Are you sure about that? Because the way Bozo acted since finding out that you were attacked, it seems like he's in love with you, and more than a friend."

My heart skips a beat. "How has he been acting?"

Hayley chimes in. "He's ready to burn the world down, Grá. He's not going to stop until he finds out who hurt you, constantly checking in with Jerry for updates. He's beyond pissed that Jerry never told him about you being injured."

I feel a pang of guilt. "I didn't want to worry him," I murmur.

Chloe shakes her head. "Honey, I get that. I really do. But that man is so in love with you. I think he always has been."

I feel my heart racing at their words. I want it to be true. I have loved Connor long before I really knew what it meant. Our friendship has been something I have cherished, but loving him is different. I know he said he loves me, but I'm not sure if it's real or if he's just afraid to lose me completely.

"I don't know," I whisper. I'm scared, terrified that this is just a reaction from him because he's worried about me, and that he's not truly in love with me. This is too much. I can't think properly. Hell, I can't even breathe without fear gripping me tight. "I think it's best if I go back home." I don't want anyone to get hurt, and me being here could cause them all to be caught in the crossfire of whatever the hell those men want from me.

Ailbhe leans forward, her voice gentle. "Grá,

honey, I know you're scared, but pushing away the people who care about you isn't the answer. Especially not Bozo."

"She's right," Mallory adds. "When I was going through my own shit, I tried to push everyone away. I kept everyone at arm's length. It only made things worse. Having Raptor by my side made me stronger."

I feel tears welling up in my eyes again. "I just don't want anyone to get hurt because of me," I whisper.

Chloe squeezes my hand. "That's not your decision to make, sweetie. Bozo's a big boy. He can decide for himself if he wants to be involved."

Mallory nods emphatically. "And trust me, he wants to be involved. That man is head over heels for you, Grá. Don't push him away because you're scared."

I take a deep breath, trying to process their words.

"I just... I don't know what to do," I admit, my voice barely above a whisper.

Hayley leans in, her eyes soft with understanding. "Talk to him, Grá. Really talk to him. Tell him how you feel, your fears, your hopes. Give him a chance to do the same."

"And if it doesn't work out?" I ask, voicing my deepest fear.

Ailbhe shrugs. "Then at least you'll know. But, honey, I've seen the way that man looks at you. I'd bet my last euro that it'll work out just fine."

Just then, the clubhouse door swings open with a bang. We all turn to look, and my heart nearly stops. Connor stands there, his eyes scanning the room until they land on me. The intensity in his gaze takes my breath away.

"Grá," he says, his voice rough with emotion.

The girls all exchange knowing looks. Mallory gives my hand a squeeze, offering me support. "Go to him, Grá," she whispers.

I rise to my feet as Connor approaches. He reaches out for my hand and I don't hesitate in taking it. He leads me outside, the wind howling as we step out of the clubhouse. It's cold and miserable, but thankfully, it's not raining.

"Are you okay?" Connor asks, his voice low and husky. His eyes never leave mine, and I can see a mixture of concern and tenderness in them. My heart races.

"Sunshine," he says thickly. "Please don't lie to me. Are you in pain?" His hand comes up to cup my cheek, his thumb gently caressing the bruised skin. I wince slightly at the touch, and his eyes darken with anger.

"A little," I admit. "But I'm okay."

"I'm going to find who did this to you," he says, his voice a low growl. "And when I do, they'll wish they'd never been born."

I swallow hard, torn between the warmth his protectiveness brings and the fear of what might happen. "Connor, I—"

"No, Grá," he cuts me off, his voice firm but not unkind. "I know what you're going to say. You don't want me to get hurt, that you don't want me to do something that could get me into trouble. I understand that you want to protect me, but baby, it's my turn to protect you."

The hurt in his voice makes my heart ache. I reach up, placing my hand over his where it rests on my cheek. "Connor, I'm scared," I admit softly. "Not just of what happened, but of... this. Us."

His eyes soften, and he pulls me closer, wrapping his arms around me. I sink into his embrace, feeling safe, just as I do whenever I'm in his arms. "I know, Sunshine. I'm scared too," he murmurs into my hair.

I pull back slightly, looking up at him in surprise. "You are?"

He nods, a rueful smile on his face. "Terrified.

I've never felt this way about anyone before, Grá. The thought of losing you fucking kills me."

My breath catches in my throat. "Connor..."

"Let me finish," he says, gently. "I know I've been an idiot. I've wasted so much time, trying to convince myself that what I felt for you was just friendship. I made things even worse by fucking you and walking away. Friends with benefits was never going to work. It's always been more than that. I've loved you for years, Sunshine. I was just too scared to admit it."

Tears well up in my eyes as I listen to his words. "Why were you scared?"

He sighs, running a hand through his hair. "Because you deserve better than me, Grá. You deserve someone who can give you everything you want, someone who isn't broken."

I shake my head vehemently. "You're not broken, Connor. You're an amazing man who has the biggest heart I know. You've always protected me. You've always been someone I can rely on, someone to lean on."

"My dad—"

"Is a fucking dickhead," I hiss, cutting him off. I watch as he raises a brow, a smirk playing on his lips. "He was a vile man who got off on bullying you. You are so much better than he ever was, Con. You're smart—hell, you're practically a genius—but that man made you think it was a curse, when the truth of it is it's beautiful. You're beautiful. I just wish you'd see that."

Connor's eyes soften at my words, and he pulls me closer, resting his forehead against mine. "You always see the best in me, Sunshine. Even when I can't see it myself."

I reach up, cupping his face in my hands. "That's because I love you, Connor. All of you. The good, the bad, and everything in between."

He closes his eyes, taking a shaky breath. When he opens them again, they're filled with a mixture of love and determination. "I want to be better for you, Grá. I want to be the man you deserve."

"You already are," I whisper.

He shakes his head slightly. "No, I'm not. But I want to be. I want to face my demons and give you a life you deserve. A family."

My heart soars at his words, but I can't help the small seed of doubt that lingers. "Are you sure? This is a big step, Connor. I don't want you to feel pressured—"

He cuts me off with a gentle kiss. "I've never been more sure of anything in my life, Sunshine. I love you. I want you. All of you."

I can't stop the happy tears from falling. "I love you too, Connor. So much."

He wipes away my tears with his thumbs, his touch impossibly soft and tender. "I promise you, Grá, the man who hurt you won't ever do so again. I'm not going to stop searching until I find him."

I nod, knowing there's no point in arguing with Connor when he's this determined. "Just... be careful, okay? I couldn't bear it if something happened to you because of me."

Connor's eyes soften, and he brushes a strand of hair behind my ear. "Nothing's going to happen to me, Sunshine. I promise. But I need you to promise me something too."

"Anything," I say without hesitation.

"No more secrets," he says firmly. "No more trying to handle things on your own. We're in this together now, Grá. You're not alone. I'm always right here beside you."

I feel a warmth spread through my chest at his words. "I promise," I whisper.

He leans down, capturing my lips in a kiss that's both tender and passionate. When we finally break apart, we're both breathless.

"Come on," Connor says, taking my hand. "Let's

go back inside. I'm sure the girls are dying to know what's going on."

I laugh softly, allowing him to lead me back toward the clubhouse. "They seem pretty invested in our relationship."

Connor chuckles. "I bet they are."

As we approach the door, I hesitate. "Con... what do we tell them? About us, I mean."

He turns to face me, his expression serious. "Whatever you want. It's no one's business, and anyone who has a problem with that can go fuck themselves."

I can't help but laugh at his bluntness. "Always so eloquent," I quip.

He grins, that cocky smile that I've always loved. "You know it, Sunshine."

We walk back into the clubhouse hand in hand, and I can feel all eyes turn to us. Connor looks at me, his eyes filled with warmth and love. "I've got a meeting with Jer. I'm hoping we'll have some answers soon."

I nod. "Go. I'm okay here."

"I know you are, Sunshine, but I fucking hate leaving you."

I smile, unable to hide it. I love that he's being so open. "Go," I urge.

He presses a kiss to my lips. It's soft and quick, something I love, but I wish it was longer. "I won't be long," he promises me. He gives me a lingering look before he exits the clubhouse, Raptor and Preacher following him.

"It's about damn time!" Ailbhe laughs as I move back to where we were seated before. "That man loves you something fierce, Gráinne."

I can feel the heat rising to my cheeks as I sit back down with the girls. Their knowing smiles and expectant looks make me both nervous and excited.

"SO," Mallory says, leaning in conspiratorially. "Spill. What happened out there?"

I TAKE A DEEP BREATH, trying to gather my thoughts. "We talked," I say softly. "Really talked. He... he told me he loves me." Yesterday was chaotic, and I know that he said it then, but I wasn't sure if he truly meant it. Today, I know he did.

THE GIRLS LET out a collective squeal of delight, causing me to laugh despite my embarrassment.

. . .

"I KNEW IT!" Chloe exclaims. "The way he's been acting, it was so obvious."

HAYLEY NODS IN AGREEMENT. "It's about time he admitted it. We've all seen how he looks at you, Grá."

"AND?" Ailbhe prompts, raising an eyebrow. "What else did he say?"

I BITE MY LIP, still processing everything that just happened. "He said he wants to be better for me. That he wants to face his demons and... and give me the life I deserve."

MALLORY REACHES out and squeezes my hand. "That's huge, Grá. It means he's all in."

. . .

I NOD, feeling a mixture of excitement and trepidation. "I know. It's just a lot to take in. Everything's changing so fast."

"CHANGE CAN BE SCARY," Hayley says softly. "But it can also be amazing. Especially when it's with the right person."

"AND BOZO IS DEFINITELY the right person for you," Chloe adds with a grin.

I CAN'T HELP but smile at their words. "I hope so. I really do love him."

"WE KNOW, HONEY," Ailbhe says. "It's written all over your face every time you look at him."

I finally have what I have always wanted, but there's such a terror that lingers beneath the surface within me. The men who hurt me aren't going to stop. What happens if they hurt Connor?

That's not something I could ever live with. He's

always been my rock, the man who has always had my back.

I don't want to lose him.

I can't.

TWENTY-THREE
BOZO

"You good?" Preacher asks, his American accent thick and heavy. We're at Jerry's house. He called and asked for a meeting. I'm fucking hoping it means that he has some news.

"I'm good," I lie. I'm far fucking from it. Grá's bottling up how afraid she is and it pisses me the fuck off. She shouldn't have to hide away in the clubhouse because of some motherfucking bastard who couldn't get his fucking job done. There's no doubt in my mind that they were meant to kill Antoine, but he somehow escaped and ended up in the emergency room, and that's how Gráinne ended up tangled up in this fucking mess.

Every lead that we seem to get ends up being a

dead end. Nothing pans out and it's beyond fucking frustrating.

"You're not," he says. "But you will be. Once we have a location on these fuckers, we're going to ensure that they die and that it'll be painful and slow."

I nod grimly at Preacher's words. He's right, I won't be okay until we find these bastards and make them pay for what they did to Gráinne.

We enter Jerry's house, finding him pacing in his living room. He looks up as we enter, his face grim. He does this a lot when he's angry, when something is happening that's out of his control.

"What've you got?" I demand, not bothering with pleasantries. There's no use for them, not with Jer. We both want to find these cunts, for Gráinne's safety. I trust my brothers. I know that they have my back. But Jer's different. He views my woman as his daughter. He's going to go all out to find out what the fuck is going on and where these bastards are hiding.

Jerry runs a hand through his hair. "One of my contacts in Romania came through. They've got intel on Dragomir Popescu."

My heart rate picks up. Finally, some real information. "And?"

"He's bad news, Bozo. Really bad news," Jerry

says, his voice grave. "He's not just involved with The Revenant—he's their leader. He runs their entire operation."

"Fuck," Raptor mutters beside me.

Jerry nods. "Yeah. And that's not all. Apparently, he's in Dublin right now."

My fists clench at my sides. "What the fuck is he doing here?"

"Expanding their territory, from what my contact could gather," Jerry explains. "The Revenant is making a big push into Western Europe. Ireland is their gateway."

The pieces start falling into place. "And Gráinne overheard them talking at the hospital and they've concluded that she overheard their plans."

"It could seriously fuck up their operation," Jerry finishes. "That's why they're so desperate to get to her. She's a loose end they can't afford."

A wave of rage washes over me. "They're not getting anywhere near her again," I growl.

Jerry holds up his hands. "I know, Bozo. That's why I called you here. We need to make a plan. This is a fucking tight knit operation. There's no fucking way we're getting close to them, unless we plan it to the fucking T."

Preacher steps forward. "What do you suggest?"

Jerry takes a deep breath. "We need to draw Dragomir out. Make him think we have information that could compromise their operation."

I raise an eyebrow. "And how do we do that?"

"We set a trap," Jerry says, his eyes glinting. "Use one of our own as bait. Someone who could believably have overheard something important."

The implication hangs heavy in the air. I shake my head vehemently. "No. Absolutely fucking not. We're not using Gráinne as bait."

Jerry sighs. "Bozo, I know you want to protect her, but—"

"But nothing," I snarl, stepping closer to him. "She's been through enough. I won't put her in danger again."

Preacher puts a hand on my shoulder, holding me back. "Easy, brother. Let's hear him out."

I take a deep breath, trying to calm myself. "Fine. What's your plan?"

"Her place is being watched, as is the hospital. Which means going to either place alone is a fucking huge hell no. I'm not letting them get to her, Bozo. They won't hurt her again," he growls. "But we could have her collect some clothes, or have someone else do it for her and lead them into the trap."

I clench my jaw, considering Jerry's words. As

much as I hate the idea of using Gráinne in any way, I know we need to do something to draw these bastards out. This way, she's not in their line of sight and we're drawing them out.

"And then what?" I ask, my voice tight with barely contained anger. "We just wait for them to make a move?"

Jerry shakes his head. "Not exactly. We'll set up surveillance on them, have our guys watching them. Whoever follows you—us—will be brought in for questioning."

Raptor nods slowly. "It could work. But it's risky as fuck."

"Everything about this situation is risky," Jerry counters. "But if we do nothing, they'll keep coming after her. This way, we control the situation, and we keep her safe."

I pace the room, my mind racing. The thought of putting Gráinne in any kind of danger makes me sick, but I know Jerry's right. We need to end this, and fast.

"Fine," I growl finally. "But I want every fucking precaution taken. And I'm going to be there every step of the way."

Jerry nods. "Of course. We'll have eyes on her at

all times. And we'll make sure she's never actually in harm's way."

Preacher nods, already pulling out his phone. "I'm letting Prez know what's going on. He's going to want to ensure that we have men on the clubhouse and women."

"I'll call in my men too," Jer says with a dark grin.

I leave them be and step outside for a moment, needing some air. I'm worried that this could all be for nothing, that it could end up backfiring on us and Grá will be hurt despite everything.

I pull out my phone, staring at Gráinne's number. I should call her, tell her what's happening. But the thought of hearing the fear in her voice again makes me hesitate.

"You okay?" Jerry's voice comes from behind me.

I turn to face him, my expression grim. "No, I'm not fucking okay. The woman I love has a fucking bastard after her who wants her dead."

Jerry's eyes soften. "I know. But we're going to make her safe. We've got a plan and it's our best shot at ending this quickly."

I nod, knowing he's right but hating it all the same. "If anything happens to her..."

"It won't," Jerry says firmly. "We'll make sure of it."

I take a deep breath, steeling myself for what's to come. "Alright. Let's do this."

As we head back inside to finalize the plan, I can't shake the feeling that we're about to step into something much bigger and more dangerous than we've ever faced before. But for Gráinne, I'd face down the Devil himself.

I'M LIKE A CAGED ANIMAL, prowling the warehouse that Jerry owns. It's out in the docklands, and I'm waiting with my brothers for that motherfucker to be brought to us. I went to Grá's apartment to get her clothes just as we'd planned, and to no one's surprise, that motherfucker was waiting on her. It didn't take me longer than a second to see that it was Étienne, the man who was at the poker game in Spain. He's also the fucker who Grá described as the man who attacked her.

He watched from across the street as I entered her apartment and was still there when I left. I saw the twisted fucking grin he had when we made eye contact. He's not stupid; he'll know we're the ones who are hiding Gráinne. If he's sensible, he'll stay the fuck away from the clubhouse. Jerry had Maverick and Emmanuel follow him when he left Grá's apartment. From there, they followed him across town to another apartment complex in Rathmines, where Jer has more of his men currently watching, while Maverick and Emmanuel continue to follow Étienne. Soon, they should have him cornered and be bringing him to me.

I want answers and I'm done playing around.

The warehouse is silent except for the sound of my boots on the concrete floor. Preacher and Raptor stand nearby, their faces grim. We're all on edge, waiting for the moment when Maverick and Emmanuel bring that piece of shit Étienne to us.

I check my phone for what feels like the hundredth time. No messages. No updates. The waiting is fucking killing me.

"They'll be here soon," Preacher says, his voice low and reassuring. "Maverick knows what he's doing."

I nod, but I can't shake the tension coiling in my gut. Every second we wait is another second that Gráinne could be in danger. I know she's safe at the clubhouse, surrounded by our brothers, but it doesn't stop the worry gnawing at me.

Suddenly, the warehouse door creaks open. We

all snap to attention as Maverick and Emmanuel drag in a struggling figure. It's him. Étienne.

They throw him to the ground in front of us. He looks up, his eyes wild with hatred and fear. Good. He should be fucking terrified.

"Well, well," I growl, stepping closer. "Look what the cat dragged in."

Étienne spits at my feet. "Fuck you," he snarls in a heavy French accent.

I don't hesitate. My fist connects with his jaw, sending him sprawling. "That's not very polite," I say, shaking out my hand. "And here I thought we were going to have a nice chat."

Preacher and Raptor move to flank me as I crouch down to Étienne's level. "Now, you're going to tell us everything you know about Dragomir Popescu and The Revenant. And you're going to tell us why you're after my woman."

Étienne glares at me, blood trickling from his split lip. "I'm not telling you shit."

I smile but there's no warmth in it. "Oh, I think you will. See, we've got all night, and I've got a lot of frustration to work out." I pull out my knife, letting the blade catch the light. "And trust me, by the time I'm done with you, you'll be begging to talk."

Étienne's eyes widen slightly, but he tries to

maintain his bravado. "You don't scare me. You have no idea who you're dealing with."

I lean in close, my voice dropping to a dangerous whisper. "No, you don't know who you're dealing with. You fucked with the wrong woman, and now you're going to pay for it."

I stand up, nodding to Maverick and Emmanuel. "Tie him up. Make sure it's tight."

As they secure Étienne to a chair, I turn to Preacher and Raptor. "Are you boys ready for a long night?"

They both nod, and Raptor grins maniacally. "This is what we do, brother. We don't let anyone harm what's ours."

I turn back to Étienne, who's now securely bound to the chair. His eyes dart between us, a hint of fear finally breaking through his tough facade.

"Last chance," I growl, leaning in close. "Tell us what we want to know, and maybe we'll go easy on you."

Étienne spits in my face. "Fuck you and your whore."

Red clouds my vision. Before I can stop myself, my fist connects with his face again, and again. I feel bone crunch under my knuckles, but I don't care. All

I can think about is Gráinne, terrified and hurt because of this piece of shit.

"Bozo," Preacher's voice cuts through the haze of rage. "Easy, brother. We need him conscious."

I step back, breathing hard. Étienne's face is a bloody mess, but he's still conscious, glaring at me through swollen eyes.

"Now," I say, wiping blood off my knuckles. "Let's try this again. What does Dragomir want with Gráinne?"

Étienne stays silent, but I can see the fear in his eyes now. Good. He's starting to understand the situation he's in.

Raptor steps forward, a wicked grin on his face. "My turn," he says, pulling out a set of pliers. "You know, I've always wondered how many teeth a man can lose before he starts talking."

Étienne stares at him with blank eyes. Raptor doesn't care. He holds the pliers, something he brought along with him—in his to-go bag, as Preacher calls it, and it contains every fucking weapon you could ever imagine—and grabs Étienne's hair. He pulls it backward, jerking his head back.

Raptor's whistle fills the air as he yanks out Étienne's front tooth. He doesn't stop there. Tooth after tooth he pulls from the Frenchman's mouth. It's something akin to a horror scene. Raptor's face is covered in blood splatter and his grin is satanic.

"Wait," Étienne gasps as Raptor goes to pull yet another tooth. "Wait, I'll talk."

I hold up a hand, stopping Raptor. "We're listening."

Étienne takes a shuddering breath. "Dragomir... he's paranoid. The girl overheard something at the hospital. Something about a shipment coming in."

"What kind of shipment?" I demand.

"Women and children," Étienne snarls. "Big shipment. Coming in through Dublin port next week. It's supposed to be The Revenant's foothold in Western Europe."

I exchange a look with Preacher. This is big. Bigger than we thought. Fucking animals are trafficking not only women but children. Cunts.

"And Gráinne?" I ask, my voice dangerously low. "What were your orders regarding her?"

Étienne hesitates, and I can see the fear in his eyes grow. "We were supposed to bring her in. For questioning."

"Bullshit," I snarl, grabbing him by the throat. "You were going to kill her, weren't you?"

Étienne struggles to breathe, his eyes bulging. I loosen my grip slightly, allowing him to speak.

"Yes," he gasps. "Dragomir doesn't leave loose ends. She overheard us. She needed to be stopped."

I release him, stepping back. My whole body is shaking with rage. She didn't fucking hear that. She has no idea what these motherfucking animals have planned. "Where's Dragomir now?"

Étienne shakes his head. "I don't know. He moves around; never stays in one place for long."

I grab him by the hair, yanking his head back. "Don't fucking lie to me. Where. Is. He? We know he's in Ireland."

Étienne's eyes dart around, looking for an escape that doesn't exist. "Okay, okay! He... he has a safe house. In Howth. Big place overlooking the sea."

Preacher pulls out his phone, likely to relay this information to Jerry. I keep my focus on Étienne.

"Address," I demand.

Étienne rattles off an address, his voice shaking. I nod to Raptor, who writes it down.

"Now," I say, leaning in close. "You're going to tell us everything you know about The Revenant's operations. Every detail, every name, every location. And if I think for one second that you're holding back..."

I let the threat hang in the air. Étienne nods frantically, blood and saliva dribbling down his chin.

For the next hour, we extract every bit of information we can from him. By the time we're done, we have a clearer picture of The Revenant's operations, their key players, and their plans for expansion.

As Étienne finishes talking, slumping in his chair, I turn to Preacher and Raptor. "What do you think?"

Preacher nods grimly. "Sounds legit. Matches up with what Jerry's sources have been saying."

"So, what now?" Raptor asks, cleaning blood off his pliers.

I look back at Étienne, my jaw set. "Now, we end this. We hit Dragomir hard, shut down their operation before it can take root here."

"And him?" Raptor nods toward Étienne.

I consider it for a moment. Part of me wants to end him right here, make him suffer for what he did to Gráinne. But we might need him.

"Keep him alive," I decide. "For now. He might have more information we need."

I turn to leave, but Étienne's voice stops me.

"You're dead," he croaks. "You and your bitch. Dragomir will find you, and when he does…"

I had planned on keeping this cunt alive until we had Dragomir and the Revenant brought down, but fuck that shit. He's proved time and time again that he doesn't know how to shut the fuck up.

I spin around, my fingers clasped around my knife, and I take a few steps closer to him. "No one is going to touch her," I growl, my voice low and deadly as I slice my blade along his throat.

He's dead within seconds, his throat slit, blood pouring from him like a fucking river.

One down, too many more to fucking go.

But I will make it safe for Gráinne. I won't stop until I do.

"Let's go," I growl to my brothers. "We've got work to do."

As we exit the warehouse, I pull out my phone to call Jerry. We need to move fast now. The clock is ticking, and Dragomir Popescu's days are numbered. I'll make sure of it.

TWENTY-FOUR
BOZO

Thanks to some handy hacking skills from Denis' daughter-in-law, Melissa, we've been able to identify a lot of the key players within The Revenant. Not to mention their whereabouts. The majority of them are in Ireland. The fuckers are trying to make a big splash here, but it's not going to work. No fucking way.

"Butch and his men are currently in Kildare dealing with those fuckers," Denis tells us with a grin. "The Revenant has purchased a couple of buildings there. Looks like they're wanting to set up a base of sorts."

Butch is the president of the Devil Falcons motorcycle club. He and his brothers are helping us out. Chloe is Butch's niece—of sorts. Callie and

Maverick are his actual niece and nephew. He's family, which means it's all hands on deck. We've got the Devil Falcons MC, the Gallaghers and their men, the Houlihan Gang, and us. We're going to ensure that The Revenant does not leave Ireland alive. It's time to dismantle their entire organization and take out every single heavy hitter they have.

Pyro nods grimly at Denis' words. "Good. That'll keep them distracted while we focus on Dragomir."

Every brother is here. We need all hands on deck. The prospects are at the clubhouse with the women, not to mention a few of Denis' men and Jer's men. We want our women safe and we're going to ensure they stay that way.

Jerry spreads out a map on the table, pointing to Howth. "According to our intel, this is where Dragomir's safe house is located. It's a fortified compound with at least a dozen armed guards at any given time."

"Sounds like a fucking fortress," Raptor mutters.

"It is," Jerry agrees. "But every fortress has a weak point. We just need to find it."

I lean in, studying the map. "What about access from the sea? Could we approach from there?"

Jerry nods. "It's possible. The property backs

onto a private beach. It's rocky and treacherous, but it could work if we're careful."

"I like it," Pyro says. "They won't be expecting an attack from that direction."

Jer straightens. I can see in his eyes that he's forming a plan. "Alright, here's what we'll do. We'll split into two teams. One group will create a diversion at the front gate, draw their attention. The other will come in from the beach."

"I want to be on the beach team," I ground out, my voice hard. "I want to be the one to put a bullet in Dragomir's head."

Denis claps me on the shoulder. "You got it. I'll lead the diversion team."

We spend the next hour hammering out the details of our plan. By the time we're done, everyone knows their role. We'll strike at dawn, when the changing of the guard should provide us with a moment of confusion to exploit.

As the others file out to prepare, Jerry pulls me aside. "You sure about this, Bozo? It's going to be dangerous as hell." I know he's only asking because of Grá. He doesn't want her hurt, and if something happens to me, she'll be devastated.

I meet his eyes, my resolve unwavering. I'm not backing out. This is who I am. No one harms

Gráinne. Not fucking ever. "I'm sure. This ends tonight, one way or another."

Jerry nods, understanding in his eyes. "Alright. Just be careful out there. Gráinne needs you to come back in one piece."

The mention of Gráinne sends a pang through my chest. I haven't told her what's happening. I couldn't bear to see the fear in her eyes, knowing I was walking into danger. She's got the biggest heart of anyone I know and she'd be worried if she knew.

"I'll be careful," I promise. "And Jerry? If something happens to me—"

"Nothing's going to happen," Jerry cuts me off firmly. "But if it does, I'll make sure she's taken care of. You have my word."

I nod, grateful. "Thank you."

As I head out to gear up, I pull out my phone. I should call Gráinne, hear her voice one last time before we go in. But I know if I do, I might lose my nerve. Instead, I type out a quick text.

Me: *I love you. Stay safe. I'll see you soon.*

I hit send before I can second-guess myself.

THE BEACH IS quiet as we approach. It's dark out and the wind is howling, which helps to deafen our footsteps. I can make out the silhouette of Dragomir's compound looming above us. Pretentious prick.

Pyro signals for us to halt, his hand raised. We crouch low, hidden among the boulders. In the distance, I hear the faint rumble of engines. Denis and his team are right on schedule with the diversion.

"Remember," Pyro whispers, his voice barely audible over the wind. "We wait for the signal. When those guards at the back gate start moving, that's our cue."

I nod, gripping my weapon tighter. Adrenaline courses through my veins, every nerve on high alert. This is it. The moment we've been working toward.

Suddenly, an explosion rocks the air. Shouts and gunfire erupt from the front of the compound. The diversion is underway.

"Now!" Pyro hisses.

We move swiftly, scaling the rocky incline toward the back of the property. Just as we reach the fence, I see two guards rushing toward the front, leaving their post unattended.

Raptor makes quick work of the lock, and we slip inside. The grounds are chaos, men running in all directions, shouting orders. In the confusion, we manage to make it to the main house undetected.

Gunfire begins, and I know that Denis and his men are more than capable of taking care of the guards and anyone else who tries to take them on. The Gallaghers are a force to be reckoned with.

Inside, it's eerily quiet compared to the mayhem outside. We move room by room, clearing each one methodically. My heart pounds in my chest, knowing that with each step, I'm getting closer to Dragomir.

As we round a corner, gunfire erupts. I dive for cover behind an overturned table as bullets spray the wall behind me. Pyro and Raptor return fire, and I hear a grunt of pain as one of Dragomir's men goes down.

"Bozo, Preacher," Pyro shouts over the chaos. "Second floor, he's up there. Go get him."

I nod, understanding. While they hold off the guards, Preach and I will go after Dragomir.

This ends now.

I take the stairs two at a time, my gun at the ready. Preacher is right behind me every step of the way. At the top, I hear movement behind a closed door. Without hesitation, I kick it open.

There he is. Dragomir Popescu., The man responsible for all of this. He's alone, frantically shoving papers into a briefcase. He looks up as I enter, his eyes widening in surprise and fear.

"It's over," I growl, leveling my gun at his head.

Dragomir raises his hands slowly. "You don't want to do this," he says, his Romanian accent thick. "You have no idea who you're dealing with."

I take a step closer, my finger tightening on the trigger. "No, you don't know who you're dealing with. You fucked with the wrong people," I snarl. "You targeted the wrong woman."

Dragomir's eyes narrow as understanding dawns. "The nurse," he spits. "This is about that fucking nurse?"

My grip on the gun tightens, rage boiling inside me. "Her name is Gráinne," I growl. "And yeah, this is about her. But it's also about all the other lives you've destroyed. The women and children you traffic. The families you've torn apart."

Dragomir laughs, a cold, mirthless sound. "You think killing me will stop anything? The Revenant is bigger than me. We have operations all over Europe. You can't—"

His words are cut off by the sound of my gun firing. The bullet catches him in the shoulder, and he stumbles back with a cry of pain.

"I don't give a fuck about your operations," I snarl, advancing on him. "Tonight, it ends for you."

Dragomir clutches his bleeding shoulder, his eyes wild with fear and anger. "You're making a mistake," he gasps. "I have connections, power. I can make you rich beyond your wildest dreams."

I laugh darkly. "You think I want your blood money? You think anything you could offer would make up for what you've done?"

Dragomir lunges for a desk drawer. But Preacher is faster. He tackles Dragomir to the ground, pinning him there.

"Nice try, asshole," Preacher growls.

I crouch down next to Dragomir, pressing the barrel of my gun to his forehead. "Any last words?"

Dragomir glares at me, defiant to the end. "Fuck you," he spits.

I smile coldly. "Wrong answer."

The gunshot echoes through the room. Dragomir's body goes limp, his eyes staring blankly at the ceiling.

For a moment, there's silence. Then the sound of footsteps thundering up the stairs. Pyro and Raptor burst into the room, guns at the ready.

"It's done," I say, standing up. "He's dead."

Pyro nods grimly. "Good. The rest of his men are

dead, other than three of them. We want answers, so we want to ensure we have them all. Denis and his team have them secured."

I take a deep breath, feeling the adrenaline start to ebb. It's over. We did it. Gráinne's safe.

"Let's get the fuck out of here," I say. "I need to see Gráinne."

As we make our way out of the compound, I can't help but feel a sense of relief wash over me. The nightmare is finally over. Gráinne is safe.

As I look at the chaos around us, the bodies of Dragomir's men littering the ground, I pray that this is the end of The Revenant. But there's a niggling in my stomach telling me we've missed something.

As we make our way out of the compound, I hear sirens in the distance, growing louder by the second.

"We need to move," Pyro barks. "Now."

We all scatter, jumping into whichever vehicle is free at the moment. Our bikes are miles away. We came from a boat that's left on the shore. As the vehicle I'm in speeds away from Howth, I feel the tension in my body start to uncoil. We did it. We took out Dragomir and dismantled a major part of The Revenant's operation.

But that niggling feeling in my gut won't go away.

Something about this feels too easy, too clean. The Revenant has always been one step ahead of us.

Could we really have caught them off guard like this?

I push the thoughts aside as we approach where our bikes are left. It doesn't take long until we're riding home. Right now, all I want is to see Gráinne, to hold her in my arms and know that she's safe.

As we pull into the lot, I see her standing at the door, her arms crossed over her stomach. She's wrapped in one of my hoodies, looking small and vulnerable. The moment she sees me, she starts running.

I barely have time to dismount before she crashes into me, her arms wrapping around my neck as she buries her face in my chest. I hold her tight, breathing in her familiar scent. Christ, this woman is fucking everything to me.

"You're okay," she whispers, her voice muffled against my cut. "You're really okay."

I pull back just enough to look into her eyes. They're red-rimmed and puffy, like she's been crying. "I'm okay," I assure her, cupping her face in my hands. "It's over, Grá. It's over."

She nods, tears spilling down her cheeks. I wipe them away with my thumbs, then lean in to kiss her softly. When we break apart, I rest my forehead against hers.

"I love you," I murmur. "So fucking much."

"I love you too," she replies, her voice thick with emotion.

I continue to hold her, needing to touch her. I hear Denis approaching. I turn to face him, keeping one arm around Gráinne.

"Good work tonight," Denis says, his voice gruff. "But we're not done yet. We've got those three prisoners to deal with, and we need to make sure we've truly cut off the head of the snake."

I nod, feeling that unease creep back in.

"You're right. We can't let our guard down yet," Pyro growls. "Wrath got the papers that fucker Dragomir had in the briefcase. He and Preach are going over them as we speak."

Denis grins. "Get some rest. We'll regroup this afternoon and figure out our next move. Let those bastards stew for a bit."

As Denis walks away, I turn back to Gráinne. She's looking up at me, worry etched across her face.

"What is it?" she asks.

I hesitate, not wanting to worry her further, but I've promised to always be honest with her. "It's just something doesn't feel right. Taking out Dragomir was almost too easy."

Gráinne's brow furrows. "You think there's more to come?"

I nod grimly. "I think The Revenant might be bigger than we realized. Dragomir said they have operations all over Europe. We may have cut off one head, but—"

"They might grow two more," Gráinne finishes, understanding in her eyes.

"Exactly," I say, pulling her closer. "But whatever comes next, we'll face it together. I promise you that."

Gráinne nods, burying her face in my chest again. "I was so scared," she whispers. "When I got your text, I knew something was happening. I couldn't sleep. I just kept imagining the worst."

My heart clenches at her words. "I'm sorry, Sunshine. I didn't want to worry you, but I couldn't leave without saying something."

She looks up at me, her eyes fierce despite the tears. "Next time, be honest. I'd rather know what's happening than be left in the dark, wondering if you're alive or dead."

I nod, knowing she's right. "That I can do. I may not be able to give you everything, but I'll let you know what I can. We're in this together."

Gráinne smiles, a small but genuine smile that makes my heart skip a beat. "Together," she agrees.

As we walk into the clubhouse, my arm around her waist as she leans heavily against me, I can't shake the feeling that this is just the beginning. The Revenant may be wounded, but they're far from defeated. And something tells me that the real battle is yet to come.

For now, though, I push those thoughts aside. Tonight, I'm going to hold my woman close and be grateful that she's safe. Tomorrow, we'll face whatever may arise.

TWENTY-FIVE
GRÁINNE

The second we're in his room, he's on me, his lips hot and heavy against mine, his hands gently skimming along my body. I melt into his embrace, my fingers tangling in his hair as I pull him closer.

His touch sends shivers down my spine, igniting a fire deep within me. It's been a while since we've been this close, and God, I've missed it. We stumble backwards until my legs hit the edge of the bed. He breaks the kiss, his dark eyes burning with desire as they lock onto mine. For a moment, we're both breathless, chests heaving. Then he's lowering me onto the mattress, his body covering mine as his lips find my neck.

I arch into him, a soft moan escaping my lips. His hands slide under my shirt, calloused fingers tracing patterns on my skin. I tug at his shirt, desperate to feel his bare skin against mine. He pulls back just long enough to yank it over his head before capturing my lips again in a searing kiss that leaves me dizzy and wanting more.

My hands roam over his now-exposed chest, relishing the feeling of taut muscle beneath my fingertips. He groans into my mouth, the sound sending a jolt of electricity through me. His fingers fumble with the buttons of my blouse, his usual control lost in his eagerness. I can't help but smile against his lips, amused by his impatience.

Finally, he manages to undo the last button, pushing the fabric aside. His mouth leaves mine to trail kisses down my neck, across my collarbone, lower still. I gasp as his lips brush against the swell of my breast, my back arching off the bed. His hands slide around to my back, quickly unhooking my bra.

"God, you're beautiful," he murmurs, his voice husky with desire as he drinks in the sight of me.

I pull him back down to me, craving the feel of his skin against mine. Our kisses grow more urgent, hands exploring one another with need.

His fingers ghost along my sides, leaving goosebumps in their wake. They pause at the waistband of my jeans, a silent question in their hesitation. I nod, breathless with anticipation. He smiles, a mixture of tenderness and hunger in his eyes as he slowly, torturously, begins to undo the button.

He's so gentle as he touches me, and I know it's so he doesn't hurt me. My injuries are still fresh, but I need Connor right now. I need him so much it hurts.

"Grá," he growls as he lowers his mouth on mine once again.

Connor's fingers work deftly, sliding my jeans down my legs. His touch is feather-light over my bruises, a stark contrast to the intensity of his kisses. I wince slightly as he presses a kiss against my bandage where I was stabbed, and he immediately pulls back, concern clouding his features.

"Are you alright, Sunshine? We can stop if—"

I silence him with a kiss, pouring all my need into it. "Don't you dare stop," I breathe against his lips.

He hesitates for just a moment before nodding, his eyes dark with barely restrained passion. His hands resume their exploration, but now there's an added layer of care in every caress.

I reach for his belt, fumbling with the buckle in my eagerness. Connor chuckles softly, the sound vibrating against my skin where his lips are pressed to my neck. He helps me, and soon we're both free of the last barriers between us.

As he positions himself above me, Connor pauses, his gaze locked with mine. In that moment, I see everything—his love, his worry, his desire. "I love you," he murmurs, the words carrying the weight of a vow.

"I love you too," I whisper back, my heart swelling with emotion.

Then he's entering me, slowly, carefully. The world narrows down to just us, the feeling of him inside me, the sound of our mingled breaths, the taste of his skin as I press my lips to his shoulder.

We move together, finding our rhythm. It's gentle at first, mindful of my injuries, but as the pleasure builds, so does our urgency. I cling to him, my nails digging into his back as waves of pleasure crash over me.

Connor buries his face in my neck, his breath hot against my skin as he whispers endearments against me.

I can feel myself getting close, teetering on the edge of bliss. "Connor," I gasp, my voice raw with need.

He understands, his movements becoming more purposeful. One of his hands slips between us, and with a few expert touches, I'm falling apart beneath him, crying out his name as ecstasy washes over me.

Connor follows me over the edge moments later, his body tensing as he finds his release. He collapses on top of me, careful not to put his full weight on my injuries. For a long moment, we simply lie there, breathing heavily, our bodies still connected.

Finally, Connor lifts his head, his eyes meeting mine. There's a softness in his gaze that makes my heart skip a beat. He brushes a strand of hair from my face, his touch impossibly tender. "Are you okay?" he asks, his voice laced with concern.

I nod, unable to keep the smile from my face. "More than okay," I assure him, leaning up to press a soft kiss to his lips.

He returns the smile, relief evident in his features. Slowly, he withdraws from me, and I sigh at the loss of connection. He rolls to the side, pulling me with him so that I'm nestled against his chest. His arms wrap around me, holding me close, and I revel in the warmth and safety of his embrace.

We lie in comfortable silence for a while, Connor's fingers tracing lazy patterns on my skin. I can hear the steady beat of his heart under my ear, a soothing rhythm that threatens to lull me to sleep.

"I'm sorry, Sunshine," Connor murmurs

suddenly, his voice barely above a whisper. "That I worried you," he trails off, his arms tightening around me.

I press a kiss to his chest, right over his heart. "I know, but it's okay. Everything's going to be okay."

He sighs, his breath ruffling my hair. "I need you to tell me if anything makes you uneasy, if anything or anyone scares you."

I prop myself up on an elbow, looking down at him. His face is etched with worry. "Hey," I say firmly, cupping his cheek with my hand. "It's going to be okay."

He nods, his hand sliding into my hair. "Promise me, Sunshine."

I swallow hard, knowing that he needs me to do this. "I promise, Con. You'll be the first one to know if anything feels off."

He nods, seemingly relieved that I agreed without much of a fuss.

"Sleep, Grá," he says, his voice thick and hoarse. "You're safe here."

He has no idea that I'm always safe whenever he's with me. He's always made it that way. I close my eyes and snuggle closer to his body, loving the warmth of him next to me. "Night, Con. I love you," I whisper.

"Night, Grá," he says. "Love you too, Sunshine."

When I fall asleep, I do so with a huge smile on my face. This is all I have ever wanted.

I'M SITTING on the bed, wearing his tee as he gets dressed. "What's the plan for today?" I ask, wondering if I'll be confined to the clubhouse once again.

"We'll be dealing with the aftermath of yesterday," Connor tells me distractedly as he pulls on his cut. He turns to me, his eyes assessing me. "Grá, there's nothing to worry about."

I breathe a sigh of relief. "Okay, good. I don't think I could face another day being cooped up here."

He moves toward me, his fists planting on either side of me on the mattress, his eyes glinting with barely concealed anger. "I get that you're used to working and doing what you want, whenever you want, but, Sunshine, these fuckers wanted you dead. They beat you, stabbed you, and they would have killed you."

I swallow hard, my heart racing as I meet Connor's intense gaze. The memories of that terrifying attack flash through my mind. I can almost feel the phantom pain of the knife slicing into my skin.

"I know," I whisper, my voice trembling slightly. "I just... I feel so helpless, Connor, like I'm not in control of my own life anymore."

His expression softens, and he cups my face gently with one calloused hand. "I get it, Grá. But right now, keeping you safe is my top priority. Our top priority."

I lean in to his touch, drawing comfort from his warmth. "So, what exactly does 'dealing with the aftermath' entail?"

Connor's jaw tightens, and I see the dangerousness return to his eyes. "We're going to send a message."

A shiver runs down my spine, both from fear and a twisted sort of excitement. I know I should be horrified by the implications of his words, but a part of me feels vindicated. Protected.

"Will you be gone long?" I ask, trying to keep the neediness out of my voice.

He leans in, pressing a fierce kiss to my lips. "Not if I can help it. But I need you to promise me something, Sunshine."

I nod, breathless from his kiss. "Anything."

"Call me if you need me." I have a feeling that's not what he was going to say.

I want to argue, to insist that I can take care of myself, but the memory of helplessness, of pain and terror, is still too fresh. So instead, I nod again. "I promise. If I need you, I'll call you. Can I go to my apartment?"

Connor's eyes narrow slightly, and I can see him weighing the risks in his mind. After a moment, he sighs. "Alright, but you're not going alone. I'll have Jerry have two of his men escort you there and back."

I bite back a protest, knowing it's futile. Instead, I force a small smile. "Thanks. I just need to grab a few things, maybe water my plants if they're not already dead."

He nods then leans in to press his forehead against mine. "I know this isn't easy for you, Grá. But I need you safe. You're... you're everything to me."

The raw emotion in his voice makes my heart clench. I wrap my arms around his neck, pulling him closer. "I know. You're everything to me too."

We stay like that for a moment, just breathing each other in. Then Connor pulls away, his expression hardening as he slips back into Bozo. There's a difference between the two. I have always gotten

Connor. But the hard eyes and angry glint tells me that Bozo is never far beneath the surface.

"Jerry will have men here as soon as he can, okay? Stay in the apartment, don't linger, and come straight back here. Understood?"

I nod, trying not to feel like a chastised child. "Understood."

As Connor leaves the room, I start to get dressed, my mind racing. I know he's just trying to protect me, but I can't help but feel trapped.

Thirty minutes later and I see Brendan and Ruairí waiting for me. I've known Brendan for a while, and I'm shocked to learn that Ruairí is Ailbhe's brother who now works for Jer.

"Grá," Brendan says with a small nod. "You okay?"

I force a smile, trying to appear more composed than I feel. "I'm fine, Brendan. Thanks for asking."

Ruairí eyes me sceptically, his gaze lingering on the fading bruises on my face. I resist the urge to touch them self-consciously.

"Let's get going," I say, eager to leave the confines of the clubhouse.

The ride to my apartment is tense and silent. Brendan drives while Ruairí sits in the back with me, his eyes constantly scanning our surroundings. I feel a mixture of gratitude and frustration at their vigilance.

As we pull up to my building, a wave of nostalgia washes over me. It feels like ages since I've been here, though it's only been a few weeks.

"We'll come up with you," Brendan says as he parks the car.

I nod, knowing there's no point in arguing. We make our way up to my apartment, and I fumble with my keys, suddenly nervous.

When I open the door, the familiar scent of home hits me, and I feel a lump form in my throat. Everything is exactly as I left it, yet it feels different somehow. Like it belongs to a different version of me. My heart races as I remember the attack that happened here. I hate that my home will always be tainted by what that animal did to me.

"I'll just be a few minutes," I tell the guys, my voice sounding strained even to my own ears.

As I move through the apartment, gathering clothes and personal items, I can't shake the feeling of being watched. Not by Brendan and Ruairí, but by someone else.

I water my plants, most of which have miraculously survived my absence, and pause at my desk. My laptop sits there, untouched. I hesitate for a moment before grabbing it and shoving it into my bag. Maybe I can do some paperwork, feel a little more like myself.

As I'm zipping up my bag, my phone buzzes. It's a text from Connor.

Connor: Everything okay?

I type out a quick reply. ***Me: All good. Heading back soon.***

Just as I hit send, I hear a crash from the living room, followed by Ruairí's shout. "Get down!"

My heart leaps into my throat as Brendan bursts into the bedroom, his gun drawn. "We need to go. Now."

I fumble with my phone, remembering the promise I made Connor. I quickly text as best as I can as I rush after Brendan.

Me: Not sure what's going on but something's not right.

I hear a gunshot and instinctively duck, my heart pounding in my chest. The sound is followed by a man grunting and something heavy hitting the ground.

Brendan grabs my arm, pulling me toward the fire escape. "Move!" he yells, shoving me through the window.

I scramble onto the metal grating, my hands

shaking as I grip the railing. The sound of more gunshots echoes from inside the apartment, and I hear Ruairí shouting something I can't make out. I pray that he's okay.

Brendan follows me out, his body tense as he scans the alley below. "We need to get to the car. Stay close to me, understand?"

I nod, unable to form words. We start descending the fire escape, the metal clanging beneath our feet. I'm acutely aware of how exposed we are, my eyes darting around for any sign of danger.

Suddenly, a figure appears at the end of the alley. Even from this distance, I can see the glint of a gun in their hand.

"Shit," Brendan mutters, pushing me behind him. I watch in horror as the man who appeared in the alley points his gun at Brendan and shoots him.

I release a horrified scream as Brendan crumples to the ground, blood blossoming on his shirt. My mind races, torn between the instinct to help him and the desperate need to run.

"Go!" Brendan gasps, his face contorted in pain. "Get out of here!"

Tears blur my vision as I turn and sprint down the alley, away from the gunman. My heart pounds in my ears, drowning out everything but the sound of footsteps behind me. I don't dare look back, focusing solely on escape.

I round a corner, nearly losing my footing on the slick pavement. My lungs burn as I push myself harder, faster. I need to find help. I need to get somewhere safe.

Suddenly, a hand grabs my arm, yanking me into a narrow space between two buildings. I open my mouth to scream, but a large hand clamps over it.

"You should know," I hear my captor growl as they start dragging me toward the parking lot. "I love the chase. It's been five years now, Gráinne."

I sob against the hand pressed over my mouth as I realize who has me. Mike. He was my friend. Why is he doing this?

He reaches his vehicle and throws me into the trunk. "You should have just accepted one of the dates, Grá," he grunts with a wicked smile as he slams the trunk door down, sinking me into darkness.

Oh God, what is he going to do to me?

TWENTY-SIX
BOZO

I stand against the wall, my arms crossed and legs planted as I watch Pyro, Jer, and Denis Gallagher question the men we took from the house last night.

The interrogation room is dimly lit, the air thick with tension. This is one of Jer's many locations around the city, a run-down hotel that's seen better days. The three prisoners are bound to chairs, their faces bruised and bloodied from the fight. I can see the fear in their eyes as they face down the imposing figures of Pyro, Jer, and Denis.

"Let's try this again," Denis growls, leaning in close to one of the men. "Who else is involved in The Revenant's operation?"

The man spits blood onto the floor. "I told you, I don't know anything. I'm just a hired gun."

Denis straightens up, his face a mask of cold fury. He nods to Jer, who steps forward, cracking his knuckles.

I wince as Jer's fist connects with the man's jaw. The crack echoes through the room, followed by a pained groan.

"Wrong answer," Pyro says, his voice dangerously soft. "We know you're more than just muscle. Dragomir kept you close for a reason."

The man's eyes dart between the three of them, panic setting in. "Please," he whimpers. "I can't tell you anything. They'll kill me."

"And what do you think we'll do if you don't talk?" Denis snarls.

I shift against the wall, itching to join in and beat the information out of them. We need this information. We need to make sure The Revenant is truly finished.

Suddenly, one of the other prisoners speaks up. "Wait," he says, his voice shaky. "I... I know something."

All eyes turn to him. He's younger than the others, barely more than a kid really. Fear is written all over his face.

"Talk," Pyro commands.

The young man swallows hard. "Dragomir... he

wasn't the top. There's someone else, someone higher up."

My blood runs cold. I knew it. I fucking knew it was too easy. I fucking knew there was more to this than what there appeared to be. Dragomir went too easily. Too fucking easy.

"Who?" Denis demands.

"I don't know his name," the kid says quickly. "But I've heard them talk about him. They call him the Puppetmaster."

Jerry and Denis exchange a look. I can see the wheels turning in their heads. That's not a name I've heard before, but I'm wondering if Jer and Denis have?

"Where can we find this Puppetmaster?" Jer asks.

The young man shakes his head. "I don't know. But..." He hesitates, glancing at his friends. "They're supposed to be after someone, or something that they need to make the Revenant bigger, better than before."

"Where is he?" Denis presses.

"Here in Ireland," the kid whispers. "That's all I know, I swear."

The room falls silent as we all process this information. It's not over. Not by a long shot.

Pyro turns to me, his expression grim. "Looks like we're no closer to finding out the truth."

Frustration doesn't even fucking cover it right now. Christ, what the fuck is going on? I quickly send a text to Gráinne, making sure she's okay.

"Do you know who the Puppetmaster is?" I ask Jer and Denis.

I watch as Denis nods grimly. "I've heard about him. He's a low-key player here in Ireland, but he's got a lot of connections in Europe. It's where he makes his money."

Jer nods, his jaw tight. "Damien Hammond is the Puppetmaster."

I frown. Am I supposed to know who that is?

"Bozo," Jer says, his voice tight. "The guy who asked Grá on a date? He works in the hospital with her. He's been a friend since she started college. Mike Hammond is the son of Damien Hammond."

I clench my jaw, staring at him dumbfounded. "You let some fucker close to her?" I snarl. "How the fuck was he able to get that fucking close to her?"

Jer's eyes flash with anger at my accusation. "We didn't know he was part of this shit. Had I known, he would never have been anywhere near her."

I take a deep breath, trying to calm the rage

building inside me. "So what now? We go after this Puppetmaster?"

Denis shakes his head. "Not yet. We need more information. If we move too quickly, we could spook him and lose our chance."

"And in the meantime?" I ask, my voice tight with frustration.

"We keep Gráinne safe," Pyro says firmly. "And we dig deeper. Find out everything we can about Damien Hammond and his operations."

I nod, my mind racing. "What about Mike? He's still close to Gráinne. We need to get him away from her." She hates being confined to the clubhouse, and I know she's dying to get back to work, but he's also there and that's not something I'm comfortable with.

Jer runs a hand through his hair. "We can't just snatch him up. That'll raise too many alarms. We need to be smart about this."

"I don't give a fuck about being smart," I growl. "I care about keeping Gráinne safe."

"And we will," Denis assures me. "But we need to play this carefully. If we tip our hand too soon, we could lose everything."

I clench my fists, hating the logic in his words. Every instinct in me is screaming to hunt down Mike

Hammond and beat the truth out of him. But I know they're right. We need to be strategic.

"Fine," I snarl as I reach for my cell and see two messages from Gráinne.

Grá: All good. Heading back soon.

But not even minutes later, I see she messaged again.

***Grá*: Not sure what's going on but something's not right.**

I lift my head and see Jer watching me. "What?" he asks, his voice tight.

"Call Brendon and Ruairí," I snarl as I hit dial on Grá's number. "Find out what the fuck is going on."

Her cell rings and rings, but there's no answer. Over and over again I call her, but to no avail. She's not fucking answering.

"Where the fuck is she?" I hear Jer roar into the phone.

Fear unlike anything I've ever felt before grips my heart as I hear Jer's words. My mind races with worst-case scenarios. Has Mike Hammond gotten to her? This has to be the Puppetmaster's doing!

"Fuck!" I roar, slamming my fist into the wall. The pain barely registers through my panic.

Pyro is already moving, barking orders into his

phone. "I want every available man out looking for her. Now!"

Denis grabs my arm, his grip like iron. "We'll find her," he says, his voice low and intense. "We'll tear this city apart if we have to."

Gráinne has worked for Denis since Jerry took her under his wing. She's family to everyone. It's hard not to love Grá. She's the sweetest woman you'll ever meet and she cares about everyone.

I nod, trying to focus. "We need to check Mike's home," I say, my voice shaking with barely controlled rage. "He could have taken her there."

Jer's already heading for the door. "I'm on it. I'll have every man I have working this."

Exiting the run-down hotel, I can't think straight. My mind is a mess with all the things that asshole could be doing to Grá. Never have I felt as fucking helpless as I do right now.

The cool air does nothing to calm the fire burning in my veins. If anything's happened to Gráinne, there won't be a force on this earth that can stop me from raining hell down on those responsible.

As I climb onto my bike, my phone buzzes. For a split second, hope flares in my chest. But it's not Gráinne. It's an unknown number.

The message is simple, chilling, and fucking taunting.

Unknown: The game has changed. Your move.

Attached is a photo that makes my blood run cold. It's Gráinne, unconscious and bound, in what looks like the trunk of a car.

I show the phone to Pyro, who curses violently. "They're playing with us," he growls.

"Then let's show them how we play," I snarl, gunning the engine.

As we tear through the streets of Dublin, I make a silent vow. I will find Gráinne. I will bring her home safe. And then, I will unleash a reckoning upon the Puppetmaster and his entire operation that will shake the very foundations of their world.

God help anyone who stands in our way.

The roar of our bikes echoes through the streets as we race toward Mike Hammond's place. My mind is a whirlwind of rage and fear, the image of Gráinne bound and helpless seared into my brain. I can barely focus on the road, my hands gripping the handlebars so tightly my knuckles are white.

Jer's voice crackles through the com in my helmet. "Just got word from one of my guys. Mike's car isn't at the hospital. He's supposed to be working a double shift, but he left early. No one has seen him in hours."

"Fuck!" I snarl, swerving around a slow-moving car. "So, where the hell is she?"

"We'll figure it out," Pyro's calm voice comes through. "Stay focused. We can't help her if we crash."

I take a deep breath, trying to steady myself. He's right, but it doesn't make it any easier. Every second feels like an eternity, knowing Gráinne is out there, scared and alone.

We screech to a halt outside Mike's apartment building. Before the bikes have even stopped, I'm off and running toward the entrance. Jer and Pyro are right behind me.

The lock on the front door is no match for my foot. I kick with every ounce of power I have and the fucking thing splinters. We burst in, guns drawn, ready for anything.

But the apartment is empty. Silent. Undisturbed.

"Search everything," Pyro orders, already moving toward the bedroom. "There has to be something here. Some clue."

We tear the place apart. Drawers are emptied,

furniture overturned, every possible hiding spot examined. But there's nothing. No sign of Gráinne, no evidence of any connection to the Puppetmaster.

"Fuck!" I roar, slamming my fist into the wall. The plaster cracks under the impact, but I barely feel it. I feel utterly fucking useless. I have no idea where she is or what that fucking cunt is doing to her.

Jer puts a hand on my shoulder. "We'll find her," he says, his voice low and intense. "We won't stop until we do."

Suddenly, Pyro calls out from the living room. "Guys, you need to see this."

We rush over. Pyro is holding a small notebook he found hidden behind a loose baseboard. As he flips through it, my stomach turns.

It's filled with notes about Gráinne. Her schedule, her habits, even details about her relationship with me. This wasn't just surveillance, this was obsession. Not to mention pictures, hundreds upon hundreds of pictures of her. Some up close and others taken at a distance. She has no idea the camera is even there.

"That sick fuck," Jer growls, his face pale with anger.

Before we can discuss it further, my phone

buzzes again. Another message from the unknown number.

Unknown: Tick tock. The clock is running out for your precious Gráinne.

Attached is another photo. This time, it's Gráinne awake, her eyes wide with fear. She's in some kind of dark, damp room. A basement, maybe. There's a newspaper in the frame, today's date clearly visible. Proof of life.

My stomach churns. "We need to find her. Now." I can't fucking lose her. No way. I just can't. She's my fucking everything.

Jer's already on his phone, barking orders. "I want every abandoned building, every warehouse, every fucking hole in the ground searched. Now!"

Pyro's studying the photo intently. "Wait," he says suddenly. "Look at the wall behind her."

I peer closer, trying to see past the terror on Gráinne's face. And then I see it. Faded, barely visible, but unmistakable. A logo.

"That's the old textile factory," Denis says, his voice tight. "It's been abandoned for years."

"Let's go," I growl, already heading for the door.

As we race toward the old factory, I can feel the adrenaline coursing through my veins. We're close. So fucking close. Hang on, Grá. We're coming.

We kill the engines a block away, not wanting to alert anyone inside to our presence.

"Remember," Jer says as we approach, "we need to be smart about this. We don't know how many of them are in there."

I nod, but my mind is singularly focused. Get to Gráinne. Everything else is secondary.

We move silently, weapons drawn. The lock on the side door is no match for Pyro's skills. Within seconds, we're inside.

The factory is massive, filled with shadows and echoes. Every sound seems amplified; the creak of the floor, our muted breathing. We move carefully, checking each room, each corner.

And then we hear it. A muffled cry. My heart leaps into my throat. Gráinne. Fuck, she's alive.

We follow the sound, moving faster now. As we round a corner, we see a figure standing guard outside a door. Before he can even react, Jer has him in a chokehold. The man struggles briefly before going limp.

I'm at the door in an instant, kicking it open with all my strength. The sight that greets me makes my blood boil.

Gráinne is there, tied to a chair. Her face is tear-stained, but her eyes light up when she sees us. Mike

Hammond stands behind her, a gun pressed to her head.

"One more step," he snarls, "and I'll blow her fucking brains out."

Time seems to stand still. I can see the fear in Gráinne's eyes, but also a flicker of hope. She trusts me. Trusts us to get her out of this.

"Let her go, Mike," I say, my voice low and steady, trying to buy time as I assess the situation. Mike's hand is shaking slightly, his eyes wild with desperation. He knows he's cornered. There's no way out for him. Not anymore. He crossed the line when he took her. I'm going to enjoy killing him.

"You don't want to do this," I say, taking a small step forward. "Think about what you're doing."

Mike's grip on the gun tightens. "Stay back!" he shouts. "I'll do it, I swear!"

From the corner of my eye, I see Jer and Pyro spreading out, flanking Mike. Good. We might have a shot at this.

"Your father put you up to this, didn't he?" I ask, trying to keep him talking. "The Puppetmaster. This was all his idea."

Mike's eyes widen in surprise. "How do you—"

That moment of distraction is all we need. In a blur of motion, Pyro lunges forward, tackling Mike from the side. The gun goes off, the sound deafening in the enclosed space. My heart stops for a moment, but the bullet embeds itself in the wall, missing Gráinne by inches.

I'm on Mike in an instant, my fist connecting with his face again and again. All the fear, all the rage of the past few hours pours out of me. It takes both Jer and Pyro to pull me off him.

"Enough," Jer says firmly. "We need him alive."

I nod, still shaking with adrenaline. I turn to Gráinne, who's watching the scene with wide eyes. In a heartbeat, I'm at her side, untying her bonds.

"Are you okay?" I ask, my voice hoarse with emotion. "Did they hurt you?"

She shakes her head, tears streaming down her face. "I'm okay," she whispers. "I knew you'd come."

I pull her into my arms, holding her tight. For a moment, the world fades away. She's safe. She's here. Nothing else matters.

But reality crashes back in as Pyro speaks up. "We need to move," he says urgently. "The Puppetmaster will know something's wrong by now."

I nod, helping Gráinne to her feet. She's shaky but determined. "What about Mike?" she asks, glancing at the unconscious man on the floor.

"We're taking him with us," Jer says grimly. "He's got a lot of questions to answer."

As we make our way out of the factory, I keep Gráinne close, my arm around her protectively. This isn't over, not by a long shot. The Puppetmaster is still out there, and now he knows we're onto him.

TWENTY-SEVEN
BOZO

"Now," I begin, my fists clenched as I get down on my haunches and come level with Mike. He's tied to a chair, and we're back at Jer's abandoned hotel once again. "Where is your dad?"

Mike shakes his head, his eyes barely open from the beating he took from me.

"I told you," Mike slurs, blood dripping from his split lip, "I don't know where he is. My father doesn't share that kind of information with me."

I grab his chin, forcing him to look at me. "You expect me to believe that? After what you did to Gráinne?"

Mike's eyes flicker with something—fear, maybe guilt. "That wasn't... it wasn't supposed to go down like that. I was just supposed to watch her, report back. Things got out of hand."

"Out of hand?" I snarl, my grip tightening. "You kidnapped her, you piece of shit!"

Jer places a hand on my shoulder, pulling me back slightly. "Easy," he murmurs. "We need him talking, not unconscious."

I take a deep breath, trying to rein in my rage. Jer's right, but every time I look at Mike, all I can see is Gráinne bound and terrified in that warehouse.

"Alright," Pyro says, stepping forward. "Let's try this again. Your father, the Puppetmaster, what's his endgame? What's he after?"

Mike shakes his head again, but there's hesitation in his eyes now. "I... I don't know. He keeps me in the dark about most of it."

"But you do know something," Denis presses, calling out his bullshit. "Talk."

Mike swallows hard, glancing between us. "He... he's been working on something big. Something that'll change everything in Ireland's underworld."

"What is it?" I demand.

"I don't know the details," Mike says quickly. "But I've heard him talking about a shipment. Something coming in from Eastern Europe. Weapons, maybe drugs. Whatever it is, it's valuable enough that he's willing to risk everything for it."

Jer and Denis exchange a look. "When?" Jer asks.

"Tonight," Mike says. "I think. That's why he wanted me to keep tabs on Gráinne. He knew you'd be distracted if she was in danger."

The revelation hits me like a punch to the gut. We've been played, manipulated from the start. And Gráinne got caught in the middle of it all.

"Where's the shipment coming in?" Pyro asks.

Mike shakes his head. "I don't know. I swear. My father doesn't trust me with that kind of information."

I clench my fists, frustration boiling over. We're still no closer to finding the Puppetmaster or stopping whatever he has planned.

"It's time to cut the fucking bullshit, Mike. We know that you're up there with your father. It's why you took Grá," Denis asks. "Now, where's the shipment coming in?"

Mike hesitates, fear flickering across his face. "I... I can't. If he finds out I talked..."

"You should be more worried about what we'll do if you don't," I growl. "You hurt the woman I love. You think I'll take it easy on you if you don't fucking speak?"

Little does he know that I'm going to kill him no matter what. He went after the wrong person.

Mike's eyes dart around us. His body trembling. "The docks," he breathes. "They're coming into the docks tonight at eight."

I glance at my cell and see that's less than two hours from now. We don't have much time.

"The docks," I repeat, my mind already racing with plans. "Which part?"

Mike hesitates again, but a sharp look from Denis makes him continue. "There's an old warehouse there, hasn't been used in years. That's where the exchange is happening."

Jer's already on his phone, barking orders to gather our men. Denis moves to secure Mike, ensuring he can't escape.

I turn to Pyro. "What do you think? Could be a trap?"

Py nods, his expression grim. "Could be. But we can't afford to ignore this. If the Puppetmaster is bringing in something big enough to change the game, we need to stop it. If it's that big, it'll take out the Gallaghers and Jer. That's not happening."

"Agreed," I say, checking my weapon. "But Gráinne stays here, under guard. I'm not risking her again."

"Of course," Jer says, rejoining us. "I've got our best men on it. She'll be safe."

I nod, grateful. "Alright, let's move. We've got less than two hours to get set up."

As we head out, I can't shake the feeling that we're walking into something bigger than we realize. The Puppetmaster has been one step ahead of us this whole time. We can't afford any mistakes now.

The ride to the docks is tense, the weight of what's coming hanging heavy in the air. As we approach Pier 14, I see the old warehouse Mike mentioned. It's a hulking, rusted structure, perfect for clandestine meetings.

We park our vehicles at a safe distance away and proceed on foot, using the cover of darkness and the maze of shipping containers to our advantage. Our men are already in position, creating a perimeter around the area.

"Remember," Jer whispers as we near the warehouse, "we need to identify the shipment before we move in. We can't risk losing it in the chaos."

I nod, my grip tightening on my gun. The anticipation is killing me, every nerve in my body on high alert.

Suddenly, we hear the rumble of engines. Two

large trucks are approaching the warehouse, followed by a sleek black car.

"That'll be the Puppetmaster," Denis murmurs.

We watch as the vehicles come to a stop. Men begin to pour out, armed and alert. And then, from the black car, a figure emerges.

Even from this distance, there's something commanding about him. This must be Damien Hammond, the Puppetmaster himself.

"Hold positions," Pyro orders over the comm. He's leading this; everyone else is too fucking emotionally invested. "Wait for my signal."

We watch as the men begin unloading crates from the trucks. Whatever's in there, it's heavy. They struggle with each box.

And then, unexpectedly, Damien Hammond turns and looks directly at our hiding spot. A chill runs down my spine. Somehow, he knows we're here.

"We've been made," I say on a rumble. How the fuck did that cunt know we're here?

"Shit!" Jer hisses. "How the hell did he spot us?"

Before anyone can respond, gunfire erupts. Bullets ping off the metal containers around us, forcing us to duck for cover.

"So much for the element of surprise," Pyro

growls. "Everyone move! Do not let those trucks leave! We want Hammond contained."

We spring into action, returning fire as we advance on the warehouse. The night air fills with the deafening sound of gunshots and cries of pain as the bullets hit intended targets.

I see Damien Hammond retreating toward his car, surrounded by a protective circle of men. Rage surges through me. This is the bastard behind it all, the one who put Gráinne in danger.

"He's leaving!" I shout to Jer, already sprinting toward Hammond's position.

Bullets whiz past me as I weave between the shipping containers. I can hear Jer cursing behind me, followed by heavy footsteps.

My focus narrows to a single point: Damien Hammond.

As I round the corner of a container, I come face to face with one of Hammond's men. Without hesitation, I fire, dropping him before he can raise his weapon.

Hammond is almost at his car now. I put on a burst of speed, desperation fueling my movements. He's not getting away. Fuck no. I won't let him.

"Hammond!" I roar.

He turns, his eyes meeting mine. For a moment,

time seems to slow. I see the cold calculation in his gaze, the slight smirk on his face. This is a man used to being in control, to always being one step ahead.

But not this time.

I raise my gun, ready to end this once and for all. But before I can pull the trigger, something heavy slams into me from the side. I go down hard, my weapon skittering away across the concrete.

As I struggle to my feet, I see one of Hammond's men advancing on me, his fist already swinging. I dodge the blow, countering with a vicious uppercut that sends him staggering back.

I hear the sound of a gunshot fill the air and it's followed by Jer's maniacal laughter. "Did you really think you could escape, Hammond?"

I breathe a sigh of relief. He has him cornered. I know that Jer's men will be at his side, making sure Jer's secured and that cunt doesn't escape.

Hammond's man advances on me again, but this time I'm ready for him. I slide my hand into the back of my jeans, my fingers closing around the other gun I have. Within seconds, I fire off a shot and the fucker crashes to the ground, a bullet hole in his chest.

I don't waste another second, sprinting toward where I last saw Hammond and Jer. As I round the corner, I see Jer has Hammond on his knees, gun pressed to the back of his head. Hammond's men lie motionless on the ground nearby.

It's over. Everyone is gathered around the cunt, watching him. He's not as cocky as he was mere moments ago.

"It's over, Damien," Jer growls. "Your little empire ends here."

Hammond chuckles, a sound that sends chills down my spine. Even now, facing death, he seems unnervingly calm. "You think this is the end? You have no idea what I have created."

I approach cautiously, my gun trained on Hammond. "Really? The Revenant is done, finished. There's no one of importance left. Dragomir, gone. Antoine, gone. Étienne, gone. Marcel, gone. Not to mention, your son. Mike." His eyes flash with anger and pain. Good. "You shouldn't have gone after Gráinne."

Hammond's eyes flick to me, a cruel smile playing on his lips. "Ah, the protective boyfriend. How touching. Tell me, how is dear Gráinne? I hope Mike didn't rough her up too badly."

Rage surges through me. Before I know it, I'm in front of Hammond, my fist connecting with his jaw.

He sprawls backwards, blood spurting from his split lip.

"Enough," Jer says sharply, pulling me back. "We need him talking, not unconscious."

Hammond spits blood, his eyes gleaming with malice. "You want to know what's in those crates? Power. The kind of power that will reshape this country. Weapons, yes, but more than that. Technology. Information. Everything needed to control not just the underworld, but the government itself."

"You're insane," I growl.

"Am I?" Hammond laughs. "Look around you. The world is changing. Those who control the flow of information control everything. And I was so close—"

Suddenly, the night is split by the wail of sirens. Police. Somehow, they've found us.

"Fuck," Jer curses. "We need to move. Now."

I look at Hammond, still kneeling before us. We can't let him go, not after everything he's done.

Jer nods to his men. "Throw him into the back of the van. It's time to get the hell out of here."

"This isn't over," Hammond hisses as Jer shoves him toward one of our waiting vehicles.

"You're right," I growl, leaning in close. "It's not.

Because I'm coming for you. For what you did to Gráinne. For all of it."

Fear flickers in Hammond's eyes for the first time. Good. He should be afraid.

The sound of sirens grows closer as I climb onto my bike. I finally feel relieved. This is it. This is the end. Fuck.

EVERYONE IS GATHERED at the abandoned hotel. It's hours later and we've been waiting on Denis to arrive.

"I had Melissa and some of my men go through the crates," he tells us as he enters the room. "Those fuckers had some intel that was stolen from NASA, not to mention every fucking name of a crooked cop, federal agent, judge, and politician in the world. Someone has been doing their homework."

I let out a low whistle. "Jesus Christ. No wonder Hammond thought he could control everything."

"That kind of information..." Jer shakes his head, looking stunned. "It's beyond valuable. It's fucking dangerous."

Pyro leans forward, his expression grim. "What

are we going to do with it? We can't just sit on this kind of intel."

"We can't use it," Denis suggests, his eyes glinting with rage. "Think about it. With this information, we could have everyone in our pocket. Politicians, judges, cops... We'd have every fucking corrupt asshole after us, not to mention every criminal wanting that information."

"So we destroy it," Pyro says firmly. "We don't need it."

Jer looks at him, seemingly impressed. "I agree. It would be too fucking much heat on us."

"By destroying it, we're making sure no one else can use it either," Denis says. "No one else gets it."

Jer nods. "Alright. We destroy it. All of it. But first, we have to deal with Hammond and his fucking son. They crossed a line coming after my family."

I grin, a vicious satisfaction coursing through me. "I like the way you think."

"So, who gets the honor of killing him?" Pyro asks.

I feel my fists clench involuntarily. "Me."

Jer nods, understanding in his eyes. "I get my shot first, then he's all yours."

I nod, a grim smile on my face. "Fair enough."

We make our way down to the basement where

Hammond is being held. The air grows thicker, heavier with each step. This is it—the moment we've been working toward for months.

As we enter the room, I see Hammond tied to a chair, bruised and bloodied but still defiant. His son, Mike, is in a similar state nearby, fear evident in his eyes.

Jer approaches Hammond slowly, his presence filling the room. "You know, Damien," he says conversationally, "I've been in this game a long time. Seen all kinds of men come and go. But you? You're something else."

Hammond spits blood, glaring up at Jer. "Is this the part where you try to break me? Save your breath."

Jer chuckles, the sound devoid of humor. "Break you? No, Damien. I'm going to destroy you."

Without warning, Jer's fist connects with Hammond's face, the crack of bone echoing in the small room. Hammond's head snaps back, a groan escaping his lips.

"That's for coming after my family," Jer growls.

He continues his assault, each blow punctuated by a reason. For the lives ruined, for the chaos caused, for thinking he could play God with people's lives.

By the time Jer steps back, Hammond is barely conscious, his face a mess of blood and bruises. Mike is sobbing quietly in the corner, unable to look away.

Jer turns to me, wiping blood from his knuckles. "He's all yours now."

I step forward, my heart pounding. This is the man responsible for Gráinne's suffering, for the fear and pain she endured. I want him to suffer, to feel even a fraction of what she felt.

"You know," I say, my voice low and dangerous, "I've been thinking about this moment for a long time. Imagining all the ways I could make you pay for what you did."

Hammond's eyes flutter open, focusing on me with difficulty. "Do... your worst," he manages to slur.

I lean in close, my voice barely above a whisper. "My worst? No, Damien. I'm going to do to you exactly what you did to Gráinne. I'm going to make you feel helpless, terrified, unsure if you'll live to see another day."

I straighten up, looking at Jer. "We're going to need some supplies."

Jer smiles, and within minutes, there's an assortment of knives at my disposal. I pick up the sharpest and begin to stab shallow holes over Hammond's body. Not enough to kill him, but enough to hurt like a motherfucker.

Hours pass, and the fucker's almost dead. He's been slowly bleeding out as I've stabbed him. "You shouldn't have touched her," I growl as I slide the knife into his stomach. "You should never have gone after her."

When it's finally over, I turn to Mike, who flinches away from my gaze. "Your turn," I say, my voice flat and emotionless.

Mike's eyes widen in terror. "Please," he whimpers. "I didn't... I never wanted—"

"Shut up," I snap, cutting him off. "You had your chance to make this right. You could have helped Gráinne. You could have told us the truth from the start. But you didn't."

I step closer, looming over him. "You kidnapped her. Terrorized her. And for what? To impress Daddy?"

Mike shakes his head frantically, tears streaming down his face. "I'm sorry! I'm so sorry! Please, I'll do anything..."

"Anything?" I echo, a cruel smile twisting my lips. "Alright then. Tell me everything. Every detail about your father's operation. Every name, every contact, every dirty little secret. And maybe, just maybe, I'll make it quick."

For the next hour, Mike spills his guts. He tells us about hidden bank accounts, secret allies, contingency plans we hadn't even considered. By the time he's done, he's a sobbing mess, but we have more information than we ever hoped for.

I look at Jer, raising an eyebrow. He nods, a silent understanding passing between us.

"Thank you, Mike," I say, my voice deceptively gentle. "You've been very helpful."

Relief washes over Mike's face, quickly replaced by confusion as I raise my gun.

"Wait! But you said—"

The gunshot drowns out the rest of his words. Mike slumps in his chair, a neat hole in his forehead.

"I said maybe," I mutter, turning away from the body.

Jer claps a hand on my shoulder. "It's done," he says quietly. "It's over."

I nod, suddenly feeling the weight of everything we've been through. "Yeah. It's over."

Now it's time to go home to Grá and let her know that she's safe. This shit won't ever touch her again.

TWENTY-EIGHT
GRÁINNE

It's been two days since I was taken by Mike. I'm heartbroken that my friend would do that to me, but I'm glad he can't hurt me anymore. I hate that he was so deceptive, that he was able to hide who he truly was. I've learned a lot about him over the past two days. Both he and his father were monsters. They trafficked women, drugs, and guns. They had plans on blackmailing as many officials as possible and using them to do inhumane things.

I'm back in Connor's room at the clubhouse, my body aching and my mind reeling. Connor hasn't left my side since they rescued me, his protective instincts in overdrive. I love that he's no longer hiding how he feels. I feel even more connected to him than before.

"Grá," he says softly, pulling me from my thoughts. "You need to eat something."

I look at the untouched plate of food on the nightstand and feel my stomach turn. "I'm not hungry," I mutter.

Connor sighs, sitting on the edge of the bed. "I know you're hurting, Sunshine. But you need to keep your strength up."

I meet his eyes, seeing the worry and anger in them. "How could I have been so blind?" I whisper, feeling tears well up. "He was my friend, Connor. I trusted him."

Connor's jaw clenches, and I can see him struggling to control his rage. "None of this is your fault, Grá. Mike fooled everyone, not just you."

I nod, but the guilt still gnaws at me. "What's going to happen now?"

"We're going to live happy," Connor says, pressing a soft kiss to my lips. "Nothing else is going to happen."

God, I love this man. "Love you," I breathe, needing to tell him.

I watch as his eyes dilate. "Never doubt it, Sunshine, it's only ever been you."

My heart races at his words. This is everything

I've ever dreamed of, and it's come true. Connor loves me and I love him.

His lips slant against mine and my blood heats. God, I need him. Connor's kiss deepens, and I feel the familiar heat building between us. His hands roam my body. As his fingers brush against a tender spot on my ribs, I wince involuntarily. Connor immediately pulls back, his eyes clouding with concern and barely concealed fury.

"I'm sorry," he murmurs, his voice rough with emotion. "I didn't mean to hurt you."

I shake my head, reaching for him. "You didn't. It's just... I'm still a bit sore."

Connor's expression darkens. "I should have killed him slower," he growls, and I know he's thinking about Mike.

A shiver runs through me, and not entirely from fear. Part of me is horrified at the casual way he speaks of murder, but another part—a part I'm not entirely comfortable acknowledging—loves his protectiveness.

"It's over now," I say, as much to convince myself as him. "He can't hurt anyone else."

Connor nods, but I can see the tension in his shoulders. "I won't let anyone hurt you again, Grá. I swear it."

I believe him. After everything we've been through, I know Connor would move Heaven and Earth to keep me safe.

"Please, Connor," I whimper as he watches me. "I need you."

I watch the slow grin form on his face, and his eyes darken with desire as he looks at me. "Are you sure, Sunshine? I don't want to hurt you."

I nod, pulling him closer. "I'm sure. I need to feel you, to know this is real."

He searches my face for a moment, then leans in to capture my lips in a searing kiss. His touch is gentle, mindful of my injuries, but I can feel him holding back.

I moan softly as his hands roam my body, carefully avoiding the tender spots. My own hands find their way under his shirt, tracing his muscular back.

Connor breaks the kiss, his breathing ragged. "Tell me if it's too much," he says, his voice husky with desire.

"I will," I promise, already missing the feel of his lips on mine.

He slowly peels off my shirt, his eyes roaming over my exposed skin. I see a flash of anger as he takes in the bruises marring my flesh, but it's quickly replaced by a look of such tender love that it makes my heart ache.

Connor's touch is soft and gentle as he traces the outline of my body, his calloused fingers leaving trails of fire on my skin. He leans down, pressing soft kisses to each bruise, each mark left by Mike's cruelty. It's as if he's trying to erase the pain with his love.

"You're so beautiful," he murmurs against my skin. "So strong, Grá."

Tears prick my eyes at his words. After everything that's happened, I've felt anything but strong. But here, in Connor's arms, I start to believe it again.

I reach for him, needing to feel his skin against mine. He helps me remove his shirt, and I run my hands over his chest, tracing the familiar pattern of his tattoos.

Connor's breath hitches as I explore his body. His eyes, dark with desire, never leave mine. "I love you," he says, his voice rough with emotion. "More than anything in this world."

"I love you too," I whisper back, pulling him down for another kiss.

He pushes my thighs open. "Please be ready for me," he begs.

I'd laugh if I weren't so needy. "Always," I

whimper as he runs his cock along my folds. I'm always ready for him.

I gasp as Connor slowly enters me, my body stretching to accommodate him. I feel so full, but God, it feels so fucking good.

"Okay?" Connor asks, his voice strained as he holds himself still.

I nod, wrapping my legs around his waist to pull him closer. "More than okay," I breathe.

He starts to move, setting a gentle rhythm that soon has me panting. His lips find mine again, swallowing my moans as he gradually increases his pace.

I lose myself in the sensation, in the feel of Connor's body moving with mine. There's no pain, no fear, only love and pleasure.

"God, Grá," Connor groans, his hips snapping forward. "You feel so good."

I arch into him, meeting his thrusts. "Don't stop," I plead, feeling the familiar tension building inside me.

Connor's hand slips between us, his fingers finding my most sensitive spot. I cry out as he rubs tight circles, pushing me closer to the edge.

"Come for me, Sunshine," he urges, his movements becoming more erratic. "Let go."

His words, combined with the delicious friction,

send me over the edge. I shatter around him, calling out his name as waves of pleasure crash over me.

Connor follows soon after, burying his face in my neck as he finds his release.

Connor lifts his head to look at me. His eyes are soft, filled with so much love it makes my heart fill with warmth. "I love you," he says again, pressing a gentle kiss to my forehead.

I smile, so unbelievably happy. "I love you too." I sink against him. "Thank you," I murmur, pressing a kiss to Connor's chest.

He tightens his arms around me. "For what?"

"For loving me. For saving me. For everything."

Connor tilts my chin up, making me meet his intense gaze. "You don't need to thank me for that, Grá. You're my everything. I'd do anything for you."

He holds me tight, pressing a kiss against my head. I close my eyes, blessed to have him with me.

"We're going to shower and then you're going to eat," he says sternly as he gets off the bed and pulls me with him.

"Fine," I sigh. "But I want to go to Jerry's house and check on Brendan and Ruairí."

Connor's expression softens at my request. "Of course, Sunshine. We can go after we eat. Jerry's been asking about you anyway."

I nod, feeling a mixture of relief and anxiety. I need to see with my own eyes that Brendan and Ruairí are okay. I haven't seen them since they were both shot. Thankfully, from what Jer said, they're doing okay.

We shower together, Connor's hands gentle as he helps me wash. The hot water soothes my aching muscles, and I feel more human by the time we step out.

As promised, Connor makes sure I eat before we leave. The food sits heavy in my stomach, but I know I need the strength. I just feel a little helpless and guilty. Both Brendan and Ruairí got shot because of me and I hate that.

The ride to Jerry's house is quiet, Connor's hand resting protectively on my thigh. I watch the familiar streets pass by, trying to quell the rising panic in my chest. Connor seems to sense my unease, giving my leg a reassuring squeeze.

"I've got you, Grá," he murmurs. "Brendan and Ruairí are dying to see you."

I nod, but I feel worried sick. What if they hate me for getting them hurt?

Connor helps me out of the car, keeping a protective arm around me as we approach the front door. Before we can knock, it swings open, revealing Jerry's worried face.

"Ah, loveen," he says, pulling me into a gentle hug. "I'm glad you're home. Are you okay? Let's get you inside."

I return the hug, feeling tears prick at my eyes. "I'm okay," I assure him, though my voice wavers slightly.

Jerry ushers us inside, leading us to the living room. I'm shocked to see both Brendan and Ruairí sitting down. My heart clenches at the sight of them. Brendan's arm is in a sling, and Ruairí has a nasty cut above his eye. His face is pale and he's leaning heavily on his left side, but they're alive.

"Grá," Brendan says, standing up carefully. "Thank God you're alright."

I move to hug him, mindful of his injury. "I'm so sorry," I whisper, feeling guilty for the pain they endured because of me.

Brendan shakes his head. "Don't you dare apologize. We're just glad you're safe."

Ruairí nods in agreement. "That bastard shouldn't have hurt you," he says, his voice gruff with emotion. "He's gone now."

Connor's hand on my lower back grounds me, reminding me that I'm safe. "How are you both healing?" I ask, trying to change the subject, the doctor in me coming out. I need to do something.

As Brendan and Ruairí fill me in on their recoveries, I feel some of the tension leave my body. They're okay. We're all okay. It'll take some time before they're fully healed but they will heal.

As Connor talks with Brendan and Ruairí, I move to Jerry, who's watching me with so much concern that I want to cry. Instead, I reach him and lean against his side.

"I was so worried," he admits. "When you went missing, I wanted to lose it, but I knew I had to find you. Bozo and I wouldn't have stopped looking for you."

I feel tears welling up in my eyes at Jerry's words. The love and concern radiating from him is overwhelming. "Thank you," I whisper, my voice choking with emotion. "I don't know what I'd do without you all."

Jerry wraps an arm around me, pulling me closer. "You're family, loveen. We take care of our own."

I nod against his shoulder, letting his words sink in. Family. It's been so long since I've truly felt like I belonged somewhere, with people who would do anything to protect me.

"How are you really doing?" Jerry asks quietly, his eyes searching my face.

I take a deep breath, considering my answer. "I'm coping," I say finally. "It's hard. He was my friend. But I'm trying to focus on the fact that it's over now."

Jerry nods, his expression serious. "It is over, Grá. And we'll make damn sure nothing like this ever happens again."

There's a steely determination in his voice that both comforts and unnerves me. I know these men are capable of violence, of doing terrible things to protect their own. Part of me is grateful for that protection, while another part worries about the cost.

"I just want to move forward," I admit. "To feel normal again."

Jerry squeezes my shoulder gently. "It'll take time, loveen. But you're strong. You'll get there."

I give him a small smile, feeling a surge of affection for this man who's become like a father to me. "Thanks, Jer."

Our conversation is interrupted by Connor, who approaches us with a concerned look. "Everything okay?" he asks, his eyes flicking between Jerry and me.

I nod, reaching out to take his hand. "Yeah, we're good. Just talking."

Connor relaxes slightly, but I can see the protective instinct still simmering beneath the surface. I know it'll be a while before he truly lets his guard down with me not being around him.

"We should probably head back soon," Connor says, his thumb rubbing circles on the back of my hand. "You need to rest."

I want to protest, to insist that I'm fine, but the truth is I am tired. The emotional toll of the past few days is catching up with me.

"Okay," I agree, turning back to Jerry. "Thanks for everything, Jer. And please, let me know if there's anything I can do to help Brendan and Ruairí."

Jerry nods, a small smile on his face. "Of course, loveen. You just focus on taking care of yourself for now."

We say our goodbyes, and for the first time in years, I realize that it's hard to leave my home. Jer is my dad. He may not be by blood, but he's a better father than my actual dad was.

"You okay, Sunshine?" Connor asks once we're in the car.

I nod. "Yes, more than okay."

I've never felt so loved and cared for. This is everything I could have ever wanted. My life is better than I could have ever imagined, and I'm loved.

TWENTY-NINE
BOZO

Three Months Later

It's been three months since the shit went down with Hammond and The Revenant. Thankfully, that shit's dead in the sand and there's no coming back from it. Everything that was in the crates was burned. There's no fucking way we'd let the names of the corrupt high officials into anyone's hands.

Grá stays with me here at the clubhouse. She never returned home to her apartment. Something I'm pleased about. I want her with me, always. The woman is my everything, and as soon as she's ready,

I'll be knocking her up. I see the way she looks at the other brothers' kids. She's especially fond of Eva, Wrath and Hayley's daughter.

I can't wait to have what my brothers have. But I'm more than fucking happy with having Grá in my life.

"You good, brother?" Cowboy asks as he slides onto the stool beside me. "Where's Grá? I've not seen her today."

My eyes narrow on him. "Why are you looking for my woman?"

He laughs. "Just asking. Everyone knows she's yours. I don't poach my brothers' women."

"She's working for Jer today. Jer called her early this morning saying he needed her."

Grá found it hard going back to the hospital, so she now works as a doctor at a local clinic. Thankfully, she's able to work whatever hours she wants and was supposed to be off today anyway.

"Oh, it must be the women Jer found," Tank tells us as he joins us.

"What women?"

Tank leans in, lowering his voice. "You haven't heard? Jer's men busted a human trafficking ring last night. Found a bunch of women locked up in a warehouse on the outskirts of town. You've got to be a scumbag to be involved in that shit."

My grip tightens on my glass. Even after taking down Hammond and The Revenant, there are always more cunts rising to the surface.

"Shit," Cowboy mutters. "No wonder Jer called Grá in. Those women are gonna need medical attention, not to mention some serious psychological help."

I nod, a mixture of pride and concern washing over me. Of course Grá would drop everything to help. It's who she is. But the thought of her dealing with the aftermath of such brutality makes my stomach churn.

"Any idea who was behind it?" I ask Tank.

He shakes his head. "Not yet. Jer's men are still investigating. But Jer's beyond pissed, from what I heard from Jason."

Jason's Tank's cousin and works for Jer. Of course he's going to know the ins and outs of what's going on.

"Fuck," I growl. Just when we thought it was over.

Cowboy puts a hand on my shoulder. "We all know that this shit doesn't happen here. Once the news hits Prez and the Gallaghers, I'm just going to say good luck to whoever the fuck is behind it."

At once, our cells buzz, which could only be one thing. Prez.

Prez: Meet me at Jerry's. ASAP.

"Looks like we're about to find out more," Tank says, sliding his phone into his jeans pocket.

It doesn't take long for us to get to Jerry's house. The second we're off our bikes, Pyro's there. "This shit is some of the worst that I've seen," he growls.

Jer's face is grim as we approach. "Glad you're here. We're going to need all hands on deck."

"Is it a trafficking ring?" I ask.

He nods. "Sort of. The women we rescued? They're not just random victims. They were targeted."

"Targeted?" Cowboy asks. "What do you mean?"

Jer runs a hand through his hair—a sign of frustration I've rarely seen from him. "Basically, someone pays a fucking lot of money for someone, they give a detailed description, and then they're delivered to that person."

The implications hit me like a punch to the gut. "How young are we talking?"

Pyro shakes his head. "Think the youngest Jer's men found was six months old."

Fucking hell. What the fuck?

As I walk into Jer's home, I see Gràinne talking to a young brunette woman. The moment Grà sees me, her shoulders slump forward and she gives me a soft smile. "Hey, Con," she greets me.

I move to her, needing to hold her and make sure that she's okay. I wrap my arms around Grà, feeling her tense body relax against me. She buries her face in my chest for a moment, taking a deep breath before pulling back to look up at me.

"It's bad, Con," she whispers, her eyes haunted. "These women, these children... what they've been through..."

I stroke her cheek, wishing I could take away the pain I see in her eyes. "I know, Sunshine. But you're helping them now. That's what matters."

She nods, squeezing my hand before turning back to the young woman she was talking to. "Caoimhe, this is Connor. Con, this is Caoimhe. She's one of the women Jer's men rescued last night."

Caoimhe gives me a wary look, shrinking back slightly. I keep my distance, not wanting to frighten her further.

"Nice to meet you, Caoimhe," I say softly. "You're safe here. No one's going to hurt you."

She nods but doesn't speak. Grà puts a gentle

hand on her arm. "Why don't you go rest for a bit? I'll check on you later, okay?"

As Caoimhe walks away, Grà turns back to me, her face set with determination. "We need to find who's behind this, Con. These bastards can't get away with it."

"Caoimhe?" I hear Cowboy growl.

Turning, I watch as my brother storms toward the frightened woman and hauls her to him.

"Ciarán." The woman shudders against him. "Ciarán," she whimpers.

"I've got you, Caoimhe," he says gently, something that I've never heard him do before. "You're coming with me," he says, his tone brooking no arguments. He turns his stare to Jer. "I want to know everything," he snaps, before walking away with Caoimhe in his arms.

"What just happened?" Grá asks, her eyes wide and her lips parted. "Is she okay?"

"He's not going to hurt her," I tell her. There's no way he'd do anything to her other than protect her. I've never seen Cowboy even remotely protective of anyone. Until now.

Whoever the fuck has done this, God help them. Cowboy is going to tear them a-fucking-part.

COWBOY AND CAOIMHE'S story is up next: https://geni.us/CowboyFVD

BOOKS BY BROOKE:

The Kingpin Series:

Forbidden Lust

Dangerous Secrets

Forever Love

The Made Series:

Bloody Union

Unexpected Union

Fragile Union

Shattered Union

Hateful Union

Vengeful Union

Explosive Union

Cherished Union

Obsessive Union

Gallo Famiglia:

Ruthless Arrangement

Ruthless Betrayal

Ruthless Passion

The Houlihan Men of Dublin:

The Eraser

The Cleaner

The Silencer

The Thief

The Fury Vipers MC NY Chapter:

Stag

Mayhem

Digger

Ace

Pyro

Shadow

Wrath

Reaper

Haunted by the Storm

The Fury Vipers MC Dublin Chapter:

Preacher

Raptor

Bozo

Cowboy

The Saint's Outlaws MC: Boston Chapter:

Ghost's Redemption

Rogue's Reckoning

Standalones:

Saving Reli

Taken By Nikolai

A Love So Wrong

His Dark Desire*

ABOUT BROOKE SUMMERS:

USA Today Bestselling Author Brooke Summers is a Mafia Romance author and is best known for her Made Series.

Brooke lives with her daughter and hubby on the picturesque west coast of Ireland. There's nothing Brooke loves more than spending time with her family and exploring new cities.

Want to know more about Brooke? www.brookesummersbooks.com
Subscribe to her newsletter: www.brookesummersbooks.com/newsletter
Join Brooke's Babes Facebook group.

Printed in Great Britain
by Amazon